D1558975

Enjoy your power!

PURSUIT

BOOK 1: YA KUWINDA

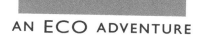

AN ECO ADVENTURE

PURSUIT

BOOK 1: YA KUWINDA

ONE TINY PLANT IN THE CONGO WITH
THE POWER TO CHANGE EVERYTHING

ONE BRAVE WOMAN'S QUEST
TO FIND IT AND SAVE IT

A NOVEL

BRANDON WIGGINS

2ND EDITION
VISION WORLD PRESS
CARMEL

PURSUIT
Book 1: Ya Kuwinda

Copyright © 2015-2018 Brandon Wiggins
All rights reserved

Revised Second Edition 2018

Published by Vision World Press
Carmel, California
www.brandonwigginsauthor.com

ISBN: 9780692195451

Second Edition designed and produced by
Lucky Valley Press, Jacksonville, Oregon
www.luckyvalleypress.com

Originally published in 2015 as "*Pursuit*"
Original 2015 cover design by Gene Harris,
with edits by Joyce Krieg

Printed in the United States of America on acid-free paper that meets the Sustainable Forestry Initiative® Chain-of-Custody Standards. www.sfiprogram.org

Heroes aren't born. They're cornered.

\- Mickey Rooney

PROLOGUE

2010 August
North Kivu Province
Democratic Republic of Congo
Africa

The girl's chest heaved as she stumbled through the dense jungle. Survival. That was all that mattered. Outrun her pursuers and survive. She had no weapon, only fear—and the fierce desire to avenge her people.

The marauders figured she'd be easy prey. After all, weren't they entitled to take whatever they wanted? And so they laughed at her clumsy attempts to outrun them and traded crude jokes as to what they'd do with her when she was caught. Surely they would capture her—it was only a matter of time.

They hadn't counted on the girl's ability to avoid panic under severe circumstances, a vital survival skill on the subcontinent. She understood she couldn't outrun them and to try would be suicide. Her inner resolve told her she could outsmart them as long as she was in control of her emotions and they were out of control of theirs.

Control was everything. But just when she needed it the most, she lost focus, her emotions running wild. She had just witnessed the massacre of her entire family, seemingly on the whim of her adolescent would-be captors. She knew she was the last in her family to survive and the burden made her body feel unbearably heavy.

The girl crouched behind a large stone outcropping to catch her breath and regain rational thought. As she hid, her pursuers temporarily lost track of her position. They slowed to smoke the local weed and tell their outrageous stories.

She shivered, hearing every word, and slunk behind a large boulder.

The boys advanced, slowly and deliberately. The girl groped behind her, desperately searching for a weapon to stage her last defiant and surely hopeless defense. Instead of the expected rock her hand found a hollow spot, a tiny indentation in the soil. She quickly reached around with both hands to clear away the dirt. Perhaps there would be an opening large enough to bury and cover herself with leaves—the slimmest of chances, but the only one she had.

The space opened up into the root structure of a giant African mahogany tree with a twisted underground root system, just wide enough for the slight girl to shimmy in and hide among the tendrils and branching nodes. She crawled under the outcropping and covered the entrance with small rocks and debris.

Heart pounding, she held her breath as the predators passed by without a clue.

PART ONE

CHAPTER 1

Big Sur, California, 2010

Dense fog and treacherous curves make California's Highway One one of the most perilous roads in the nation, but Harper Morgan Smith didn't mind. She careened over the twists and turns with the skill and nerve of a Le Mans racer. As far as she was concerned, she and her 1972 Karmann Ghia were not only negotiating with danger, they were actually defying it.

She turned the convertible up a steep dirt driveway and came to a screeching halt on a flat parcel overlooking an azure sea. Harper climbed out of the sports car and headed to the edge of the precipice to feel the ocean breeze fondle her face. She sighed as she turned away from the sea and headed toward the cabin and her desk. She had a report to file and she was already late.

At her Mac, she found an email from an unfamiliar source: Pharmco. org.

The subject line made Harper's blood race a little faster. 'Your time has come to save the world.'

Harper normally didn't open emails from unknown sources, but it hadn't been caught by her sophisticated spam filter, so she looked at the message. She actually did want to save the world, although she wasn't sure how a simple email would make that happen.

Dear Ms. Smith:

Please accept a meeting with me to discuss a highly classified venture regarding a most rare and unusual plant material. You will find the subject matter of the utmost importance. My associate will be contacting you directly, as time is of the essence.

Due to the immensely sensitive nature of this endeavor, please delete this email immediately and tell no one of this proposal.

At your service,

Dr. Traven Vandervere, Pharmco, UK

"My horoscope said this would be a day the winds would change," she murmured under her breath. She did not actually believe in horoscopes, but was open to the whole 'ohm' of the universe. A painful and recent bout with heartbreak had left her ready for a change in the 'winds.'

They met the first day of graduate school. He noticed her long before she was even aware there were other students in the science wing of UC Santa Cruz. She fought long and hard for her scholarship and wanted no distractions from her immersion in botany and academia.

Andrew came from wealth and privilege. He graciously forced himself into her life with ease, making her feel loved. She had no male role models growing up and he seemed ideal. Sometimes she wondered why he was even interested in her.

When Andrew left Harper to be with Analise three months ago, a situation mired in a Madame Bovary-style drama, she concluded that most men were primitive beasts and could not be trusted.

Even the most well-bred, perhaps especially the well-bred, succumbed quickly to sexual overtures by any woman. She was finished with men— unpredictable and unreliable— an unaffordable luxury.

Her Big Sur cabin was small but comfortable, the wainscoted walls and efficiency kitchen quaint. She had a break on the rent in exchange for landscaping advice and a substantial amount of manual labor on the seven-acre property overlooking the ocean. She kept her monthly expenses low. Any extra money went to support her mother's extravagant lifestyle in southern California. Her mother, a financial disaster, was prone to excessive spending on luxuries then delighting in having her daughter pay for the damages.

The real treasure was the view. The bay window looked out from the Ventana Wilderness high above the ocean to an endless sea of whales and dolphins. Her favorite time was early evening during stormy weather, when the sea took on a teal, iron, and gold-prism palette meant only for her eyes. She loved the ocean and had studied marine biology until she found she got incurably seasick. She selected a more terrestrial science interest, but the ocean still reached out for her.

She breathed deeply as her father's voice took her back to the one summer she spent with him…

Although not a plant per se, as there is no real root system, sea kelp is the perfect instrument of photosynthesis. Most people don't know or care much about kelp species, although many of the products they use on a daily basis, such as toothpaste and shampoo, are made with kelp ingredients.

In fact, most botanists are not even aware that kelp forests have both annual and perennial members. Nereocystis *and* Agarum *display a very similar growing habit to your basic cyclical terrestrial forest.*

Growing up to six inches a day under the most strenuous of circumstances, kelp is the most sustainable organism on this planet.

The kelp's most amazing attribute is the 'holdfast.' Not a root, mind you, a holdfast. Just because the root structure is not conventional doesn't mean it is not superbly suited to its function.

Without your own 'holdfast,' Harper, you will float away and get caught up with the torrents and predators of life. Due to circumstances beyond your control, you have no proper root structure. You must develop your own 'holdfast' —and it must be strong.

Extremely strong.

She was abruptly jolted from her thoughts by insistent thuds on the front door.

Shit, who could that be? She checked herself to make sure she didn't have her shirt on inside out or sprouts between her teeth and opened the heavy redwood door. A large black car was parked in the driveway.

"Harper Morgan Smith?"

"I am."

"I have been sent to collect you for your appointment with Dr. Vandervere."

The large man spoke with an accent. Harper placed it as South African. She had the gift of language. With just a few spoken words, she could identify the general origin of most people. She never let on her uncanny ability to learn any language.

His accent was very slight, but his stature was not. Though she stood a full five feet, seven inches, at 125 pounds she felt as small as a child answering a parent's door.

She was struck by the vague image of "Magnus somebody," a South African strong man, who Harper once saw on TV pulling airplanes with his bare chest. She focused on his speech to distract herself from his size.

"You must be kidding," she smirked to the hulk at her door.

The look on his face told her that he was definitely not kidding.

"You are to come with me now."

"Sorry, Magnus. I have work to do."

"Your work has changed. Get your things."

"Magnus, I am not going anywhere with you," she said, even though she knew she couldn't dissuade this Zimbabwean Neanderthal from anything that might cross his fancy. She was completely isolated in the middle of seven acres on a thousand-foot ridge at the top of Big Sur. The most intimidating weapon she had was a pair of Corona pruners. It occurred to her she could use another type of Corona to her advantage, but she needed time to think.

"Geez, lighten up. You look warm. Why don't you come in and have a beer?"

The fog had lifted and suddenly the day was warm. He grumbled but his demeanor softened. "The heli has no air conditioning. No need at high altitude, but it seems bloody hot for northern California." Sweat silhouetted his large jaw line.

"This isn't northern California, it's the Central Coast," she said, handing him a beer. "Um, heli? As in helicopter?"

The comment jarred his attention. He downed his beer as his focus returned. "We will go now. Dr. Vandervere is waiting."

He still wasn't kidding. She heard an increasingly loud whirling noise as an unmarked corporate helicopter touched down in the clearing in front of her cabin.

"The pilot is waiting," the hulk growled.

Harper Morgan Smith had an associate degree in horticulture and plant science, a bachelor's degree in botany, a minor in micro-biology, and a master's degree in eco-botany. Based on her outstanding academic record and impressive field experience as a teen, Cornell gave her a full-ride scholarship in her senior year of high school. But due to other financial obligations incurred by her mother, she was unable to attend, and continued her education in the less-expensive UC system. Harper was currently working toward a doctorate program and looking for a suitable topic for her thesis, a process that could take years to complete.

A remarkable thesis could launch her career—and insure her financial security.

She had nothing to lose. Her ex-boyfriend was enjoying the fruits of another woman and her mother the fruits of Harper's own labor. She took small inconsequential jobs just to survive, with no chance to contribute what she knew in her heart was her destiny. Plus, this opportunity with Vandervere might offer her the ideal topic for her thesis.

Not to mention saving the world.

CHAPTER 2

Harper was inside a shrine to taxidermy. Rich mahogany walls were covered with the stuffed, preserved heads of African animals. Harper recognized the common chimpanzee, the mountain gorilla, the bonobo and okapi. Also in the room were a mix of snakes, an odd armadillo-like creature and a menagerie of iridescent beetles. If the disembodied heads had a collective human-like expression, Harper would call it confused astonishment. The once-living animals seemed to know they were doomed to hang in perpetuity on plaques in some rich guy's office.

The one that both offended and amused her most was the large animated wild boar. The huge tusks gave the impression of eternal drool, invisibly dangling above her captor's dark greasy head.

"I am not in the habit of being abducted from my home, Mr. Vanderwhatever. I would appreciate an explanation."

"The name is Dr. Vandervere, Ms. Smith. Thank you for coming under these most unexpected circumstances." His mouth moved to form something related to a smile. "I assure you the utmost secrecy is necessary regarding this project, thus the necessity of absconding with you immediately, lest you discuss the intrigue."

Durban—or perhaps Capetown. An unmistakable vernacular—a dialect mixture of English, Dutch and Apartheid ancestry.

His accent told much about him, but she kept her expression innocent and guileless.

The wiry man wore a suit with a pinstriped vest. His black hair was slicked back, exposing cold, gray eyes. His pale skin was pockmarked and sallow, like someone who never slept.

"The endeavor we are about to undertake requires that no one be aware of our intent. There are many interested parties who would do anything required to intervene. I daresay," he added slowly, "anything."

"Please get to the point, Mr. Belvedere," she said.

He winced. "Miss Smith, Pharmco is an international think tank whose only interest is in the betterment of humanity. There are representatives from each of the giants in the industry in our fold. We are the combined brains behind all the top pharmaceutical corporations worldwide, collaborating to eradicate disease on this planet." His elbows perched on his large gilded French partner's desk as he absentmindedly wrung his hands.

"Go on." Harper cocked her head very slightly and raised one eyebrow. She felt as helpless as one of those lifeless beasts of prey hanging on the walls, and didn't like it.

"We have discovered a plant in a very remote and dangerous part of the world that may not only cure certain forms of the most insidious worldwide disease but could be a preventative vaccine."

His eyes were an unsettling shade of steel—his demeanor even colder.

Harper had been raised on the road, every turn an unknown. Her mother moved Harper from town to town, school to school. Arriving at each new locale, Harper reluctantly embraced the task of re-establishing herself, only to start again after her mother's next dramatic termination or break-up. Harper's childhood taught her how to size up any new situation quickly and make the best of it.

The gift had served her well—never more so than now.

"Mr. Vanderbilt." He winced when she mangled his name again. "Do you expect me to believe that an organization which you purport to represent would hire me, practically an undergrad, to locate and deliver an important botanical and medicinal discovery?"

"No, Miss Smith. I do not. I do, or should I say we do, expect you and a team of other specialists in their fields to track down, locate, and deliver a specimen to us so we may analyze and duplicate the plant's life-saving capabilities."

He sat back smugly in his large, tribe-crafted zebra chair.

She again focused on the carcass of the boar on the wall above him. *Funny, he looks just like the pig. Father was right—one should always look up.*

"It sounds intriguing Mr. Vandergelder. What's in it for me?"

"Five hundred thousand dollars upon delivery, as well as one percent of all global revenue." His tone was all business.

She tried not to gasp. That kind of money would not only pay off her massive student debt, it would fund her thesis research, guaranteeing acceptance to the finest doctoral programs on the planet. She would also finally be rid of the perpetual burden of scraping together money to bail out her mother from her escapades.

Harper tried to conceal her thoughts, but was not doing very well. "Dr. Vandervere …."

He had her. Still, she asked one more question. "What disease? What miracle cure might I have a hand in delivering that could ease human suffering?"

"A myriad of insidious forms collectively called cancer."

CHAPTER 3

"Ezekiel, please fetch Miss Smith some tea."

A large black man appeared out of the woodwork. He wore a traditional butler's uniform, complete with white gloves.

"Yes sir, Dr. Vandervere." He averted his eyes as he asked Harper in a very deep and heavily accented voice, "What kind of tea would Mademoiselle prefer?"

Harper's mind still raced with the possibilities posed by the money and by the challenge of finding the rare plant. Tea? Who cares about tea at a time like this? Her keen mathematical brain was busy calculating "one percent globally." She knew at least a half billion people worldwide suffered from some form cancer at any given moment and more would get sick as global population and toxicity increased.

The butler continued to hover. "Um, hot?" she finally replied.

Vandervere sank back into his chair. "Perhaps I should elaborate on the expedition. You and your team will be flown to Kinshasa and trans—"

"The Congo?" She interrupted him. "As in the Democratic Republic of Congo, formerly known as Zaire? I am so not going anywhere near the DRC. Do you know what they do to women over there? I listen to NPR, you know!"

"I applaud your knowledge of geography. Yes, the Congo, the third largest country in Africa. We believe it's the only place the plant resides." He stood up and paced the area behind his desk, caressing each African artifact. His attention was captured by a small shriveled head.

"Harper, I assure you, what you have heard is not the full story. You know how the news media sensationalizes everything. May I call you Harper?"

"No."

The black man in white gloves magically appeared again, placing the tea on a small table. "Your tea, Mademoiselle."

Hmm, Nairobi. Born in the west, the Ivory Coast perhaps, the slight French accent telling, but raised in the Nairobi area by South Africans.

She smiled smugly as if she had just figured out a tricky answer on Jeopardy.

"I assure you will be completely safe at all times. You will be escorted by armed guides carrying the finest GPS and equipment, and Pharmco will be in close contact every moment."

She tried to engage Ezekiel's glance to gauge his opinion of an American woman venturing into the Congo. She sensed he'd been working for "Mr. Vanderjerk" a long time. If the butler spoke again, she would pick up a few syllables consistent with his employer's speech, the doctor's thoughts completely meshed with his own. However, Ezekiel refused to meet her gaze.

Like she was in some strange version of a Joseph Conrad novel, she sipped her tea and considered the proposition. She looked down, pretending to be distracted by a crack in her nail.

"Miss Smith. We have chosen you specifically for your unique talents for plant location and identification. Your extensive studies in eco-botany and the fact that you speak French—and at least six other languages—make you possibly the only person on this planet able to complete this crucial mission." Vandervere was sitting lightly on his chair now, leaning toward her.

Pandering to my ego, very effective.

Harper knew about the Congo – over seventy thousand square miles of undisturbed virgin forest. Virgin forest! What every eco-botanist on the planet dreams of exploring—leaf by leaf, flower by flower. Now here she was, an obscure grad student, being handed the opportunity of a lifetime, fully funded with the highest quality equipment and staff. She would be the envy of every eco-scientist in her field.

Her father would have been proud.

"How do you know such a plant exists and that it lives in the DRC?" She was almost on the hook but still didn't want this unpleasant man to know.

"Another scientist has confirmed its existence and general location. The last time we spoke to Dr. Merrill—"

"Dr. Merrill?" she interrupted.

"Do you know of Dr. Merrill?" he asked, sounding surprised.

"He was my undergrad botany professor, not to mention my mentor. I've been emailing him for months now with no response. I've been worried sick about him."

She had shown a hint of vulnerability and Vandervere pounced.

"Yes, Harper. We have been trying to locate him for some time. You see, he refused our help in his search for the plant. He was unprepared and poorly equipped. I am afraid he is missing. If you leave immediately, perhaps you will encounter him."

The final carrot, dangling right in front of her eyes.

"There will be a contract outlining the terms, of course," she said, doing her best to disguise her excitement by sounding business-like.

"I would expect nothing less from you, Miss Smith. Our legal counsel in London will deliver your contract when we stop to pick up some of other team members."

Harper's gaze made one more tour of Vandervere's office as she thought things over. The offer seemed credible; the doctor as sincere as a man such as he could be. The plant—if it could be found, and if it really did possess amazing healing properties—would be a tremendous boon to humankind.

What have I got to lose?

She locked eyes with Vandervere. "I'm in."

Dr. Vandervere smiled. It was an expression without warmth or joy, as cold and lifeless as the animals decorating the walls of his office.

CHAPTER 4

"Doctor Vandervere says you will be comfortable here," Ezekiel said as he opened the door to a suite: a palace atop a hill. Long crimson velvet drapes framed huge gilded windows offering a view stretching from the Golden Gate Bridge to Coit Tower. The baroque furniture reminded Harper of Sally Stanford's Valhalla Inn in Sausalito, where her mother took her when she was a child. This was old San Francisco. She relaxed in the familiar surroundings.

"Doctor Vandervere was right," she said, speaking as much to herself as to the butler.

He delivered the small duffle bag she packed before Magnus had hustled her into the helicopter.

"Does Mademoiselle have any other baggage?" He came slightly closer.

"Not that fits into a carry-on, Ezekiel, but thank you." She looked sidelong at him. "How long have you been with Dr. Vandervere?"

"My father was in the employ of his father in the Cote d'Ivoire."

"But you were schooled in Kenya, Nairobi to be exact."

"How does Mademoiselle know that?" For the first time, Ezekiel made direct eye contact with her.

"Call it a hunch. So this Vander-guy is OK?"

He immediately looked away as if he had already said too much. "Mademoiselle will rest now until the others come."

"Others?"

"The physician for your vaccinations and an outfitter for your travel gear. Doctor Vandervere will supply everything you will require for your journey. I will be returning with your dinner. You must rest. You leave first thing in the morning."

He closed the door without looking back. She tried to ignore the creeping feeling of dread.

"It's natural to feel nervous. I am going to the Congo," she said aloud.

Between interruptions by the medical man with the needle and the woman who took her measurements and returned later armed with shopping bags, Harper studied the landmarks from the suite's large bay window. She must be on California Street at the top of San Francisco's luxurious Nob Hill. The limousine's tinted windows on the ride from the airport to Vandervere's mansion gave her little clue as to where she was taken.

When Harper was very small, her mother dressed her up with hats adorned with ribbons and placed her tiny hands in delicate gloves. She'd then parade her around downtown San Francisco showing her off to the man-du-jour. It all seemed so glamorous. There was a time when Harper worshipped her mother.

She knew the truth about her mother now but the charms of the City-by-the-Bay had not faded in Harper's heart. The wide-eyed little girl inside could still be enchanted.

Ezekiel returned with a tray, placing it on a dining table overlooking North Beach and the Marin Headlands, just as the city lights blinked on for the evening. Harper preferred starlight, but this brightly lit urban skyline was special. These lights belonged to her.

"Mademoiselle is hungry now?" Ezekiel asked, opening a sterling silver dome to reveal a large artichoke, a filet mignon laced with roasted garlic and a salad of mixed greens and heirloom tomatoes. A menu printed in elegant calligraphy on parchment revealed what Harper had already suspected, that these were her favorite foods from her beloved Central Coast—an artichoke from Castroville, the filet from cattle raised in Cachagua, garlic from Gilroy, and salad ingredients harvested from Earthbound Farms in Carmel Valley.

"The prisoner's last meal?" she murmured. Even though it was disturbing that Vandervere had so much personal information about her, it didn't stop her from picking up her knife and fork.

Ezekiel softly smiled at her, revealing brilliant white teeth. "You will need your strength, Mademoiselle. *Bon appétit et une bonne nuit de sommeil.*"

"*Merci beaucoup,* Ezekiel." She realized her guard was falling fast. "*Peur être sincere ...* I am afraid."

"*Peur* can be your ami, Mademoiselle." He placed the napkin on her lap.

Fear can be my friend? How can that possibly be?

CHAPTER 5

Harper was just congratulating herself for being the luckiest person on the planet as she luxuriated in Vandervere's suite, half-asleep in cool, 1,000-thread count sheets, when she heard a gentle knock on the door.

Morning already?

"Mademoiselle, I have come to deliver your breakfast and your effects." Ezekiel's voice sounded apologetic.

Harper leaped from the bed and hastily wrapped herself in the thick terrycloth robe she'd found laid out on her bed the night before. As she hurried to the door, she remained partially immersed in the dreams of the night, both promising and terrifying.

"Just like my life," she murmured.

Before she quite knew what was happening, Harper was dressed, fed and bundled into a black sedan heading through the early morning fog to a private airport in South San Francisco. Magnus was silent during the ride and she was glad of it. The giant man opened the car door for her while an attendant transported her small bag to an unmarked plane. She started toward the stairs, then hesitated before entering the jet. She looked back over her shoulder.

"Thanks for everything, Magnus," she said with a smile.

He grunted and nodded in her direction.

A stunning black woman in a navy blue flight attendant's uniform stood at the cabin door. She gave Harper a broad, warm smile. "Welcome to the Pharmco Boeing BBJ, Miss Smith," she said in a velvety South African voice.

"Thank you." Harper stepped into the cabin and gushed like a teenager. "Sheesh, you guys know how to travel in style!"

The teak-paneled cabin was inlaid with ivory designs. Harper counted two large leather couches and six overstuffed leather chairs, as well as a brass bar and a state-of-the-art media center.

"My name is Ursula and I am at your service." The flight attendant projected an air of calm self-assurance. The graying temples in her short wiry hair were the only clues to her true age. Her uniform clung to an athletic body and her dark skin had few wrinkles.

"Very nice to meet you, Ursula. Please call me Harp."

They exchanged smiles as Harper chose a large chair by the window.

"So … where we are going?" Harper asked. "Straight to the Congo?"

"You will be briefed on every aspect of your mission in due time. But to answer your question – our next stop will be Boston, where we will pick up the first of your team members. Our flight time to Boston will be approximately five and a half hours. We will pick up the rest of the team at different locations on our way to the Kinshasa N'djili Airport. We will not reach our final destination for over twenty-four hours, so you will have plenty of time to prepare."

Ursula directed Harper to follow her to the rear of the plane. "This will be your cabin."

My own room—on a jet! Harper had never heard of such luxury. The room Ursula displayed to Harper was small but exquisitely appointed, from bed with down pillows to copper sink. A small desk was bare except for an oversized envelope with the Pharmco corporate seal, addressed to Ms. H. M. Smith and stamped "Confidential."

"I think I can hang out here for a couple of days," Harper said with a smile.

"Prepare for takeoff," the pilot's voice boomed over the intercom system.

French. Southern France. "Let's hope he hasn't been sipping the Beaujolais this morning."

Ursula smiled. "Please take your seat Miss Harper; we will be leaving shortly."

They both buckled themselves in as the jet hurtled down the runway and lifted into the sky—and the greatest adventure of Harper's young life.

CHAPTER 6

A large flat screen from the jet's media center displayed the humorless and slightly disturbing face of Vandervere.

"Welcome to the Pharmco Boeing BBJ. You will meet your team members soon. It is important you are aware of your co-workers' special talents, as you work as a cohesive unit."

"All this money, you'd think they could hire someone a little more entertaining. How about Ben Affleck? I like him," Harper said with a smirk.

Ursula smiled.

"As you know, your mission is to locate, harvest and deliver a rare plant material from an unpopulated area of the Democratic Republic of Congo. Once your team assembles, you fly to a private area of the Kinshasa N'djili Airport where you will be transported by Jeep then by helicopter to the country's interior. From there you will proceed on foot."

Vandervere's face darkened, causing Harper to tense, her forehead creasing, lips pressed together. "In the Congo on foot, you have got to be kidding me!" She tried to suppress panic with humor. "Good thing I left my stilettos at home."

Ursula smiled to herself as she stepped behind the bar. "May I offer you a drink, Miss Harper?"

"The Congo on foot? Better make it a double Patron Viejo."

Vandervere's voice continued to drone on the video. "Your team will be fully equipped with state-of-the-art technology. Locating the plant material will be relatively simple, thanks to Dr. Merrill and his last known location."

Harp's chest tightened at the mention of her beloved mentor. What had happened to him?

"Your team members have been carefully chosen for their skills and expertise. Let's meet them now, shall we?"

"Nothing worse than someone trying to be cute—who definitely isn't," Harper said with a roll of her eyes. Ursula stifled another giggle.

"The first member of your team, Sergeant David Murano."

A photo appeared: a man of good stature, dark piercing eyes, heavy black eyebrows and a shaved head. He had a friendly smile with one silver tooth on the left side. Harper thought he looked capable.

"Mr. Murano is an ex-Green Beret and has served in the southern Sahara regions for over a decade. His expertise is in personnel and tribal management as well as jungle terrain skills."

"Oh good, my jungle terrain and tribal management skills seem to be lacking," Harper smirked.

"The next team member ...." Harper reached for her tequila. Just what the doctor ordered.

Looking back at the screen, she saw a photo of herself. *What the ...? Where in the hell did Vandervere get that?*

It was a profile shot of her in the pine forest of Carmel. She didn't remember anyone taking a photo of her at work. The tequila warmed her pleasantly as she recalled the moment the photo must have been taken. She was walking through the Monterey pine and cypress forest, head bent, stooping deeply while inspecting the soil. She remembered what her father had told her, "Always remember to look up." She hadn't fully comprehended what he had meant; her nose was always to the grindstone. *Always remember to look up? What kind of advice is that?*

The coastal pine forest in Central California was an incredible place, almost holy—the soil a deep chocolate mélange of organic materials, a fusty, rich womb of fundamental creation. She embraced it every morning: the dawn with perfectly descending sunlit fingers, toying with wisps of fog and ferns as they casually touched down upon a pristine landscape, like the forest was immaculately tended by tiny invisible terrestrial gardeners.

The smell of the land, the soft indirect lighting and the slight chill in the air, even in the summer, had enticed her onto her life's path. She felt most at home in the arms of Mother Nature. Living for the moment in that forest and remembering her father's words, she did look up, just out of curiosity. She saw a grove of the structurally impressive Cupressus macrocarpa, the legendary Monterey cypress, and marveled at its architecture.

She spied a spectacular 100-foot Pinus radiata—a Monterey pine. This stately tree should have been extinct years ago and, as such, the species was riddled by countless insidious pests. Wood boring beetles, viruses, and a host of other denigrators had caused this large, 150-year-old specimen to topple onto a lower sapling. The young tree lay at a 45-degree angle, smothered by the ancient, dying pine. The tip of the sapling was stubbornly raising its head up to the sky, perpendicular to the forest floor.

Harper's memory wandered back to that precious summer with her father so long ago.

Every human strives to be upright whether they are aware of it or not. Even if he or she has had the worst possible situations descend upon them, forced to the ground, they will struggle to stay upright. Look around you in the forest, child; you will see it happen over and over. You can see the young saplings leaning, stretching, and clamoring to find their place in the sun. When they get established in their own particular spot, they reach for the sky in perfect harmony with the light, the earth, and in alignment with sheer gravity.

This is what you must do, my little sapling. Take the blows dealt to you and use them to support your stature. The upright life you lead will be a beacon for the rest of the forest.

She smiled softly as she sipped the tequila. She would have given anything for more time with her father. But she refused to allow herself to wallow.

Her attention returned to the Boeing BBJ and the video. "... is Ms. Harper Morgan Smith, botanist. Ms. Smith will be identifying the plant material and logging its exact whereabouts and habitat." She was surprised she was second on Vandervere's list.

"Ms. Smith is crucial to our mission. All team members are to assist Ms. Smith in any way possible."

Shameless flatterer ... adds to his charm. Harper felt herself loosening up.

"Our next team member is Mike Logan, engineer. He will execute all technical functions of the mission. Mr. Logan has numerous areas of expertise including handling tropical materials and mechanical operations. Mr. Logan is the 'go to' guy on this mission."

The photo of Mike Logan showed sweat pouring from a tanned and muscular body against a dense jungle backdrop. A large crossbow draped over his shoulders. A Detroit Lions cap covered most of his brown hair and his face was obscured by sunglasses and beard stubble.

Harper stared. Now there's a manly guy. Up until now, she'd been attracted to academic types, men who disappointed her in the end. Maybe time for a change?

"Get over yourself, Harper!" she said out loud. The pain returned to the pit of her stomach when she thought about her boyfriend and his recent betrayal. "You are so finished with that shit!" she declared as she returned her attention to the video presentation.

"Our mission requires a botanical chemist, Chris Housdorf. Dr. Housdorf will analyze the plant material so we may not only be sure of the phytochemicals we are looking for, but also analyze the soil in that particular habitat. You may encounter several subspecies and Dr. Housdorf will establish which variety most appropriately suits our chemical needs."

Looks a little scrawny to be going into the jungle on foot.

Harper chided herself that looks can be deceiving, and she was living proof. She'd been told more than once she'd be perfect for the role of trophy wife and that she'd fit right in with the idle rich in Pebble Beach. Her long, thick hair was an unusual mix of strawberry and gold. She wore it straight and in a ponytail most times, but on a job site in an exotic location, the humidity transformed her locks into large curls. Her eyes were sea green with yellow ringing the irises and flecks of brown scattered throughout. Andrew said her eyes reminded him of the islands in Fiji.

Still, Harper felt she could take out Dr. Housdorf in a fist fight.

"Sid Lembowsky will be our communications operator. His specialty is wireless global positioning systems worldwide. It may be tricky to use the GPS effectively under the heavy foliage canopy which obscures the sky for days at a time. Without visuals such as sun or stars, it will be impossible to navigate without it. It is crucial we know your position at all times."

Lembowsky was balding with a small crown of fuzz surrounding the perimeter of his head. He wore wire rim glasses and had a slight build. His eyes were set close. Harper noticed a substantial tuft of hair emanating from each ear and nostril.

Harper was wondering if she was the only female on the expedition when the photo of a lovely woman with light brunette hair and whiskey-colored eyes came on the screen. She looked to be in her mid-40s and aging very well.

"Dr. Claire Guthrie will be the staff physician. She recently ended a tour with Medicine Sans Frontiers, also known as Doctors Without Borders. She has extensive experience with all types of tropical medical situations."

Harper was relieved there would be an experienced woman with her, experienced with the darkness that might lie in the hearts of men when subjected to such primitive situations.

"Your guide will be Hermann Zmbaliu, a native of the DRC with firsthand knowledge of the indigenous peoples. He will assist in leading your team when you embark on the final phase of your journey into the deep rainforest. His thorough understanding of local language, customs and beliefs will be invaluable in your mission."

Something struck the botanist about Zmbaliu's face on the screen but she couldn't put her finger on it. She thought perhaps dealing with the struggles of life in central Africa could cause a person to become permanently riddled with anxiety. But, she might be reading too much into his facial expression.

"Sergeant Murano will train you on the proper use and care of your equipment. Dr. Guthrie will brief you on what to watch out for in the jungle regarding your health and welfare. Please remember your primary mission is paramount and at all times you must act accordingly. There will be no reward for failure."

How cold is that? Harper's dislike for Vandervere grew. He's like the public relations guy for the Equatorial Gestapo.

"Good luck." Vandervere signed off with a semi-salute.

Oh, brother. Harper rolled her eyes out of habit as Ursula emerged from the galley.

"Time for lunch, Miss Harper." Ursula placed a silver tray on the mahogany dining table. Harper was famished. Was it from the excitement of the journey? Or the thought that her rations might not be so grand in the very near future?

"Lobster and champagne—are you trying to fatten me up, Ursula?"

"You must eat and perhaps take a short nap, Miss Harper. It would be wise to gather your strength." Ursula topped off Harper's glass and disappeared into the cockpit. Harper dipped a piece of lobster into melted butter and looked out the window. Butter oozed from her mouth. She once heard true enjoyment meant life's juices dripped down one's chin, a concept she began to understand. She felt perched on the edge of greatness, however dangerous that precipice might be.

Benjamin Franklin defined success as "when opportunity meets pre-paredness" and Harper felt she was definitely prepared, like all she had endured throughout her life prepared her for this moment. Even if she failed, she had reached a turning point.

And while a turning point was definitely good thing, she agreed with the unpleasant Dr. Vandervere on one thing: Failure was not an option.

CHAPTER 7

Her father stooped over the beautifully clustered *cineraria stellata* and offered a rare smile.

My old friend Dr. Wiseman at the University of Hertfordshire did a study on why some people are lucky. He told me that among those people he tested, the ones who rated themselves as lucky scored markedly higher in the area of extroversion. Their extroversion significantly increased the likelihood of having a lucky chance encounter.

So-called lucky people are more likely to notice chance opportunities, even when they are not expecting them. They are open to new experiences and like the notion of unpredictability.

She giggled like any twelve-year-old girl at the thought of her stern father an extrovert. She was even surprised he had an old friend as he only occasionally socialized, and then only with his botanical colleagues.

"Father, why do you think of that when you are with the cineraria?"

Harper, you are a perceptive little one. Our lovely stellata is the horticultural embodiment of the conceptual state of luck. She lives in clusters with her sisters, languishing sublimely in the under-story of large, shady protectors. She harbors collections of bright, small star shaped flowers, thus her name stellata, and has a free and easy growing habit.

When stellata finishes her mirthful display, her seed pods float away in a feathery shower with the others, in a sleepy respite, secretly promising an amazing spring. The many clusters of flowers and resulting seed pods increase her chances of successful replication in her environment with many serendipitous opportunities to thrive in suitable locations.

Stellata has every advantage to enhance her luck and is tenacious in her pursuit to thrive. It would be wise to apply her credo to our daily lives in the knowledge that luck is what we make it.

A light knock came on the cabin door, rousing her from her reverie. "Miss Harper, we are approaching Boston. Please prepare for landing."

Harper was still smiling, aglow from the memory of her father's look. It was odd that such an analytical man would even understand a concept such as luck. The fact that he was so abstractly eloquent was even more remarkable. Harper's seeds were definitely cast. But then she remembered that luck is what you make of it.

She splashed water on her face and buckled up in the large leather chair. She looked forward to meeting Sergeant Murano. She had not spoken to anyone regarding this adventure and couldn't wait to compare notes with a fellow team member.

The Pharmco jet touched down at a private airport. Even with the luxurious surroundings, Harper was eager to get off the plane and stretch her long legs. She unbuckled her seatbelt and headed for the cabin door.

Ursula beat her to it. "I am terribly sorry, Miss Harper. You will not be permitted to deplane until we reach Kinshasa."

"Excuse me?" Harper looked at the flight attendant with widened eyes and cocked her head. "I was just going to stretch a bit." Harper hated the feeling of being trapped.

"Dr. Vandervere insists all team members stay on the plane once they board. The secrecy of this mission cannot be compromised," Ursula said. The once-friendly flight attendant was strictly business.

"I'm not going to call CNN. I'm just going to get some air."

"I have my orders, Miss Harper." Ursula looked apologetic as she focused her attention on the oncoming passenger.

"Sergeant Murano, so glad you could join us," Ursula said, her gorgeous smile returning.

The large man grinned as he ducked into the cabin.

"Damn glad to meet you, ma'am," he said after Ursula made introductions. His large hand reached for Harper's, practically crushing her fingers with his handshake.

"Likewise, Sergeant." Harper looked him in the eye and liked what she saw. He had an imposing presence, assured and strong. Her father must have had that same kind of presence as a young man. She only knew her father in his older years but she could imagine the strength of his youth.

"Passengers, will you please take your seats?" Ursula's firm voice made it clear this was not a request.

They'd spent less than fifteen minutes on the ground. Harper did her best to hide her disappointment. She wanted to visit Boston and New York. Cornell University, the Holy Grail for most botany students, wasn't too far away.

Harper buckled up next to Dave and asked Ursula about their next destination.

"New York. We will be picking up two team members there."

"What suckers from the Big Apple do we get to torment?" Dave asked. Harper was already appreciating his attitude.

"Dr. Housdorf and Mr. Lembowsky will be joining us."

The plane leveled off and Ursula headed toward the galley. "What may I offer you to drink, Sergeant Murano?"

"Will you share my champagne, Sergeant Murano?" Harper asked. "If we're going to be denied the basic necessities of life in the near future, we might as well enjoy it now."

"Thank you so much, Miss Smith. However, every time I drink, I break out in handcuffs," Dave said with mock seriousness, causing Ursula and Harper to laugh.

CHAPTER 8

The cabin door opened after a rough landing on the private tarmac of JFK International.

"Get your hands off me, Neanderthal. Who the hell do you think you are, freak?"

Magnus pushed Sid Lembowsky into the cabin. The large man didn't even bother to hide his disdain for the GPS expert.

Lembowsky threw his backpack at Ursula. "Take care of this and get this hulk away from me," he bellowed.

Ursula fumbled with the pack and tried to smile graciously. "Yes, Mr. Lembowsky."

Dave Murano tried to stifle a sneer as he unbuckled his seatbelt. "Here, ma'am, let me help with that," he said to Ursula as he took the backpack from her arms.

"Can you believe these assholes? They didn't even give me a chance to call anyone before they kidnapped me." The little man angled to get in Sergeant Murano's face but ended up looking directly into his muscular chest.

"Who was it you wanted to call, Mr. Lembowsky? I can't imagine a fellow like you having a long list of friends." Dave looked down at Lembowsky's balding head.

"And who the shit are you, dickhead? Some flunky sucking up to these corporate thugs?" Sid puffed up, trying to increase his stature.

"I am the sergeant here, sir. I will be in charge of this team the second we are in the Congo. You will adhere to the rules I set in order to assure your safety and the successful completion of this mission."

Lembowsky appeared to shrink as the sergeant commanded his attention. "Now sit down and shut up."

Another new passenger walked through the cabin door.

"Welcome, Dr. Housdorf." Ursula's smile returned. "Please take a seat; we will be taking off shortly."

"Thank you so much." Dr. Chris Housdorf was also a small man, but there the resemblance with the cranky Lembowsky ended. "What a great adventure! Isn't it exciting?" Housdorf's boyish face looked like a small child anticipating Christmas morning.

"Where are we off to now, Miss Ursula?" Dave asked cheerfully. Dr. Housdorf's optimism lifted the overall mood on the jet.

"London. We'll be picking up Dr. Guthrie, who will brief you on the mission's medical safety procedures."

She instructed the new passengers to watch Vandervere's video, adding, "Our flight time to London is approximately six hours. It is advised that you get as much rest as possible."

Harper used the time to review the materials in the big envelope marked "Confidential" she'd found on the desk in her cabin.

"TO: Miss Harper Morgan Smith, Botanist:

As you may know, Ms. Smith, Dr. Merrill was working on the chemical properties of Podophyllum peltatum. The chemical agent podophyllin is responsible for the anti-cancer activity of the resin found in the rhizomes.

Dr. Merrill's research showed that the resin is not sufficient to have an overall effect on disease. A heavy nitriloside and thiocyanate component must also be present as in Dr. Krebs' research. Of course, the beta-glycosidase enzyme must be in perfect proportion, ratio-wise, for the compound to be effective."

Harper devoured the research data, immersing herself in the world that kept her sane throughout her crazy, unpredictable life. Science was a wondrous place filled with unlimited natural potential. To her, the gifts of nature were perfect, pristine and absolute. The never-ending surprise of the wild astonished her. This was her personal connection with the supreme plan. She returned her attention to the document.

"Albert Schweitzer's medical missionary expedition in 1913 encountered many cancer-free tribes in Gabon and sub-Saharan countries. In fact, there were no known cancer cases in the native African peoples when the tribes adhered to their original diets where millet, cassava, yams, sorghum were the staples, all high in nitrilosides and thiocyanates. This was not the case in all other parts of the world at that time.

Our research indicates that tribes reported in the general area of Dr. Merrill's findings were utilizing a botanical variety of Podophyllum to ward off the disease.

Your mission, Ms. Smith, is to locate the chemical cross of the podophyllum *and the high nitriloside and thiocyantate species with the proper ratio of the beta-glycosidase. We have been unsuccessful in reproducing any compound in the laboratory that resembles the necessary chemical composition. We rely on the natural molecular compounds to display the appropriate formula. With the help of Dr. Housdorf and his chemical analysis, you must deliver the natural specimen that completes these requirements. Attached are Dr. Merrill's last known notes and diagrams."*

The text was signed by Vandervere and a PhD whose name Harper didn't recognize.

"Is that what we are looking for Miss Harper?"

Harper startled at the sound of Dave's voice, scattering a pile of notes scribbled on cocktail napkins from her lap.

"I'm not sure," Harper said, scrambling on the floor to retrieve them. "Right now, I'm just doodling an amalgam of notes, botanical requirements, combined with my educated conjecture. However, I studied under Dr. Merrill for two years and know the way he thinks." She drew a sketch of a flower and a pod, then frowned. "As in most binomial nomenclature, the naming of biological entities is based on the species' reproductive technology. I am confident I can identify the species, if it exists and if it is in flower or seed."

She wrinkled her forehead. "The flowers and seeds are the plant's sexual proponents thereby its identifiable characteristics. Dr. Housdorf's chemical analysis will be crucial in identification. I only have degrees in botanically related studies. I am not qualified to make a positive chemical ID."

Dave smiled. "Miss Harper, based on what I saw on that video, I doubt there is anything for which you are not qualified. How about giving me a little botanical data pertinent to our mission?"

Harper was only beginning to assimilate the pertinent information she gleaned over the years with the new information from Vandervere's report. Right now, she happily weaved the bits and pieces into a cohesive, conversational form. For her, things made more sense when she could verbalize the conceptual ideology. With the sergeant she hoped she could really be her technically informative and assuredly boring self.

She motioned him to sit down. "If it gets too nerdy, please feel free to fall asleep." Sergeant Dave sat down in the big leather chair next to her and buckled up. He immediately dropped his head and started snoring.

"Just kidding." He smiled, showing his signature silver tooth.

Harper sat up straight and put all the available information together in her head.

"There are over three thousand plants of medicinal interest in oncology, the study of cancer."

"Three thousand?" Dave whistled in amazement.

Harper nodded and continued. "The term 'ethno botany' was coined in 1895 and refers to the use of plants for their medicinal values within traditional societies. Most of these societies have no written traditions or pharmacological resources. The success of these societies and their treatments has been imperative to the survival of our species. With me so far?"

"Absolutely," Dave said.

"Jonathan Hartwell of Harvard University began his research in the field with the five thousand-year-old Shen-Nung and followed every written reference to cancer-curing plant materials throughout history. He catalogued the three thousand species referenced for use in the treatment of cancer. As it turns out, the ancient wise men related the causes of cancer to auto-immune dysfunctions and stresses."

Harper looked thoughtful. "There is also the matter of the lost art of head-shrinking."

"You're shitting me, right?" Dave said.

"I'm serious," Harper replied. "The mysterious tannin cocktail used in that process could possibly shrink the most stubborn of tumors."

"I'll take your word for it." Dave shook his head. "Do you really think we can find what we are looking for on this mission?"

The ex-marine seemed to be looking for her leadership.

Harper felt the weight of the mission on her shoulders. She looked around the jet at the team and didn't feel very confident. Murano was obviously top notch and the chemical doctor had the credentials. As for the annoying GPS specialist, he must be competent or a big corporation like Pharmco wouldn't have hired him for so a costly and important a mission.

"I think we have our work cut out for us, Dave." Harper said.

Ursula wheeled a cart from the galley and announced dinner. The table was set with white linens and three types of wine and champagne glasses. Harper was glad her mother had insisted she learn the art of fine dining during those childhood trips to San Francisco.

"I only eat organic food." Lembowsky said with a whine.

The captain emerged from the cockpit, addressing Lembowsky with a scowling French accent. "I suggest you eat whatever fine food is served to you, Monsieur. I expect this will be one of your last civilized meals."

All passengers shifted their attention to the captain. "Let me assure you, there will be plenty of organic food where you are going, Monsieur Lembowsky."

"And I thought this bucket of bolts was on autopilot." Lembowsky mumbled as the captain disappeared back into the cockpit.

Harper said, "Interesting that the entire crew is of African origin."

"What do you mean?" Dave asked.

"Our pilot's accent was definitely from the old Zaire. Vandervere and Magnus were definitely South African Dutch. Even that darling Ezekiel was Kenyan. This entire operation seems sub-Saharan. Don't you guys think it is a little odd that a high level pharmacological conglomerate, mostly based in the states, would have a totally African crew?"

Dr. Housdorf paused from his Caesar salad. "I consider them noble in their cause and gracious in their treatment of this team and this mission. I, for one, am grateful and honored to be included in this potentially world-changing charge. I am sure they handpicked each of the crew for their specific expertise." He smiled earnestly and reached for the salmon en croute.

Sergeant Dave finished his mouthful of clam linguini. "Since we are not headed for your usual tourist destination, I would imagine they needed to hire from within, so to speak."

"I say we toast to an incredible journey and may we deliver a true gift to mankind," Harper said, raising her glass.

"Here, here!" Smiles broadened as Ursula approached the table.

"We have approximately four hours until landing in London to pick up the doctor. The barrister will also deliver your contracts for signing and your equipment will arrive, so Sergeant Murano can acquaint you with the technological aspects of your packs." Ursula was all business. "After dessert, it would be wise to retire. I will rouse you prior to landing."

Harper dabbed the corners of her mouth daintily and unbuckled her seatbelt. "Well, I do need some sleep, but I definitely don't need dessert. Ursula, you have been a beautiful hostess and I thank you for everything."

Harper headed toward her cabin, Ursula following to attend to her needs. "When do you sleep, Miss Ursula?"

"When everyone has retired, Miss Harp." Her friendly demeanor had vanished since Lembowsky had boarded.

"Don't let that little asshole bother you, Ursula."

"No worries, Miss Harp. I have handled far more beastly creatures."

"I'll bet you have." Harper smiled.

"Are you sure you won't have just a bit of something sweet? I can bring you a small plate with which to retire."

"Oh, you are a wicked girl," Harper whispered. "Well, maybe just a little of that mango cheesecake I noticed, but my hips will never forgive you."

"But I will." Ursula winked. "I will wake you before our descent."

"Ursula, if we are going to pick up the doctor in London, what about the local guide? What about Mike Logan?" Harper said, yawning as Ursula handed her a small plate with a perfect slice of cheesecake atop a white paper doily.

"Your guide will meet us at the Kinshasa airport and Mr. Logan will find you."

"Find me?"

"I have worked with Mr. Logan before and he is very resourceful. You will find him quite ... capable."

"Capable?" Harper's eyelids were at half-mast.

"Indeed. Good night, Miss Harper."

CHAPTER 9

"Dr. Guthrie, so glad you could join us!" Dave towered over the physician and shook her small hand so earnestly her head bounced.

"Very glad to meet you, Sergeant Murano." Claire Guthrie stepped into the cabin and studied her teammates. Harper watched as the newest passenger took in the opulence of the décor and seemed impressed. As she would later tell Harper, she'd been in the Sudan for two years where luxury was defined as a mosquito net with no holes.

She was slight yet sturdy with light brown hair falling in curls around her face. It was her eyes that captivated, the color of warm brandy, backlit as if by a sunset pouring through stained glass. Her shapely figure was hidden underneath a heavy khaki jacket, but Captain Lemieux had noticed.

Just as Ursula was introducing herself, Magnus came through the door carrying two large backpacks. The large South African's presence took both Harper and Dave by surprise. Harper whispered to Dave, "Where the hell did he come from?"

Chris Housdorf introduced himself to Dr. Guthrie, his childlike smile lighting up his face.

"Likewise, Doctor." Her lovely British accent only accentuated her appeal.

Captain Lemieux, his voice thick with fatigue, informed the passengers he was would be leaving. "Your new pilots will be arriving shortly. Good luck and Godspeed on your journey."

He kissed Dr. Guthrie's hand and gave Harper French-style kisses on both cheeks. He bowed slightly to Dave, Chris, and Ursula. He ignored Lembowsky, who stared out the window listening to his iPod.

Ursula informed the passengers the London barrister would be arriving soon and suggested they seat themselves to await his arrival. "Is there anything I may get for anyone?"

"Yeah, a fucking ticket to the end of this trip," Lembowsky grumbled.

"Charming as ever," Murano said. He turned to Dr. Guthrie, introducing himself and then Harper. Harper extended her hand for a shake, but Claire grabbed her shoulders to kiss both her cheeks. Already friends, Harper thought, feeling encouraged.

"This is Mr. Lembowsky, our GPS operator," Murano continued. "He's here to make sure we don't get lost in the jungle or eaten by tigers."

The GPS expert continued to ignore his fellow passengers, ear buds deeply imbedded in his tufted ears.

"Sergeant Murano, I do not believe there are any tigers in the Congo," Claire said with a smile. "However, it would not do for us to be lost in the jungle in any case."

Claire reached over to shake Lembowsky's hand. The unexpected movement startled him, spilling beer on his Hawaiian shirt.

"Shit." He paid no attention Dr. Guthrie, yelling at Ursula to bring him another beer, "and a fucking towel!"

"My apologies, Mr. Lembowsky, please let me," Claire said, calm and polite. She took the towel from Ursula and blotted his shirt.

Before Lembowsky uttered another vulgarity, a large man in a wool suit walked through the plane's cabin door.

"I am Donald Leach, corporate counsel for Pharmco." He spoke with confidence and formality. "Each of you will sign a contract detailing the terms of your employment with the corporation. Copies will be made and sent directly to your residences after they have been signed. I am here to answer any questions. However, I can assure you that the terms each of you discussed with Dr. Vandervere are exactly as you agreed."

He reached into an expansive briefcase and pulled out five large manila envelopes.

"It would be wise to keep your individual terms to yourselves. Your functions on this team are specialized but your goal is the same. The only thing that matters is the completion of your mission."

"Yeah, yeah. Fucking bring it." Lembowsky had now finished his second beer and had moved on to dark rum.

Leach distributed the envelopes and pens, and stood waiting.

"I would like to have another attorney review this contract," Harper said. "I am not a legal expert. I'm a plant person and that's pretty much it."

"Me, too. I mean, I am stuck in my own capacity," Claire said.

"I completely understand." Leach oozed false sympathy. "But we do not have time for that. This mission must be completed with all due haste. Time is of the essence."

"What's the rush?" asked Dr. Housdorf.

"There is a danger that if this chemical formula falls into the wrong hands, the gain from this expedition will be sold on the black market. The human benefit will be lost to the highest bidder. Needless to say, the potential profit is huge and our adversaries are extremely motivated."

Leach continued. "I must caution you that no one will be allowed to disembark without a signed contract, for indemnity purposes, of course."

"Of course," they grumbled in unison. Harper, Dave Murano, Chris Housdorf, Sid Lembowsky and Claire Guthrie each set upon the business of reading through the tedious legal jargon, pausing at certain paragraphs to reread. Seeing they essentially had no choice, they all scrawled their signatures on the dotted line and replaced the contracts in their respective envelopes.

"Splendid." Leach collected each envelope and said his goodbyes. The new Congolese pilots boarded the plane, hastily moving to the cockpit and making the announcements to prepare for departure.

Harper checked her watch. "That took less than twenty minutes," she said to Dave. "I didn't even know they could refuel and do maintenance checks so quickly."

"You'd be surprised, Harp." He spoke with breezy authority. "This baby is a Boeing BBJ, a business class luxury plane. It's the only jet large enough to have individual cabins for passengers. We could fly around the world and never have to refuel until we got home."

"Really?" Harper said, her eyes wide.

"The only reason we even were on the ground for twenty minutes is so they could get flight clearance."

"And so that self-important attorney could get us to sign the contracts," Harper added.

"Next stop, Kinshasa!" Dr. Housdorf announced, his voice a carrying a combination of awe and uncertainty.

Harper's feelings echoed Housdorf's tone. No matter what happened next—a wonderful adventure or terrible danger, great benefit for humankind or a tragic failure—her old life was over.

CHAPTER 10

Once the corporate jet reached cruising altitude the intercom clicked on. The captain's voice filled the passenger cabins. "Between here and Kinshasa, Mr. Murano will brief each one of you on your supplies. Our copilot, a native Congolese, will make you aware of the current state of the Democratic Republic of Congo, physically, economically, and politically. We have about nine hours to Kinshasa. Make every moment count to prepare yourselves."

Harper caught up with Ursula in the galley.

"What is it, my dear?" Ursula inquired as she opened a container of warm French hollandaise.

"Well, I really don't know how to say this …."

"Then perhaps you should just come out with it," Ursula said with a kind smile.

"Well … I … I didn't put my contract back into that envelope."

"You what?" Now Ursula looked surprised and impressed.

"I stuffed a magazine in there instead. See, if my mother were ever to lay her hands on that contract, she'd figure out a way to take all the money. I'd never be able to use the funds for my doctoral degree. By the time I got home, she would have spent it all. I guarantee it."

Harper looked at the dark carpet of the cabin floor.

"Why would you let your mother do that to you, darling?" Ursula busied herself preparing the meal, not looking at Harper.

"She's irresponsible and incapable of taking care of herself. And I'm all she has."

Ursula stopped drizzling hollandaise sauce onto steamed asparagus to address Harper directly. "In what way may I help you, Miss Harp?"

"Will you please take the contract? Put it in a safe place. I'll retrieve it from you when we return." She pulled out the contract from under her blouse and handed it to Ursula.

"I will take good care of it. Do you wish me to contact your mother and let her know that you are OK? I have a daughter, and would be horrified if I could not locate her."

Harper looked out the tiny window of the galley into the endless blue horizon. "For once, I would like her to miss me for some other reason than what I can do for her ...." She stared at the perfect white clouds, then said firmly, "No, this is my time. I do not wish to share it with her."

Ursula looked her in the eye. "As you wish, Miss Harp."

Back in the passenger compartment, Dave was on one knee opening his backpack and displaying its contents. "Your backpacks have been ergonomically constructed to fit your body," he said. "You have each been equipped with state-of-the-art supplies, including water-resistant bedding and custom outer gear, cooking and eating utensils. Of course, each of you has also been outfitted with the equipment and supplies for your particular function on this mission."

Harper buckled herself back in her seat as Dave continued, "Mr. Logan and I will be supplied with substantial weapons, while each one of you will have a Leatherman knife and tool utensil, a small dart gun with a tranquilizer, and a GPS locator. I strongly suggest you retain the locator on your person at all times. Your guide, Hermann, Mr. Logan, and I will carry the tents. There will be three two-person tents, one for the women and the other two will be shared by the men."

"Excuse me, Sargeant," Claire interrupted. "That is only six. Where will our seventh team member sleep?"

Harper loved Claire's very proper and direct accent. Harper pegged her dialect as north London, Knightsbridge perhaps.

"He won't. There will always be one man on watch. That man will be armed during that period."

"What exactly are we watching for, Mr. Murano?" Chris Housdorf looked concerned.

"What do you think?" Lembowsky grumbled with disdain. "Peter Pan? Fairies? Wild animals, of course! We are going to be deep in the African jungle."

"Well, Mr. Lembowsky, wild animals will probably be the least of our threats," Dave said with great calm. "They are shy and tend to retreat from humans unless provoked. As you will soon discover, the most dangerous jungle inhabitants are human."

Chris couldn't help giving a little smile as Lembowsky slumped in his seat, temporarily defeated.

"The natives may be superstitious and may have never seen a white man—or woman—before," Dave said. "Keep in mind, folks, we are going into uncharted territory and have no data on the indigenous peoples in this particular area."

"Oh, I'm not afraid of some jungle bunnies with blow darts." Sid smirked. His teammates cringed.

"We should not have any trouble with the locals as long as we stay clear of their tribal villages. The real danger is the Mayi-Mayi," Dave said.

Harper shuddered. She knew from reports on National Public Radio that the two battling factions in the Congo used rape and torture to control the distribution of the plundered resources of the country. If a woman were lucky enough to make it out alive and to a healthcare facility, she was disfigured and mutilated from the inside out.

"We're not going to meet any of those guys, are we?" Harper asked shyly as she and Claire instinctively moved closer to each other.

Dave put a reassuring hand on her shoulder. "We certainly hope not, Miss Smith. However, as a precaution, both Mr. Logan's and my weapons have silencers on them. We must move as stealthily through the brush as possible. Mr. Logan will use his crossbow for hunting and we will keep conversation to a minimum."

So far, no one on the team had met the mysterious Mr. Logan. For all Harper knew, he could be a ruthless and unscrupulous mercenary. Dave was a different story. She felt she could trust him to protect Claire and her.

She told herself they were fully armed and sufficiently supplied for the few days they would be in the very densest areas of the jungle. They would be in contact with Pharmco and airlifted out of danger at any time. "We'll be fine," she repeated silently like a mantra.

"Oh, there's one more thing," Dave said, winding up his presentation. "The Congo has the largest population of chimpanzees on the planet. They are cute and fun to watch, but they are also pranksters and can exhibit gang behavior. Best to avoid them and stay close to your equipment."

Ursula served coffee, telling the team the copilot would brief them on the present situation in the Congo when they reached smooth skies over the Sahara. "Please take this time to familiarize yourselves with your individual provisions," she suggested.

"Good idea," Lembowsky said. "Now I can finally find out whether Vanderfuck made good on his promise to provide a state-of-the-art GPS. I'll believe it when I see it."

Meanwhile, Chris Housdorf, crowed like a child on Christmas morning over the field lab equipment in his pack.

"Indeed, look at this!" Claire held a Bible-sized box with a girlish gleam in her eyes. "With one drop of your blood, I can diagnose over 1100 different conditions in minutes." She pulled out another container labeled First Aid, opening it to find an extensive array of syringes, pills and vials, clearly labeled with the names of the maladies for which they were intended.

Harper couldn't imagine finding any special treasure in her pack. The only tools she needed were the mental amalgam of her life's work, the notes from Dr. Merrill and her pluckiness. In the side pocket, she found a book titled Field Guide to Sub-Saharan Jungle Botanical Species. "Full color photos and everything!" she said, trying to sound upbeat but feeling a little ill-equipped.

"Where are the rations?" Lembowsky asked. Everyone looked at Dave.

"You will find energy bars wrapped tightly inside your pack, away from the sides to not attract any insolent noses. Mr. Logan and I will trap or hunt most of our meals and I feel sure Miss Harper can supplement our diet with edible plants."

Harper thought of a piece she'd heard on NPR about a turn of the 20th century Brazilian explorer. Fossett was his name. He and his team died of disease and starvation in the jungle.

Starvation in the jungle? Once again, Harper felt the weight of her role in this mission bearing down on her.

CHAPTER 11

The copilot entered the cabin and spoke to the team in a serious tone. "The Democratic Republic of Congo is a very volatile place.

"The land is large, approximately the size of Western Europe. It is the third largest country in Africa and hosts both the huge Congo River and a large chunk of the equator. There are 64 million people in the DRC with the average per capita income of about $900 US per year.

"The country has vast resources including coltan, cobalt, copper, cadmium, petroleum, cassiterite, industrial and gem diamonds, gold, silver, zinc, manganese, tin, germanium, uranium, bauxite, iron ore, and coal." He spoke with obvious pride. "The eleven provinces were recently changed to twenty-six territories in 2006 and the government is in a constant state of disarray.

"The only thing that doesn't change is the corruption. The Rwandan and Ugandan military is in collusion with the Congolese government and military and supplied with the money and munitions from other interested countries, which is all of them. It is a lawless, brutal, primitive male country where the Mayi-Mayi have their own rules and are accountable to no one.

"They sell the vast resources to the highest bidder and extort from their own people. Since 1999, three million Congolese have died, either through murder, disease or malnutrition, most of them women, children and the elderly. There are over 250 different languages and cultures in the DRC, and many of them war against each other out of desperation.

"The people are starving and denied healthcare. Fathers are forced to sell their daughters to survive." The Congolese copilot's voice saddened. "When you look into the eyes of the soldiers, you will find only emptiness." He placed his forehead in his hand. "They do unspeakable things to people."

The copilot looked down and tears began to well in his eyes. "They have lost their souls."

Dave stepped in to fill the awkward silence. "Thus the need to be completely inconspicuous. The violence is the worst in the eastern area of the country. We will be near the center, far from cities or military areas. We will be flown directly to the landing area closest to our target. There is no infrastructure within a hundred miles of this area, so there will be no roads for the military or Mayi to approach us. The minute Dr. Housdorf has verified the proper species Miss Smith identifies, Mr. Lembowsky will contact the Pharmco chopper and we will be airlifted out in a matter of hours." He smiled at Harper and Claire.

The copilot regained his composure and addressed the women. "Do not stray from your team. You must be very careful and keep your woman gods close to you." He leaned close to them and whispered. "You cannot imagine what they will do to you if you are captured."

"Now, now, enough of that," Dave said. "Everything is going to be fine. Don't worry Monsieur; we will take very good care of these fine ladies. I would sacrifice my life for their safety." He gave each of them a fatherly hug.

"Much luck on your journey. Your mission must override your fear. May God be with you." The copilot bowed slightly and ducked back inside the cockpit.

The mood in the passenger compartment was solemn. Dr. Housdorf fingered his mobile lab during the entire presentation, never raising his gaze. Without warning, he stood up and addressed the group. "We cannot change the morality and politics, or lack thereof, in the DRC. We can, however, be successful in our quest and contribute perhaps one of the greatest gifts mankind can receive in this millennia. I say we give it all we've got."

He looked eye-to-eye at Dave, Harper, Claire and Sid. "What do you say? Are we ready?"

Each team member's lower lip tightened in resolve as heads nodded in agreement. "We're ready," they said in unison.

"Nicely done, ladies and gentlemen," Ursula said. "Now I must shoo you off to sleep, everyone to quarters. This will be your last undisturbed rest for some time. I suggest you make the best of it." Ursula put her hand under Dr. Housdorf's elbow to urge him along. "You have six hours until we land in Kinshasa. Sleep well."

As the team members silently withdrew to their respective cabins, engrossed in their thoughts and trepidations, Ursula escorted Harper to her cabin.

"Ursula, do you think we'll really be all right?" Harper suddenly felt vulnerable. "I have many plans for my life and I hope to finally find some things for myself."

"Harper Morgan Smith, you have been preparing yourself for this journey your whole life." Ursula patted the bed, urging her to sit, and seated herself beside Harper. "You have strength from within that will show itself when the situation demands it." The flight attendant took Harper's hand and looked the girl directly in the eye as she fished something from her pocket. "I want to give you this."

She placed the object in Harper's hand and closed it. "My husband gave me this before he died. He said it would show me light whenever I needed to see it."

Harper opened her hand to see a well-worn brass lighter. "This is so special. I can't take this! What if I lose it?"

"It will help you see." Ursula smiled and embraced Harper. "And don't lose it! A very good friend of mine told me a long time ago, before his life was tragically taken, that life happens while you are busy making plans." Ursula exposed an intimate moment without hesitation. "Goodnight, Miss Harp."

"Goodnight Ursula—and thank you."

PART II

CHAPTER 12

The overstuffed envelope looked small in Jones' huge, black hand as he handed it to the uniformed man carrying the AK-47.

Monte Jones was a very large man, in every way. His stature was almost as big as his personality and both paled in comparison to his broad, white-toothed grin.

"Dis take care of it mon, you be havin' good time tonight, eh?" Monte said as he gave the man a vigorous slap on the back. The man almost choked on his cigarette. The soldier smiled a sparsely toothed grin, took the envelope and stuffed it in his shirt. He jumped back in his Jeep and instructed his driver in Swahili.

Monte's smile faded as he watched them leave the tarmac. The Boeing BBJ had landed in a private area of the Kinshasa airport, away from the commercial airlines. His gaze was directed to the vision standing at the top of the flight stairs. "There you are, my beautiful Nubian princess! Ursula, you know you are the burning desire of my loins." Monte spoke in his normal decibel level, easily overriding the noise of the jet. "I continue to wait for your soft kiss upon my cheek at our wedding." His boyish smile lit up the pavement.

"You are a shameless flatterer, Monte." Ursula smiled. "You know my heart has been held by another in limbo for years now," her voice was almost inaudible, but Harper caught it.

Refreshed from a few anxious but restful hours of sleep, the team gathered their packs. Harper, Claire, Sid, Chris, and Dave cautiously disembarked. Two camouflaged Mercedes Jeeps awaited their arrival, parked haphazardly on the tarmac.

"Come, my children, I will take you on the ride of your lives!" The big man spoke in a deep baritone voice that seemed to reverberate in surround sound. He laughed loudly. "My name is Monte Jones. My drivers and I will take you as far as the road goes into the interior. There are few roads past Kananga and no infrastructure in the heart. The condition of our ground route is impossible to know until we get there. I am afraid you are stuck with me until we find a spot for Captain Gauld to pick you up in the chopper."

The Boeing's engines reduced their audio assault to a minimum. The heat and humidity oppressed the team like heavy yokes as they descended the stairs and assembled into the collective engrossment of Monte. The surroundings seemed like the lost world in The Time Machine, both modern and primitive at the same time. Harper wondered what the hell she was doing there.

The lady doctor asked, "Monte, is it? If we are in such a hurry, why aren't we going to take the helicopter into the interior directly?"

Jones bit his lower lip, visibly ingesting the form of the small and sturdy, yet very curvaceous, Dr. Guthrie. An intoxicated smile crept across his face.

"I do believe you may steal my heart away from the goddess Ursula, Dr. Guthrie," he sighed with a flirtatious smile. "That is a very astute question."

The group moved in closer for the answer.

"While we are in the west, it is imperative we stay out of sight. There are others who wish to capture our prize and many more whose only desire is to confiscate our resources or hold you for ransom. A chopper would be sighted and questions asked. We must move on the back roads under the radar, so to speak. It may surprise you, but we do have access to technology here in the west, Dr. Guthrie. It would not serve us to tempt those capabilities. When we get closer to the interior, there is a complete void of any technology, barring Mr. Lembowsky's GPS, of course," he gave a smile to Sid, which was obviously appreciated. "And a chopper will be safe, barring any uncertain weather. It will be our, I mean my, sole discretion on the location of heli pick up." Monte winked at Sergeant Murano. "Captain Gauld will decide where he will drop you. Since most of the area is completely unmapped and areas are cleared and grown over in a matter of weeks, there is no way to tell until we get there, wherever 'there' may be."

"I demand you give us a little more concrete information about our game plan, Mr. Jones. I do not care to …." Lembowsky puffed up again.

Monte could see eyes rolling throughout the group. "I do not care, Mr. Lembowsky." Monte stood directly in front of Sid, magnifying their differences in size to comical proportions. "I care that we leave this tarmac before other sweaty palms wish to be rubbed. Please put yourselves and your gear in the back."

The small group, dressed in travel gear, tossed their packs into the backs of the two Jeeps. "We would have liked a single, larger covered vehicle, but I am afraid a troop transport that big would not make it through the brush. Sergeant Murano, Dr. Housdorf and the lovely Dr. Guthrie, you will travel with me tonight. Ms. Smith, you and Lembowsky will travel with Keenu. Please make sure you have everything. Salongo, alinga mosala!" Mr. Jones heartily bellowed.

Harper approached Ursula, standing square-shouldered at the base of the flight stairs. "I can't believe this is goodbye, Ursula. The last two days have seemed like a lifetime, time I have had the honor and privilege to share with you. Thank you for all you have done for me ... and the rest of the team, of course."

"It has also been a privilege for me, Miss Harp. I will treasure our moments as well as what you have entrusted to me. You will be in my prayers as well as my heart." Ursula looked at Harper eye-to-eye and hugged her endearingly. "You will be just fine, Miss Harper. You will find it."

"I will?"

"Yes, all of it."

Ursula pulled away and ascended the stairs. Harper stepped up into the Jeep next to Sid and looked over to Ursula as the flight crew prepared to close the cabin door.

Ursula stood and waved with a smile. The engine of the BBJ Jet revved up for departure as the team buckled into their assigned seats in the Jeeps. Harper felt a shudder of terror, like she might never again feel a connection with civilization or another human being. The feeling was oddly familiar.

They headed off the tarmac directly toward the surrounding jungle and were immediately engulfed in deep brush on a hidden road, which seemed unusual as the Congolese capital of Kinshasa and its immediate neighbor Brazzaville housed almost nine million people. Once they entered the sequestered path, it was not only like the past was behind them, it seemed like the portal had closed. The thick foliage and heaviness of the atmosphere immediately engulfed the Jeeps and their passengers in a shroud of primitive existence.

Here we go, Harper said to herself.

CHAPTER 13

As disagreeable as Sid Lembowsky could be, Harper was glad she'd been paired with him for the first leg of the trip, for it gave her plenty of solitude to think things over. As she came to terms with the string of events leading to her current extraordinary situation, she became enchanted by the tropical forest.

In California there were myriad plant habitats, many with adjunctive micro-climates within meters of each other: both low and high desert, multiple kinds of forest, extreme coastal and severe inland climates. If it existed, California had it. She had surfed and skied on the same day more than once.

This close to the equator, the environment was so entirely different, Harper felt she might as well have set foot on another planet. Leaves were huge, the largest she'd ever seen. Root structures she would expect to see below ground sprawled on the surface; species that were normally shrubs grew in a wild tangle of vines. Everything was larger than life, vibrant, exotic, filled with a thousand delights for the botanist.

The Jeeps bounced on a hard dirt road, a bumpy journey but bursting with so many new sights, sounds and smells, Harper didn't care. They passed a few crossroads and could see settlements and villages through the brush. Harper was mesmerized by the motion as darkness fell. She never felt so much at home, in her own element, as when surrounded by plant life. Here, she felt embraced by the lush green foliage, lulling her into a comfortable space which felt soothing after so much turmoil in her personal life. As she immersed herself in the comfort and beauty of her surroundings, she couldn't help hearing her father's voice:

The deciding factors of a tree's branching structure are both numerous and mysterious. Sunlight availability, the growth hormone and communicator auxin, as well as nutrients, genes, and sheer physics dictate branching geometry. Mathematics play a huge role in branching in that many species use the Golden Ratio and the

Fibonacci numbers to form branching structures, especially in the whorl forms.

Without the proper branching design, continuously adjusting to physical and environmental challenges, the tree not only cannot compete for sunlight but will topple in the forest. An overabundance of foliage on one side will eventually succumb to gravity.

When you grow up, Harper, you must branch out in many directions in order to achieve balance in your life. Any branch too heavy in one direction will bring you down. If you do not branch at all, you will not receive the necessary nutrients to flourish.

I know it is sometimes petrifying because you will most certainly fail. Humans unfortunately do not have the brilliant auxin as a guide. Well, in actuality we do; it is called a brain. However, humans have the misfortune of desires and ego which will perpetually cloud our branching strategies.

If you do not branch, and branch well, you will sit on the forest floor and be stunted, never showing the true beauty of a perfectly balanced person. It takes much work, Sapling, constantly stretching away from the known.

But you must.

Another jolt on a rut in the road brought Harper back to the present, her senses again engaged by the jungle surrounding her. Although not entirely knowledgeable of the indigenous species, she tried to familiarize herself with the locals. The foliage, botanical growth habits, and plant communities would be her new playground. She was stepping into her own world of botany, making friends with her cohorts.

She began to smile. Now she knew why she came. This mission was for her and her alone. Sid sat next to her, engrossed in his iPod. The driver lit a cigarette, blowing a plume of sulfur and tobacco into her face. The stench momentarily transported her back into the human world.

"Excuse me, sir," she said to the driver.

Keenu turned his head and exhaled more smoke.

"Where is our guide?" She yelled over the sound of the motor, magnified under the foliage canopy. "Where's Hermann?"

The driver responded by silently leering at Harper's chest. The Jeep hit another large pothole and Lembowsky was startled into consciousness.

"Keep your eyes on the road, asshole!" he roared.

Exactly what I wanted to say, Harper thought with grim satisfaction, deciding that Sid Lembowsky might prove a useful traveling companion after all.

As twilight deepened, Harper saw only the red tail lights of her companions' Jeep and the black jungle on both sides of her. Occasionally, she spied a small creature scurrying across the road in the headlights. The noxious diesel fumes wafting back from the other Jeep started to give her a headache and she wondered how much longer they would drive without a break. The journey felt more like an endurance marathon than a scientific expedition.

Just as she was resigning herself to endless discomfort, Monte laughed loudly and spoke the most beautiful words she'd heard in hours: "We have arrived, my children. It is time to rest!"

"It's about time!" Lembowsky peered over his glasses at the campsite and turned to Harper. "Want to bet this will turn out be a fucking nightmare?"

The Jeeps turned in to a circular area centered by a large bonfire and surrounded by small buildings part concrete, part thatch. The area was surrounded by heavy brush.

Men came out of the huts with guns raised.

"Mistah Jones, we have been waiting for you, bruddah! What fine things have you brought?" A large man clad in a tattered plaid shirt and sporting a large rifle approached the front Jeep, eyeing Dr. Guthrie.

"No, bruddah, the women are mine. I have dis for you boys!" Monte pulled out a large burlap sack from behind the seat. The man snatched it eagerly as the Jeeps finally stopped moving.

Harper climbed out, muscles stiff after sitting cramped for so long. She tottered to Dr. Guthrie. "Everything all right, Claire?"

Claire arched her back. "Jolly good, Harp, and you?"

"Jolly good!" The women laughed. Several of the local men looked at them and whispered to each other. Harper and Claire instinctively moved toward Monte and stood directly behind him.

The huge black man laughed, "Don't be bein' afraid, my darlings. Big Monte will take care of you!"

Monte showed the team members their respective huts. Harper and Claire were shocked to discover they were expected to bunk with Monte.

"Monte, you seem like a respectable gentleman, but this does not seem to be entirely appropriate," Claire said with her typical British reserve. "I am sure Miss Harper and I would prefer to have our own hut."

He responded with his characteristic hearty laugh. "Dr. Guthrie, if it does not appear you are with me, it may seem to others you are available for the taking. I do not think that would be wise, my beauty."

"Indeed." Seeing the wisdom of his words, she ducked into the big man's hut. Harper followed.

As tired as Harper was, sleep would not come. She lay awake and listened to the local men as they talked in their native language. She heard some Bantu roots and picked out some words. She knew there were hundreds of languages and dialects spoken in Africa. Some had French roots; those she could handle, but most of the tribal languages were of Bantu origin. She wondered why Vandervere hadn't supplied her with even the Berlitz tourist version of a Bantu dictionary.

A rooster crowing awakened the team after a few hours of sleep.

"Come my lovelies, it is time we go." Monte dressed in the dark and left the women's hut.

"Not exactly the Nairobi Hilton, is it?" Harper remarked to Claire as she threw on her khakis and twisted her strawberry hair into a knot.

"Ursula did try to warn us, didn't she?" Claire returned the laugh. Then her voice turned serious. "Today, I imagine we will get farther and farther from humanity. Another world awaits us."

"Well, Dr. Guthrie, in the immortal words of Sid Lembowsky, fucking bring it on!"

CHAPTER 14

Near the site of last night's bonfire, a man stood closely talking with Dave Murano and Monte. Harper surmised he was Hermann, the guide. When had he come? Surely not in the middle of the night—wouldn't that be too dangerous? Harper decided it didn't matter, she was just glad an expert on the local scene was joining the expedition.

Monte made introductions. Hermann clicked his heels together and took both the women's hands and touched them to his lips. Something made Harper pull her hand away. She immediately felt embarrassed.

Hermann laughed. "I will not hurt you, sparrow. We are on the same team."

Monte Jones picked up on the discomfort and intervened. "I will take the women with me today; it is important they be acquainted with the terrain. Miss Harper will be doing research and development on the local plant communities."

A tiny sliver of sun pierced the dense forest canopy, signaling sunrise. The day promised to be full of surprises. Faces gleamed with anticipation as the team piled into the Jeeps. The adventure had truly begun.

They spotted birds, lizards, an occasional okapi, and heard the intermittent echo of boisterous primates in the trees. The thick covering of trees and vines made it difficult to keep track of the passing time, and the stifling heat and humid atmosphere were claustrophobic.

Harper and her teammates felt euphoric, anxious and disoriented. She wished to look closer at the flowers, root structures or seed pods for positive identifications of the many unusual plants, but the rough ride made it impossible. But Harper knew this plant community. Thick, gnarly roots were exposed to both air and water and still the ancient trees thrived, embracing small gullies and cradling shallow rivers. The creatures inhabiting the creeks declared their territory with subtle splashing sounds.

The whine of the engines and the intermittent animal sounds lulled Harper into a sublime dreamlike state.

Harper was thrust back into the human world when someone sharply slapped her. She reeled and lifted her hand to her temple. "What the hell was that for?"

"Oh God, I am so sorry, Harp! A mosquito the size of a bus was biting your head!" Claire blushed at her over-reaction to the large insect.

"Jesus, did you have to hit me so hard?" Harper crinkled her nose. "My brains almost came out of my ear!"

Claire held up the palm of her hand, displaying bright red blood. "This is not good. Did you put on your mosquito repellent this morning?" The usually kindly doctor looked stern.

"Oh shit, I forgot. I was so engrossed in the plant materials I wasn't paying attention." Harper reached into her pack and dug for the repellent.

Dr. Guthrie's voice continued to scold. "Harp, I can treat malaria most of the time, even though some of the recent strains are immune to our standard treatments. However, I cannot stop dengue fever. If you become infected, it will seriously debilitate this mission."

Harper thought Dr. Guthrie was making too big of a deal out of one little insect. She looked at the doctor. "Claire, why are you here?"

Claire took Harper's hand. Gone was the brusque, business-like tone. In a whispered voice shaking with emotion, she said, "My son. My son was in a hospital in Rwanda with schistomiasis. He was in the Peace Corps, an endeavor I regret pushing him toward. While he was under their care, he was mistakenly transfused with HIV positive blood. I couldn't save him. He died six months ago."

"Oh, Claire, I am so sorry. Please forgive me for prying. I could see something in your face although I didn't know what it was. I am so sorry." Harper put her other hand over the doctor's.

Claire's eyes welled with tears. "I should have dropped everything and rushed to him. Rwanda is somewhat civilized these days; I have heard it is a rather large eco-tourist attraction. I really thought such a routine case was, well, routine. I was very selfish. I will never forgive myself."

"Oh, Claire, destiny wields her own fates. He was very fortunate to have you as his mother. I am sure he is in a better place." Harper immediately regretted uttering such a trite cliché.

The next two hours were spent in silence, the passengers engulfed in their own thoughts. Monte finally raised his hand and both Jeeps pulled off the ill-defined dirt road to a small beach by a shallow stream.

Harper had not eaten since the previous night's unidentifiable meat product and plantains. A small piece of blue was visible through the profusion of green fronds overhead, the angle of light indicating mid-morning.

The men stepped off the Jeep and immediately relieved themselves against the nearest tree trunks. Harper and Claire exchanged glances, wishing it were just as easy for them.

Both hands occupied, Monte laughed. "Ladies, please be careful if you retire into the brush. There are many things in the jungle more intimidating than these men."

Harper looked at Hermann and Sid, considering the situation. "I doubt it, sir." She reached up and grabbed a large, smooth *strelizia nicolai* leaf and tore it in half. "Come on, Dr. Guthrie, let's go."

Monte supplied the team with rations from a cooler in the back of his Jeep. Harper recognized the foliage in front of her and reached through the branches to pick the orange fleshy fruit. They had not seen anything but the occasional hut for hours. Harper performed the mental cartographical math for a visual on their approximate location. Her curiosity got the better of her judgment and she asked Lembowsky for assistance.

Sid leaned against a rock with his head bent over the equipment on his lap. "Mr. Lembowsky, have you become familiar with that cool GPS thingy yet?" She surprised herself by sincerely being interested in his response. After all, she told herself, he was here to do a job, just like the rest of the team.

"What do you think, chickie? This is what I do." With that snide response, her temporary empathy evaporated.

"I was only asking if everything was functioning to your expectations, Mr. Lembowsky."

"Hey, Miss Harper Morgan Smith, as if you needed so many names, I am pretty sure I've got it under control." Lembowsky's voice continued to drip with sarcasm. "We are right where we are supposed to be. Hey, look up Merrill's notes for the coordinates again. I need to correlate your information with mine."

"Great, Sid, thank you for being so thorough. We certainly all need to be on the same page for this mission to succeed." She favored him with a smile, since the entire team was listening to their conversation.

Monte Jones lit a Durban cigar as a charming grin came over his face. "I see we are all on track, my friends. Miss Harp is indeed correct that you must work as a team in order to reach your goal. In the jungle, each one of you will be a hero at times, so you must each act as a hero at all times, since you just don't know which time will be yours." Monte looked at each member of the team before spitting a cigar tip into the brush.

The next minutes were spent in silent chewing and swallowing, the wordless noises of hungry people devouring a long-awaited meal. They sustained themselves on Monte's provisions, saving the rations in their packs for their journey on foot.

"Monte," Dr. Guthrie said after finishing a piece of dried fish, "about that captain in the helicopter …."

"Captain Gauld?"

"Yes. When will he come to pick us up? I'm concerned about time. We don't seem to be making much progress."

Monte took Claire's chin in his hand. "Time is the only thing we really have, Madame Claire." He reached down from where his large body reclined on the small river bank and grabbed a handful of sand, lifting it up chest-high before her. "Every minute is a gift we must treasure like a precious jewel, for that moment will never be retrieved."

He carelessly let the sand sift through one hand into the other and placed the remaining granules into Claire's open palm. "It is much better to have the love of life as it is rather than life as you want it to be. Your precious memories are the essence of who you are. Celebrate the moments, with or without the persons you have lost. Those moments are your real treasure."

Claire's large brandy-tinted eyes brimmed with gratitude. She looked away, pretending to be examining her medical equipment.

Dr. Housdorf dabbed sweat off his neck with a clean handkerchief and approached Monte. "When do you anticipate being summoned by Captain Gauld?"

"I hope we will be on the other side of Kananga in the early morning. This will give us one more night to prepare and review the equipment. Have you familiarized yourself with the field lab?"

"Absolutely. I am confident with the equipment and my ability to analyze the data. I just wish I had a substance with a known chemical footprint. A control, as it were."

"Keenu, Salongo, alinga mosala!" Monte stood up and grabbed a hand-rolled cigarette from Keenu's top pocket. "I am sure you are familiar with the chemical compound THC, Dr. Housdorf?" Monte held the sample in his outstretched hand and grinned.

"From a laboratory standpoint only, of course. Every college chemistry major knows the tetrahydrocannabinol compound. I did not realize that was so readily available in Africa."

Chris took the sample and began to run data analysis with his field lab.

"Cannabis is a very big crop in Africa, Dr. Housdorf. However, almost none is exported." Monte reached for the newly lit joint hanging from Keenu's lip. "I am afraid we Africans have a very big appetite for small pleasures." He took a large puff.

Harper felt oppressed by the weight of the heat and humidity. She peeled off her safari couture, enjoying the cool comfort of exposed skin clad only in thin t-shirt and cropped khaki pants, and started to head for the creek. "We Africans, Monte? I thought I heard a slightly Middle Eastern accent, Saudi perhaps?" She smiled at him as she put her toe in the creek water to test the temperature.

"Well done, Miss Smith. You are a clever girl, aren't you? Yes, as a teenager, I came from the Yemen Peninsula through Ethiopia. My parents were missionaries from the Sudan, exiled into Saudi by the militia. My small amount of schooling was Arabian, although my academic advancement was taken from various, shall we say, nefarious locations."

"Missionaries, Monte? Are you a follower of the way of the cloth as well? It seems your 'nefarious' education is extensive, judging by your obvious vocabulary skills and field intelligence," Dr. Guthrie asked with interest.

"My lovely Dr. Guthrie, I have not believed in the church since I saw my parents beheaded with a machete." He began to clean his fingernails with his bayonet.

Claire gasped and fumbled with her backpack.

Harper looked upstream and spotted a small pool only a few meters distant. It almost called her name, promising cool relief from the heat and humidity. She crashed through the jungle in its direction.

"I would not travel too far, Miss Smith," Hermann looked up from his papers and flicked a large green beetle off his shoulder. "There are beasties in the jungle."

"Yeah, yeah, whatever."

Harper knew better than to remove her shoes and was prepared to suffer the rest of the day in squishy footwear as she waded into the knee-deep pool. It wasn't as icy as she'd hoped, but the lukewarm water still felt divine. Harper bent over to dip her head and dampen her hair. She felt something tugging on her exposed calf. It startled her, but she did not want to cry out like a frightened child in front of her teammates. She muffled a scream with her hand.

She pulled at the creature on her leg, but it was surprisingly difficult to remove. A sudden unusual noise caused her to stop and listen. Was that really metal being unsheathed?

In a split second, she turned to see a huge green snake hanging from a tree, its eyes glaring directly at her. The snake's head was the size of a football and the body the girth of the business end of a baseball bat.

In the next millisecond, she spotted another pair of eyes in the foliage staring at her and the snake. This second pair of eyes belonged to a strange man preparing to slice off the snake's head with a machete.

Harper shot up from the water. Her wet hair, now unbound, floated freely around her face. She instinctively crossed her arms to keep the stranger from seeing her nipples under the wet t-shirt.

"Who are you? Show yourself." She was proud that she spoke with authority, hiding the terror she felt inside.

The man said nothing, just pulled aside a large *Musa* leaf and stepped onto the creek bank.

Harper's pounding heartbeat returned to normal as she recognized the face from the video on the Pharmco corporate jet. "So, Mr. Logan, are you in the habit of spying on bathing women?"

"Hardly, Miss Smith. Are you in the habit of putting yourself and your team in danger? That python would have been wrapped around your pretty little neck if I hadn't come along."

He raised the machete. "Ever eaten snake meat? Tastes just like chicken."

"You cannot kill it. What if it's an endangered species?"

He crouched, readying himself to strike the fatal blow on the snake.

Without hesitation, Harper leaped, flinging herself against the chest of the blue-eyed man. The pair fell to the ground as the man's back slammed against the soft leaf litter. Harper's chest heaved against his while her wet hair and t-shirt dripped on his torso. They were eye to eye, nose to nose, exchanging breaths in momentary silence.

"You should not be out here alone, Miss Smith," Logan said softly.

"I can take care of myself." She held his gaze, focused on her. Was the jungle playing tricks on her, or did she really feel an electric current sizzle between them?

"Miss Smith, I am afraid I must insist." His attention shifted from Harper to the jungle above and behind her head. "A bush python's bite will paralyze a forest elephant in a matter of seconds." His eyes remained fixed on the same spot. "I would hate to think of what that large reptile might do to a small creature like you. By the way, I would not make any sudden moves if I were you. She is ready to strike the back of your neck."

"Well, then, I suppose we should do something about it, Mr. Logan." Her hands held his wrists, effectively pinning him to the ground.

His eyes left the snake and returned to her. She smiled at him warmly while moving her left hand to the hilt of the machete, grasping it firmly. She immediately threw her right hand over the base and in one instant leaped up and around. With one neat whack, she severed the head of the predator dangling behind her back. Its huge green head landed in the water with a large splash while the enormous body slipped off the bough onto a rock.

Harper smoothed her hair, rubbed the red sucker mark on her calf left by the long-forgotten leech and headed back to where the rest of the team gathered their gear for departure.

"Mike Logan! Great to see you, mon!" Monte said with his typical heartiness. "I see you have met Miss Smith."

Suddenly Harper felt awkward, as if everyone were staring at her wet t-shirt. She grabbed her over-shirt where she'd left it on a rock and turned her back to the group to button it. Monte introduced the group to Mike Logan.

"I have worked with Mr. Logan before and I assure you that you are in very good hands." Monte's cigar hung out of the side of his mouth. Harper wondered how he could smoke, talk and smile all at the same time.

The team shook Mike's hand as Dave Murano admired the new team member's handmade crossbow. When Monte got around to formally introducing Mr. Logan to Harper, they both sheepishly touched hands, then turned away from each other.

"Now, now, children, let's not be shy. It is past time to continue our journey. The sooner we reach the approximate coordinates I have supplied to Mr. Lembowsky, the more rest you will have tonight. Mr. Logan, please join us in the front Jeep so I may get you up to speed. Salongo, alinga mosala!"

The crew tossed their gear into the Jeeps and took off. The trails were getting rougher and they encountered few crossroads and villages. As civilization dwindled and all but disappeared, the animals became larger and more abundant. The jungle canopy grew more dense, revealing only occasional glimpses of sky.

This is it, Harper thought. *This really is the heart of the jungle.*

CHAPTER 15

H arper's thoughts bounced around in her head, keeping time with the incessant jolting of the Jeep. She wondered about Ursula and the person who held her heart "in limbo." Analyzing her feelings for Mr. Logan gave her a headache. To distract herself from that perplexing topic, she studied Dr. Merrill's notes again for a mental visual on the mysterious plant's native habitat.

The Jeeps continued to climb, the humidity decreasing as the elevation increased. The foliage was larger and the plant communities evolved from lowland forest to equatorial rain forest. She reflected that plant communities were a commonly overlooked topic in many horticultural study programs. Fortunately, Harper thought to herself, Dr. Merrill was adamant that every student grasped the importance of identifying the individual communities.

Harper pictured the dynamic Dr. Merrill leading his class. When he lectured in the areas of his passion, no professor was more riveting or intellectually stimulating. She was inspired by his presentations, enthralled by the purity of his intent:

Plant communities and their health are the crucial elements of natural survival. Take the plight of the commercially produced strawberry. Driscoll Inc. has, as we speak, 180,000 acres of strawberry fields grown with one and only one variety of fragaria. This is called monoculture: Note: this will be on the midterm.

The result in the case of predators, including fungus, insects, virus, and bacteria, is that when any plant in the group gets infected, the rest of the population is not only susceptible, but likely to succumb. The grower has to overdose the fields with methyl bromide to combat crop devastation.

The purpose for plant communities is that different varieties exhibit different growing habits, harbor beneficial predators, attract a variety of pollinators ... well, the list is endless. In the natural arena, speaking generally, one variety will house the insect or bacteria that will inhibit the pest of its neighbor. Another good neighbor may drop seed pods that can alter the local pH, stalling a bacterial infection.

Perhaps more importantly, each member of the plant community occupies a different niche. In a natural habitat, you have the arboreal members, the vining members, the low semi-herbaceous shrubs, the taller woody shrubs, the annuals, the perennials, etc. Each member inhabits its own area of expertise in order to thrive. It is imperative for the habitat that each position be filled and functioning.

Human communities are no different. If all the members of the community have the same function, who will harbor the beneficials? If we have all annuals, what will the pollinators and predators do during the dormant season without perennials? Nature is, by design, a place for all different types of inhabitants. If a habitat shuns one of its natives, the community is out of balance and will eventually expire.

I guarantee the concept of 'tolerance' was not ever an issue in a natural situation. If you fulfill your niche in your own community, you will thrive and be a crucial contribution to the whole.

Dr. Merrill made her think existentially. She believed in God, albeit it not the guy in the white robe. She believed in the miracle of creation. But, for her, Nature was the everyday embodiment of a supreme being.

The jungle absorbed Harper, ingesting her into its primordial being. She tried to meld what she already knew with what she suspected and, more importantly, what she needed to know. The picture began to take shape. Staying on task during her mission was challenging but amazingly engaging.

The Jeeps slogged on in the increasing darkness. Harper lost her sense of time and direction. Accustomed to estimating light for plants by foot-candles, her natural ability couldn't compete with the cloud cover, the dense forest canopy, and the growing twilight. Lembowsky constantly fiddled with the GPS equipment, making Harper feel slightly reassured. She had not heard a word from the guide Hermann except for his comment at the creek earlier that day. She wondered what qualified him for such an important mission.

A chaos of noise and movement erupted above them. Harper looked up to see a group of chimpanzees laughing hysterically at the humans' puny attempts to penetrate their natural habitat. The chimps became more vocal and raucous as they distracted the Jeeps to the side of the rough road. With a sudden movement, one of the chimps dipped from a low branch into the rear Jeep and grabbed Harper's backpack.

The primates screeched in hilarity as Harper scrambled after them. She stumbled as far into the jungle as she could without losing sight of the Jeeps. Logan and Murano called after her to come back. The chimps disappeared into the thick jungle as quickly as they'd arrived.

"But they got my pack!" she moaned, hanging her head as she trudged back to the Jeeps. "Oh my God, guys, I am so sorry. I let them get some of our rations. I can't believe my guard was so … well, off guard."

She must have sounded defeated and pathetic, because several of her teammates laughed out loud.

"TIA, my precious!" Monte chuckled in his usual wholehearted way. "This Is Africa. We are not the indigenous species here!"

"I hope you didn't lose anything imperative to our mission." Dr. Housdorf's tone of voice expressed genuine concern and compassion. Harper realized that even though Chris had referred to the mission, he was really asking if she was all right.

"I'm good, but I appreciate your concern." She gave him a warm smile. "Fortunately, Dr. Merrill's notes were tucked in the seat of the Jeep and not in my pack. The only things we really lost were the rations and my extra clothes."

"We are not concerned about extra clothes for you!" Sid hooted, causing snickers from some of the other men. Housdorf and Murano stayed silent, while Monte glared at his drivers when they joined in.

"You can always share my jungle couture with me," Claire said, "although our mutual wardrobe may get a little odiferous." Harper sent Claire a grateful look, not so much for the offer to share clothing, but for her gentle humor, which created a steadying and calming mood.

Dave addressed the group as the expedition continued. "We'll look for a suitable place to camp now. Monte says this will be our last night in the Jeeps and we need to seek out an appropriate location for the chopper to pick us up in the morning. He says there's a river plain ahead where the foliage has abated and the sand is not too soft for a landing."

"I daresay, Sergeant Murano, it will take a lot more than a couple of monkeys to distress us. After all, we did go into the jungle with you people." Claire was smiling slyly.

"Well, Dr. Guthrie, that you did!" Dave said. "I personally can't wait to get into the jungle on foot. Then will we be part of something from another time, something ancient."

Dave bent his head to whisper to the two women. "Frankly, I am not fond of Monte's drivers. They give me the creeps. I don't like the way they look at you girls."

"Quite. I completely agree," Claire replied. "However, I am enchanted with Monte. He seems the man of the hour."

Monte chose that moment to turn to her and smile sweetly. "We will be approaching a campsite soon, Dr. Guthrie. I would be honored to share my tent again tonight, Madame."

"You are very kind, Monte. I will treasure our last moments together." Claire returned his smile.

Watching this small, friendly exchange between two people, it occurred to Harper that when people are in uncertain situations, they come together simply on the basis of pure humanity. It gave her a warm feeling of comfort, a source of hope for the future.

The Jeeps plodded along slowly as the terrain became even rougher, making it impossible to speak to another person in the same vehicle without yelling. Harper was relieved to hear Monte declare something in Swahili to his drivers like camp was in their immediate future. The language began to take shape in her head, but without a Bantu base knowledge, it was rough going.

CHAPTER 16

Harper sat between the large Monte and the enigmatic Mr. Logan as dinner was served in front of the campfire. The plates were bandanas and the silverware nonexistent, but the ravenous Harper didn't care.

A six-inch insect resembling a cockroach scrambled in front of their feet. Silently, Logan removed a short knife from a hidden ankle strap and flung it at the cockroach, slicing off its head.

Harper swallowed quickly. "It's true what they say about cockroaches, you know."

Logan continued to shovel food into his mouth with his fingers. "What's true?"

"That the cockroach can live without its head."

"Fascinating." His tone indicated it was anything but fascinating.

"A cockroach can live for weeks without its head. In fact, the head can also live without the body for some time."

He yawned and wiped his mouth with his bandana.

"Yes, in fact, the functionality of the cockroach, *Periplaneta*, is poikilothermic, or cold-blooded. They do not expend energy to heat themselves and can get by without much sustenance, weeks actually. If you cut off their heads, the body will 'breathe' through their spiracles. The brain does not regulate that function; it is achieved by a primitive vascular system using pressure. After decapitation, they can stand, move and react to touch."

He stuffed the bandana into a pocket and ignored her.

"The lonely head can survive for a long time as well, given some nutrients and refrigeration."

Logan stood up and left. She heard him mutter one word under his breath: "Geek."

It wasn't the first time a man had called her that and it wouldn't be the last, Harper told herself as she finished her rations. She turned to the man on her other side. "Monte? Who is this Captain Gauld? Do you think he'll be able to deliver us close to the area in Dr. Merrill's notes?"

"You are in very good hands, Miss Harper. Captain Gauld is a Louisiana boy who works for Zipperco in the west. This continent is so dangerous for the oil companies that their entire staffs live on large tankers ten miles off-shore."

"No kidding!" Harper tried to imagine such a lifestyle.

"Captain Gauld transports executives and employees to and from the Kinshasa airport, delivering them to various jobsites in this ravaged country," Monte continued. He looked down at her in the firelight. "He is doing us a tremendous favor by transporting your team, although I suspect that Pharmco is paying him very well. I would imagine the other groups interested in your treasure would kill to get his knowledge of the terrain." Monte lit a half-smoked cigar.

"Who are these 'other groups' that are after this plant material? I would think that the humanitarians of the world, all countries and all peoples, would do anything to see this cure found, harvested, developed and distributed." Harp's doe-like eyes awaited his answer.

Monte laughed his wholehearted bellow, shaking the overhanging canopy and her inner core. "You are the naïve child. Focus on your task and do not worry about the exterior intentions. This is your destiny, Miss Harp, and you must succeed. The consequences of the others succeeding in this quest would be devastating to humanity and its suffering."

Harper liked this large, friendly man and appreciated his willingness to speak freely with her. "I felt a connection with Ursula on our flight. Could you tell me a little about her?"

He hesitated. In Africa, information could be a valuable commodity. He looked down at Harper and deciding she could be trusted, he kept talking. "When I first met her years ago, she was a ... well, flight attendant does not really describe her station. I want to say administrative assistant. She served on Air Force One. The White House staff never went anywhere without her. Much to my dismay, she fell completely in love with one of the Cabinet members."

"Ursula and a member of the White House staff?" Harper asked. "I pictured Ursula as the partner of someone brilliant. But I didn't think of her hooking up with someone in government, especially in the administration of the last eight years."

"Can you think of no one in government, Miss Smith, who lives up to that description? Brilliant and innovative?"

"To be honest, no."

"My darling Ursula was married to an amazing Kenyan man for many years before he was assassinated. I had the pleasure of escorting him on many a diplomatic mission. When he died, her heart disintegrated and her face became lifeless. That is when she took the job on Air Force One. She already had the highest security clearance. She worked with the Clinton administration and seemed to get her spirit back. She went along, loving and nurturing her children until … well, it happened. She fell in love. Unfortunately, it wasn't with me."

"Jeez, that sounds like a happy ending. But she told you that her heart was held in limbo. I heard her." Harper pictured her new friend and embraced the warmth of that memory.

"Yes, child. However, the love of a government official, especially one that high up, is not easily fulfilled."

"That high up, Monte? You can't tell me that any of those guys are worthy of Ursula. No way." She shook her head, her brow furrowing as she tried to recall the upper echelon of Bush-era cabinet members.

"Perhaps you may recall the incredibly brilliant Secretary of State."

"What? Did you say Secretary of State? You mean …?" The look of incredulity on her face was obvious.

"No, you heard me properly. It has haunted me every day of my life."

Monte left the fire and disappeared into the darkness. Harper felt alone in the jungle, questioning everything she thought was true.

CHAPTER 17

Harper awoke the next morning feeling queasy and tired but chalked it up to the effects of sleeping on the ground and eating strange foods.

"*Salinga, alongo mosala!*" Monte yelled. "There is work to do. Let's do it!" Harper considered his perpetual bellow annoying as well as inspiring in the pre-dawn mist.

Harper and Claire emerged from their small tent to find Chris, Dave and Sid stumbling out of theirs yawning and stretching. Hermann and Mike appeared from the brush from different directions to join the rest of the team. Monte and the drivers were at the Jeeps preparing for departure.

"And a very good morning to you, Monte," Claire said, sounding weary but cheerful. "*Salinga, alongo mosala!*"

"You are correct, Dr. Guthrie! We have work to do. So let's do it!" Monte laughed.

Harper then wished, not for the first time, that her life included a hidden soundtrack to herald what was happening, or what was about to happen. That way, just like in the movies, she could be prepared. Like the yee-haw scene in *City Slickers*. She wondered if she should be that cheerful.

The team traveled in the dawning light, Sid on his GPS and Monte on a two-way radio. Since when does he have a communication device, Harper wondered, and who is he talking to? She gnawed on dried fruit and hard bread as the Jeeps bounced on a dirt track barely describable as a road.

The terrain became more and more difficult to navigate. Harper was thinking she was glad it wasn't raining when the skies opened up and water poured down. In California rain was seasonal, tolerable, and, all in all, quite pleasurable for a terrain mostly coastal and high desert. She felt cozy in her Big Sur cabin during a downpour, curled up in her jammies in front of a fire.

This was completely different.

Within thirty seconds, visibility diminished to ten feet. After a minute, Harper could no longer see the front of the Jeep, like driving under a waterfall without ever getting to the other side. Harper pulled the neck of her shirt up over her forehead and cursed the backpack-stealing chimps.

Travel was impossible. The Jeeps pulled off the road at the first available opening in the foliage. Monte, Hermann and the drivers took out their machetes and hacked away at large *Strelizia* leaves to create makeshift lean-tos. The downpour was so violent it was tough going just climbing out of the Jeeps.

Mike and the native men efficiently assembled temporary shelters, cutting and cleaving small trees to create support stakes for the shanty roofs. Dave, Chris and Sid joined in to help. It occurred to Harper that perhaps it took a crisis for humankind, especially mankind, to work together, that only something catastrophic could bring such wholehearted effort.

When she understood the gravity of climate change, her first thought was that it could unite all humankind in a common goal. If Earth was on the verge of mortal peril, perhaps the east could be one with the west, the Middle East befriend its neighbors, and all *Gaia* inhabitants come to her rescue to save themselves.

But the longer she thought about it, the more she observed human nature, the more she doubted it.

CHAPTER 18

The rain pounded the crude shelters for hours, making conversation impossible. Harper did not dare pull out Dr. Merrill's notes to study, as the lean-to leaked in multiple and ever-changing places. She was glad Mike Logan and the native men had the good sense to select an elevated location for the huts. Even so, the run-off rapidly settled around the team and they huddled closer and closer to avoid sitting in what was at first a puddle and now a pond.

With nothing to do but wait, Harper drifted off into a semi-dreamlike state. She was awakened by the hard thump of Sid's sleeping head lolling on her shoulder.

"Let's go. We have lost precious time." Monte checked his watch. "Sid, please give me our coordinates."

Sid answered with a large yawn.

"Mr. Lembowsky!" Monte tapped his watch with impatience.

"Wait a fucking minute, dude, I'm working on it!" Sid frantically wiped raindrops off the GPS readout screen with the waistband of his underwear, apparently the only dry item on his person. Harper and Claire stifled their giggles over the "Scooby Doo" cartoon character on Lembowsky's shorts. He immediately stuffed the briefs back into his pants and gave Monte their current coordinates.

"Sid, it is imperative your equipment stay safe and dry every second of the journey." Monte stood directly in Sid's face, but his stance and voice seemed more concerned than combative. "If you cannot ascertain your direction or contact your employers, your mission has been lost, with or without your prize."

"Thanks, Monte. I'll be more careful." For the first time, Sid spoke to another member of the mission with sincerity and respect.

After the rain tapered off and they piled back into the Jeeps, Hermann told the team, "The going will be rough from here on out." He studied the path in front of them. "This used to be a poor excuse for a road. Now it is a river. In ten minutes, it will be a collection of muddy lakes."

He smoothed back his shoulder-length hair and ran his hands down his soaking shirt. "Prepare to get dirty." He flashed a boyish grin.

After waiting for the river to slacken, they took off down a road strewn with broken tree limbs, downed foliage and giant puddles, traveling fast to make up for lost time. Harper felt like she was on the Log Flume ride back home at the Boardwalk in Santa Cruz. She jostled like a crash test dummy. The men cracked crude jokes about the effects of jiggling on the female anatomy.

Remembering her father's advice to look up, Harper got a glimpse of clear blue sky for the first time in 24 hours. The jungle canopy parted briefly and the scene was breathtaking: the clouds flamingo pink and lavender with billowy puffs filling the upper atmosphere like heavy whipped cream. When she was a little girl she imagined climbing up a very tall ladder to sit on top of those fluffy clouds. There, she could be her own master and reign over her destiny.

She smiled. That time had come.

A flock of storks flew overhead, silhouettes against salmon clouds. The coloring of the sky suggested evening but Harper knew it couldn't be more than early afternoon. If they were delayed so long the chopper could not pick them up until tomorrow, the mission would fall behind schedule by a full twenty-four hours.

More storks filled the sky, low overhead. The sound of their cries made everyone in both Jeeps look up. The drivers' attentions were diverted and they lost command of the road. The front Jeep hit a pothole, throwing a wave of mud on the passengers in the trailing Jeep. The men in the front Jeep were jeering at their mud-spattered colleagues when the driver slammed into a ravine, now a raging river. The Jeep listed precariously. The crew jumped out into knee-deep water to upright the vehicle and save its contents.

The other Jeep jerked to a stop on the muddy bank as the first vehicle bobbed away in the fast-moving current. Everyone splashed into the rapids to stop it, but they were no match against the forces of nature. They watched helplessly as the vehicle was carried several meters downstream, lodging against a low tree in the middle of the churning water. The team waded through ocean-like waves to hold the Jeep upright.

Dave grabbed a coil of rope to tie the Jeep to the trunk of a large, partially-submerged tree. Chris, Claire and Harper created a chain to transport its precious cargo—rations, field equipment, medical supplies—onto higher ground. The force of the water was still too strong. The Jeep slipped away from the mooring and hurtled downstream. Dave trailed behind, tangled in the rope.

The remaining crew barely managed to scramble onto shore as more runoff joined the river, strengthening the current. Monte and his drivers rushed to the other Jeep to uncoil the winch while Dave was dragged down the river like a fish on a hook.

Claire and Harper raced downstream and climbed over the ragged walls of the ravine to keep their eyes on Dave. At first, they saw nothing but the Jeep's windshield swirling in a churning current as the vehicle bobbed up and down. With relief they spotted Dave wedged against a large log. He was no longer tangled in the rope and the Jeep was nowhere to be seen. "He's alive—he's breathing," Claire told Harper.

Dave tried to position himself upright on the slippery log. Claire and Harper could tell he was fighting the current with all his strength. He straddled the log and started laughing and waving. Claire and Harper responded with applause. The current was so loud not even a shout could be heard. They motioned to him to stay put while they went for help. He nodded and tightened his grip around the log.

The women were hiking back upstream when Claire stopped. "Shouldn't someone stay with him?" she yelled at Harper over the noise of the water.

"Right. I'll stay, you go and get help." Harper just turned to head back downstream when a loud cracking noise echoed through the ravine, almost drowning out the roar of the raging water. They watched in horror as the log broke from its wedged position and was violently tossed into the torrent.

"Dave, Dave!" Harper turned to Claire and yelled, "GO!"

Claire sprinted for help while Harper followed downstream as best as she could, climbing over rocks, getting slapped hard in the face with brush.

"Dave, are you OK?" She was yelling at the top of her lungs.

She could see him bobbing up and down in the surf like a tiny sailboat caught in a tidal wave. She got a quick glimpse of his face and he still seemed conscious and in control. *Hang in there!* she thought as she watched him grab a bramble root and hold on. He looked at her and waved.

"Hold on Dave! Help is coming!" Harper cupped her hands and hollered, returning his wave. She clambered up a boulder to see Claire followed by Monte and Keenu and the rest of the team. With a sigh of relief, she saw that Keenu had the foresight to bring rope. With a smile, she signaled to Dave to hold on—help had arrived.

Her gaze traveled downstream and her elation turned to terror.

The ravine narrowed to a small canyon. Under normal circumstances, an amusing little diversion in a kayak. But Harper had white-water rafted enough to recognize a "blender" situation when she saw it. The rapid current, coupled with large boulders, plus a substantial collection of uprooted tree trunks and brush, created a deadly situation. Anyone and anything entering that canyon slams into the wedged debris below with no means of escape.

Dave's fate was again at the mercy of the water. The root he'd been clinging to broke away. Monte scrambled down the river bed to toss the rope. The Jeep reappeared and continued to float downriver, just in back of Dave. The "blender" was less than fifty feet away, and the water-logged Jeep was sure to topple on Dave and crush him once he slipped over the edge.

Harper and Claire screamed with helpless agony while Monte tried to toss the rope in Dave's direction—and kept missing.

A strong wind whipped up whitecaps on the river's surface. Harper looked up and saw a helicopter hovering directly above Dave. Mike Logan hung in a harness from the chopper, poised at the edge of the precipice.

Just as Dave was about to disappear forever over the edge of the canyon, Mike grabbed him in a bear hug, securing him in an additional harness. The pair lifted skyward. The entire rescue took only seconds but Harper saw it in slow motion. She clapped her hands over her mouth. *Oh my God.*

Harper, Claire, Sid and Chris stared in speechless amazement while Hermann and Monte's team nonchalantly headed back to the other Jeep.

Claire finally said, "Good Lord. That must have been Captain Gauld. How did they get here and with such precision timing?"

"I saw Monte talking into a radio just a few minutes … I think it was just a few minutes ago." Chris sounded as shaken as Harper felt.

"Jesus Christ! That was just a little too fucking close!" Sid's eyes were as wide as they could get, magnified by his round spectacles. "What in the hell did we get ourselves into?"

They started to crash their way through the jungle to the remaining Jeep. Harper hung back, taking one last look at the ruined Jeep lying like a broken child's toy in the canyon, trapped in debris, partially submerged in swirling water. If the helicopter hadn't come along when it did, Dave would surely have been killed, crushed by the Jeep, his body mangled by swirling brush.

"Jesus Christ, indeed." Claire turned back to follow the others.

CHAPTER 19

When the team finally regrouped in a small clearing, Harper cheered with relief when she spotted Dave drinking coffee from a Thermos, laughing with Mike Logan and another man. An old, bulky helicopter was parked behind them, engine still whining.

"Well, what took you guys so long? Do I have to babysit you people?" Dave laughed.

He introduced Captain Gauld, who responded to the greeting by taking a swig of something from a flask, wiping his mouth with his shirt-sleeve and shaking hands.

"Damn fine to meet you," Gauld said. "I suppose you will be in my care for a while. We have a little less than one hundred miles to go from here. The chopper will be more comfortable than the Jeeps, but gathering from the last hour or so, not as much fun."

He made a noise like a laugh but to Harper sounded more like a nervous cackle. She wondered if he might be a little "off," but told herself that flying a helicopter in the Congo is not a career choice for most people. Harper appreciated people who "jogged to a different iPod," and Captain Gauld seemed to fit the description.

"Well, my lovely, I am afraid this is where we say goodbye." Monte Jones had Claire's hand to his lips. "I will treasure our moments in this wild place. Good luck to you, Dr. Guthrie." He sighed longingly and went to give farewells to the others.

Captain Gauld took charge. "OK, folks, let's get this show on the road. We are running behind due to Mr. Murano's little dip." Monte and his drivers loaded the crew's gear into the Russian MI6 helicopter and slapped the men on the back in bon voyage.

The team boarded the chopper but Harper wanted one last word with Monte. "That was some excellent timing in the rescue department. We are indebted to you for delivering us this far." Harper reached out her hand, but Monte grabbed her whole body in a bear hug, almost crushing her breasts.

"You are most welcome, my dear Harper. You have spunk, little girl. You let Mr. Logan take care of you. I am sure there is nothing he would like better. You don't always have to be the strong one, you know. " He smiled down at her and released his grip in time to see Claire's derriere at eye level as she boarded the chopper. He raised his hand to give her backside a slap, but Harper grabbed his arm.

"Now, now, Monte, you've already said goodbye." She giggled and let him boost her up into the cockpit. She joined the team in buckling in and donning their intercom headsets.

"Bye, Monte, and thank you! Salinga, alongo mosala!"

Harper waved as the chopper left the ground and watched the three men and the remaining Jeep get smaller and smaller, finally disappearing in the backdrop of the jungle.

CHAPTER 20

Any fears that Harper held about flying in an old Russian helicopter vanished as she was overwhelmed by the sheer beauty of the unfolding landscape. She saw the river that almost took Dave's life to her right, just as a herd of elephants came to its edge to drink. The sun was low in the sky but plenty of light was left to the day.

"Captain Gauld, how long 'til we get there?" Chris yelled, unaware that the intercom eliminated the need to shout over the noise of the chopper.

"Whoa there, Sparky, I can hear ya." Captain Gauld hooted his unusual laugh. "Until we get where? Since all I have are general coordinates, I won't really know where there is until we find it. Our challenge is to get there before dark so we can set up camp tonight." He switched an unmarked lever on the control panel and reached into his pack for the flask. After a long pull on the contents, he increased the speed of the helicopter.

Harper pressed her nose to the glass trying to figure out where she was by the landscape. The canopy below was a shaded tapestry of green with occasional scampers of unidentifiable animals or birds. She saw no road or clearing anywhere on the horizon, just an expanse of colors turned into a prism by the late afternoon sun. Harper was lulled into dreamland by the beauty of the unspoiled jungle and whirl of the helicopter blades.

Bang! The window beside her shattered, snapping her out of this peaceful enjoyment of the scenery. "Captain Gauld! Something hit the window!"

He looked behind to assess the situation just as Mike picked up a spent shell from the cabin floor.

"Hey, Greg, looks like someone is not happy we're here." Mike kneeled at Harper's side by the broken window and pointed to a clearing about fifty yards below.

Men poured out of caves with guns pointed at the chopper. The "men" were actually just boys, teenagers and young children, their clothes and faces covered with mud. Even from the chopper, she saw the ravages of torture and starvation.

"Yeah, fuck you Mayi-Mayi, bastards. Don't worry, we will leave you to your sordid bullshit." The pilot heaved the chopper a hard left and raised the altitude in a jolt. He took another swig and grumbled another obscenity.

"What the hell was that about?" Sid demanded, sweat and fear on his face.

"Fuckers. They recruit kids to work the coltan and cassiterite mines by threatening to gang rape their mothers and sisters. The kids are tortured and starved and their mothers and sisters get raped and killed anyway. Their favorite trick is to put kerosene rags in the women's mouths and light them during the rapes."

The Captain fiddled with some instrument with Russian markings.

Claire and Harper both clamped their hands over their mouths in horror.

"Coltan? What is that used for?" Dave asked.

His ploy to change the subject was all too obvious, but Harper appreciated his attempt to divert her attention.

"Every wireless technological gizmo on the face of this planet contains coltan," Gauld said. "Africa is always plundered for her riches. The booty du jour is coltan. The sad thing is, not one of those kids will ever see what it is they are dying for. If they survive working in the mines, they will be thoroughly brainwashed and will eventually become Mayi-Mayi. They wind up doing the same horrible things to the next generation."

"Jesus. How can they let them get away with it?" Chris asked.

"That's just the thing, there is no 'they' to stop them. The industrialized countries of the world must have the coltan to support their expanding markets. They only want the product delivered. They don't care how it gets there. In fact, they hire all sorts of disreputable criminals to fund the Mayi-Mayi, guerillas and the militias. They don't want to get their hands dirty, they only want the products." He made that eerie laughing sound again, stopping only to pull from his flask.

"These poor people, how are they ever going to stop the cycle?" Claire said aloud, lost in thought.

Captain Greg wiped his lips with his shirtsleeve. "The DRC government is knee deep with the rest of the global gluttony and will not spend any money on infrastructure or education. As things are now, there is no hope."

The team was silent, all eyes averted to places comforting to their particular owners. Harper's face was pressed against what remained of the window. The wind coming through the jagged hole offered a welcomed breeze.

Again she was lulled, but this time with a profound sense of despair. Only her father's words from long-ago broke through:

Pruning is perhaps the most important aspect of horticulture. In the horticultural world, we try to mimic nature. In the natural arena, there are frosts, drought, stampedes, insects, constant nibbling by creatures, viruses and bacterium and any number of possible assaults to decimate foliage.

This is by far the hardest thing for most people. It is difficult for them to 'hurt' the branch or cut away part of something that is living. The result is that much energy is spent on unhealthy parts that should have been removed.

In nature, the weak and unhealthy are eliminated without a hesitation. Pruning, and I mean hard pruning, enables the root and stem structure to become more established, thus retaining and distributing nutrients to the healthy parts of the plant. The plant on the whole has a chance to regenerate itself without the burden of the old and diseased material.

The most important thing to do in your life is diligent pruning. Cut off damaged parts that hold you down and take energy away from your growth. It is imperative your expenditures are directed to healthy endeavors. And when I say 'hard pruning,' Harper Morgan Smith, I mean not only do you need to cut hard, cutting away the damaged parts and disposing of them entirely, I mean it will be hard to accomplish. It will take a great deal of perseverance, and perhaps reliving the hurt, in order to rid yourself of the burden.

But it will be worth the pain.

"These children will never be able to prune those parts away. They have no tools. The damaged parts will poison the rest of what's left of their once innocent souls." Harper had taken off her headset and was talking out loud to herself.

She felt a finger wiping a tear from her cheek, and turned to see Mike gazing at her with an expression of pity and concern. His headset was off as well, making any speech except a shout impossible. No words were needed. That simple gesture warmed Harper's heart, reminding her that for all of man's inhumanity to man, there was also the possibility of communion, one human being reaching out to another in kindness and empathy.

She wondered if this strong, capable man sitting next to her was having similar thoughts.

CHAPTER 21

The chopper thundered on through the sky as the sun disappeared below the western horizon.

"We're as close as we can get, folks. As soon as I find a spot, providing there is one, we will land and set up camp." Captain Gauld drained the last drops from his flask. "We are entering unchartered territory here. I have never been this far into the interior before. Maybe we'll see Bigfoot." Again, that laugh.

Hermann, in a makeshift seat at the rear of the cabin, spoke for the first time since the helicopter took off. "Captain, clearing in the east, two o'clock."

"Are you familiar with this area, Mr. Hermann?" Harper asked through the intercom.

"No one is, Mademoiselle. There are perhaps some tribes who still live here, but hardly anyone from the outside has traveled this area on foot. Every time I have flown over the heart, I have seen nothing except green, a very dark green."

"Do you think we will see some indigenous peoples?" Chris got that wide-eyed little boy look on his face again.

Hermann looked perplexed. "Indigen-what?"

"Native tribes, Mr. Hermann." Claire said helpfully.

"Oh, one does not know when or where the tribes will be. They are very superstitious and move their camps often. It is said that they might still shrink heads. They do eat the organs of their enemies. My brother saw it earlier this year. They captured one of his team and cut off and ate his willy while he was still alive!"

The men instinctively moved their hands to protect their private parts.

"Indeed! I hope we avoid those not-so-charming natives. I prefer to keep my body parts attached and uneaten." Claire said, maintaining her plucky attitude.

"They would not eat you, Madame. As I said, they are very superstitious. They have most likely never seen women with the coloring of you and the Mademoiselle. I do not know what they would do. It will be best if we just stay out of their way. That is my job, Madame. I will be scouting the areas to make sure that all is clear as we go. I know the signs of where they have been and the direction they are headed. We may have to go a night or two with no fire, but I will take care of you, mum."

Harper heard an accent in his voice she could not place.

The chopper circled the area. Captain Greg announced, "OK, folks, this is it. We're goin' in."

Harper did a double-take spotting the tiny landing spot. "Jeez, we can't get in there, can we? Won't the blades get caught in the foliage?"

Sid, napping, woke up just as the chopper descended into the dark green oblivion. "At least the ground will be soft when we land on our asses."

"Shit, nothin' to it. I'm not drunk enough to miss a landing like this." Captain Gauld deftly moved the levers and controls. As the chopper lowered itself into the canopy, the trees blew back in the whirlwind. Harper marveled as Captain Gauld created his own landing pad with the blades.

"Welcome home, kids. Let's set up camp." The captain unbuckled his seatbelt and retrieved his pack from the rear of the cabin, its bulging side pocket providing Gauld with another flask.

The team wasted no time. Dave and Chris set up two tents, Sid and Hermann another. Claire and Harper surveyed an area just under the canopy for a food preparation area and fire pit. Mike disappeared.

"So, Captain Greg, will you be coming to get us as well?" Harper asked as she dug a hole for the fire.

"Well, Miss Harper, I have no instructions for that. My base is off the shores of Kinshasa, way in the west. Vanderfuck might have made arrangements from the north or east. However, those areas are very dangerous and untrustworthy. I doubt Pharmco would risk that. Those guys would just as soon kill you as look at you, regardless of what they were paid to do."

"Both Sid and Dave have radios for contact with Pharmco," Hermann said. "We all have tracking devices in our packs. I am sure the second we give them the signal, someone will be here to pick us up." The guide wiped sweat off his face with a bandana.

"I prefer to be in a little more civilized place. You people are fucking crazy to be out here." The pilot took a long pull on the new flask and laughed in his disturbing way.

Claire stood up. "Well done, Mr. Logan!"

Mike burst through the bush toting a small antelope and a large bunch of not-quite-ripe bananas.

"Okapi is very delicious. Excellent, Monsieur." Hermann unsheathed his knife to filet the animal.

Harper didn't even ask about the creature's status on the endangered list. Hunger triumphed over her conscience.

Dave deposited a bundle of firewood near the pit Harper had edged with small rocks. Captain Gauld opened a side panel in the ugly old chopper. "Allow me to add a few side dishes. How about some *fufu*?" He pulled out a brown bag of something resembling ground corn and handed it to Claire.

"I am afraid I am not familiar with *fufu*, Captain Gauld. What do I do with it?"

"Just add a little water until it's kind of doughy. Then warm it on the fire, roll it into a ball and indent the middle so it's kind of a scoop. *Fufu* is made from anything from yams to plantains and is the native equivalent of silverware. It's great with *tembo*, a kind of palm wine."

"Well then, we're set!" Claire said. The small group cheerfully prepared the meal while Hermann washed the blood of the okapi off his hands in a small creek.

Sid looked warily at a troop of small monkeys chattering above. "I hope they don't start throwing their shit."

"Sid, why did you come on this little adventure?" Claire asked.

"If you weren't a chick, Claire, I'd say it is none of your fucking business. But since you asked—I am here for the money, honey."

"A real humanitarian," Mike grumbled to Dave as he whittled a skewer for the meat.

"Yeah, yeah, Logan. I'm sure you are here to save the world." Sid smirked, mumbling *mercenary* under his breath.

Mike simply smiled in reply.

Gauld stood and drained his third flask. "Well, kids, this has been fun. Kumbaya." He began staggering in the direction of the chopper.

"You're leaving now?" Chris asked with concern. "It's dark ... and you have had, well, uh, a big dinner."

"Shit or rain or sleet or dead of night, whatever. I got a little thing in Kananga I want to bounce my balls off tonight." Gauld climbed into the helicopter and started the engine. Moments later, the blades spread the canopy for his exit. With one final wave, he was gone.

The wind from the chopper blew out the campfire and scattered debris. Silence and darkness descended over the tiny campsite.

"Man, and he called us crazy!" Harper said. "He was pretty hammered. Do think he'll be OK?"

"Yeah, he'll be all right," Dave said, snapping on his flashlight and aiming it at the dead campfire.

His voice grew louder and deeper as he addressed the team. "I am in charge now. Harper, you get with Sid, correlate where we are compared with where we want to be. Chris, check your equipment and run some tests if you can. Hermann, gather wood for the morning. Mike, you will take the first watch tonight."

Harper felt a chill at Dave's next words: "We have just switched to serious mode."

PART III

CHAPTER 22

"Orchids have the most highly evolved reproductive parts in botany," Harper told the team. "The flower itself has created an intricate pollinating system. Other species have evolved to accommodate the elaborate orchid lifestyle."

"Oh, God, here she goes again," Sid muttered as he swatted at tiny insects hovering around his mouth. "Damn, she is more annoying than these flies!"

They'd been on foot for several hours, slowly picking their way over roots and other obstructions to avoid falling face down in leaf litter. With no path to follow they crashed through the jungle, foliage slapping their faces as they passed.

Harper didn't care. Her attention was completely absorbed by the surrounding jungle and its glorious and intricate colors. She looked up. Her father would have loved being here. She was rewarded with a grove of catteleya orchids showing splashy pinks and purples and wafting an intoxicating scent.

"No, really!" she continued, as if Sid had never spoken. "Take the phalenopsis orchid, for example. Its pollinator is a beautiful moth. The flower has a small landing pad so the moth can get to the nectar drizzled deep in the throat. The moth must be the exact weight necessary to trigger nectar delivery.

"At the same moment as she is feeding, pollen is dropped from a cache positioned above her, landing on her shoulders. She has evolved to look exactly like the flower so the male moth comes and lands on top of her while she is feeding, thinking she is the flower itself. The pollen deposited on her shoulders will be transferred to his underside which is then applied to the next flower he visits. He will even mate with her, if she is willing. It is a very intricate and complicated process. Fascinating, really …."

Harper reveled in the awe she felt when describing the wonders of nature.

"Shit, will she ever shut up?" Sid grumbled.

"Wait, there's more!" Harper said enthusiastically. "The orchid is an epiphyte that uses the structure of the tree to wrap its roots around, benefitting from its cradle. Unlike a parasite, the epiphyte does not deplete any of its host's resources. Instead, it brings pollinators and nutrients which fall into the soil at the root systems, giving the tree a highly beneficial return in the form of fertilizer, payment for its lodging."

"Can we stop now?" Sid whined.

"I swear to God, if he asks, 'Are we there yet?' I'll kill him," Dave said to himself from his position at the tail end of the group. Aloud, he announced, "OK, Lembowsky, when we get to the next creek, we can stop. We could all use a break." He wiped the back of his neck with his bandana.

True to his word, Dave allowed a short rest stop at the next waterway. "Sid, do you have our coordinates?"

"Got it. We are headed in the right direction, but I see a severe elevation change coming up." Sid closed up his GPS and began to take his pants off.

"Sid, what are you up to?" Claire's comment was reflexive. She stopped trying to figure out Sid's motives on the Boeing BBJ.

The group shared dried rations and canteen water. Mike located a small pool in the creek where he washed his face and diluted the mosquito repellent in his eyes. Harper and Claire looked toward the pond, deciding whether or not to take a dip themselves and spotted Sid standing in the water. His private parts were wrapped in a large Bird of Paradise leaf and his Scooby-Doo underwear was crested on the top of his head.

Harper chewed on an unidentifiable processed food product as she watched Sid splash himself with murky pond water.

"I am thinking of a letter …."

Claire smirked. "Is it 'Y'?"

Claire and Harper laughed. Mike, who had his face in the water with his back to Sid, turned around just in time to see the small man with the waistband of his boxers framing his face.

"What the fuck are you doing, Sid?" Mike glared at him.

"If you must know, I washed my underwear and am drying them while I have a small bath." With the shorts still on his head, he pressed the water out of them, sending a small trickle down his chest.

"Jesus Christ, Sid, can't you hang your boxers on a branch or something?" Mike sloshed out of the pond and climbed into the brush.

"I don't know about you, but I didn't want any foreign critters crawling into my shorts."

Claire contributed her dry British humor. "I really don't think you have to worry about anything getting into your shorts, Sid." Dave, Hermann, and Harper laughed while Sid looked perplexed. Chris smiled to himself as he toyed with his portable lab.

Laughing, Harper put her hand to her forehead and winced.

"Are you all right, Harp?" Claire asked.

"Oh, I'm fine, thanks. Just a little headache."

"Roll up your shirtsleeves." Claire's voice suddenly had a serious tone.

"What? I'm fine. Let's go." Harper started to gather her pack together.

"Your sleeve, please."

"Fine. Here." Harper rolled up a khaki shirtsleeve to placate the physician.

Claire examined Harper's arm. "Just as I suspected." She reached for her medical bag.

"What?" Harper twisted to see the underside of her forearm and let out a yelp of pain.

"Joint pain, Miss Harp?" Claire asked.

"Some. It's nothing."

"Didn't I tell you to be sure to put on your mosquito repellent in a diligent fashion?"

The friendly doctor was now all-business, using a maternal I told you so tone.

She pulled her medical bag onto her lap and spoke to Dave. "It is the third day since her infection. She will be able to get through today. Tomorrow, we may very well be immobile."

Sid was in the bush retrieving his pants and overheard everything. "Fucking what? Are you kidding me? No. We've got to keep moving."

"My preliminary diagnosis is that she has dengue fever. Dengue is the most common arboviral illness worldwide; it is present in nineteen countries in sub-Saharan Africa. As recently as 1993, sixty thousand people in this area were inflicted with dengue. It is caused by infection with one of the four serotypes of the dengue virus."

The team listened with concern as Claire continued. "Initial dengue infection may be asymptomatic. Hopefully she has only the symptom complex of classic dengue fever, also known as DF. A small percentage of persons may develop endothelial leaks. This form is called dengue hemorrhagic fever or DHF; this causes bruises and sub-dermal leakage. She is our youngest member; she will be the most susceptible."

Claire looked worried as she finished. "Her rash seems severe for only this far into infection."

Dave immediately took charge. "OK, people, let's make some time today. Hustle up. We will go as far as we can tonight. When Harper gives out, we'll make camp and stay until she is able to proceed."

Claire gave Harper eight hundred milligrams of Tylenol and an antibiotic to stave off her symptoms.

"I'll be fine. Don't worry. I always get over things quickly. My immune system is in perfect shape." Harper rubbed her knees.

Dave spoke softly to the doctor. "Is she going to be okay?"

Claire pulled him off to the side. "Try not to worry, Dave. Dengue fever is curable. It is much more rampant in South America and the Pacific right now. There have actually been thousands of cases reported in the United States in recent years. Non-locals are much more susceptible than the indigenous peoples, who have developed immunity."

"What are the symptoms?" Dave asked. "Will the rest of us get it?"

"Not likely. She was infected by mosquitoes back with Monte in the Jeeps. I noticed her swatting them away and tried to remind her to stay up with her repellent. She was stubborn and distracted. That was hundreds of miles from here. We will all need to be extra careful with our repellent applications, however."

Dave pulled the mosquito salve from his pocket as she spoke. "She will experience severe headache, fever, and incredible joint pain. It is also called 'break back fever,' the pain is so intense. If she has the type two DHF, she could experience acute sub-dermal hemorrhaging. I saw slight signs of that on her right forearm. I will keep a close eye on it. Unfortunately, I can only give her drugs to make her more comfortable. I cannot give her a quick cure. Recovery time is anywhere from four to seven days normally, but since she is exceptionally healthy, and older than the normal patient, it may be as few as three."

"Three extra days? I don't like the sound of that. Anything can happen in three days." Dave's thick black brows furrowed with concern.

"Indeed."

CHAPTER 23

The team plodded on in silence, each focused on the need to cover some ground before Harper's strength gave out. The elevation gain and heavy brush made the going difficult. Mike climbed a kola nut tree to get an idea of what lay ahead, but the dense canopy towered over the sixty foot trunk. Harper felt like she was slogging through a humid cave, smothering and endless.

A pair of mountain gorillas regarded the intruders with mild interest. The huge primates with intelligent faces lacked aggression, were almost docile. "Really makes a person re-evaluate the subjective line between man and animal, doesn't it?" Claire remarked, summing up the reaction of the entire team.

Harper held out for almost eight hours before she slipped into semi-delirium. Claire signaled to Dave to make camp.

"We will be here for a while, folks," Dave announced. "We might as well make the best of it."

They pitched the tents in a triangular formation with the fire pit in the center. Hermann checked the surrounding area for signs of local in-habitants and found none. A narrow stream bordered the small clearing. A few shafts of dusty sunlight managed to penetrate the jungle canopy.

Harper was disoriented by this time and allowed herself to be put to bed. Dave and Mike made a pallet of soft brush so she would not be lying directly on the forest floor, the worst thing to do in deep foliage. Claire checked her vitals, gave her another dose of pain reliever, seemed satis-fied that Harper was comfortable, and made case notes in her journal.

Mike disappeared into the jungle to hunt while Dave and Hermann gathered any fuel dry enough to burn. Sid placed rocks in a circle around the hole he dug for the fire area. Chris took an aluminum pot to the stream for water to boil. The thin sunlight vanished and a light rain began to fall. The damp gloom mirrored the atmosphere in the makeshift camp as Harper's fever and pain deepened.

There was nothing they could do but wait.

CHAPTER 24

"Father, tell me again about the cork oak."

Harper was in and out of consciousness for thirty hours, mumbling nonsense. Claire put a damp cloth on her head to cut the fever. Harper woke in a start to see Claire sitting beside her. For the first time in many hours, Harper recognized the doctor.

"Claire, um, hi," Harper said in a hoarse whisper. "I am so glad you're here. Where are we?"

"She is once again with us. Splendid!" Claire smiled and turned the compress. "How are you feeling?"

"Like shit, thank you. Am I almost well? I want to get back on the road."

"Not so fast, Missy. We have a little ways to go. If we get you up and about too soon, you will relapse and your recovery time will be longer. Let's take it easy, shall we?"

"I'm OK, really." Harper struggled to raise herself on her elbows.

"You were talking about some kind of oak." Claire said as she gently pushed her back down onto the pallet.

"Was I? That's funny. My father told me a story about oak trees I will never forget."

"Were you close to him?" Claire was digging in her pack for more acetaminophen.

"No. I was told he died before I was born. Then he surfaced the summer I was 12. I was able to hang out with him for a while before he passed away."

Harper's coherence encouraged the doctor. She kept her patient focused for as long as she could. "You were told he was dead? Who told you that, and why in the world would anyone do such a thing to a child?" Claire shook two tablets into her hand.

"Well, you would have to know my mother. Her reasons for doing anything are always suspect. It seems my mother was having an affair, with a Blue Angel pilot, no less, during the entire eleven years of her marriage. She and her husband never conceived. After her divorce and the death of the pilot, my mother wanted to have a baby so she seduced a botany professor on a one-night stand. He was married and she blackmailed him to stay silent. Then his wife died and he was able to contact me. He was a brilliant botanist, albeit lacking in parental skills."

"Bloody hell, Harp, that story is horrific!" Claire stopped, holding the aspirin in her hand. "Your mother sounds like a real piece of work. Did you have any other male role models or fatherly influences?"

"None who didn't try to kiss me."

Harper never shared details about her personal life to anyone. She drifted back to sleep. Hours later when she woke, she vaguely remembered talking to the lady doctor about personal matters, hoping she had not divulged more than intended, but she did not remember anything specific. What was it Claire mentioned? The cork oak? Her mind traveled back in time to a picnic she prepared for her father by the Carmel River.

The majestic Cork Oak, he told her, Quercus suber, grows to 60 feet both wide and high and has an incredible bark structure. The gnarly thick cork is the bark of commerce. That lovely cabernet I enjoyed last night was protected by that mighty oak's 'skin.'

The oak displays a rich palette of color and texture. The leaves have a waxy deep green surface while the under leaf is a fuzzy grey. The cork bark can get up to a foot thick and uses the principles of torque to achieve its abstract geometrical branching form.

The very attribute this giant embraces for her notoriety, as well as her protection, is the one attribute that causes her downfall.

A common trait in humans.

Lovers and winemakers have desecrated her bark for millenniums. The vintners of ancient times only needed a primitive knife to seal their latest fermentations, while lovers carved eternal inscriptions. Nowadays, industrial wine merchants ravage her completely.

Even the industrious woodpecker takes advantage of her soft temperament to shove her own acorns into her skin, assaulting her inner anatomy as they hunt for wood boring beetles.

Each one of these assaults is small individually, but when accumulated over time, can take down the benevolent elder, the damage becoming irreversible. Each little jab, every insult, all moments of disrespect can result in disease and an eventual structural breakdown.

People's personal relationships are exactly like the life of this giant sentinel. A personal relationship is the sum of its parts. The twists and turns of human relationships result in a whole being, each event causes branching in a new direction, thus further stabilizing the overall structure. When nutrients and illumination are added, the fundamental structure will strengthen.

However, in human interaction, each small jab, every tiny insult, even if waived off with a hand, leaves a hole. The natural process can survive the myriad insults life bestows on you gladly and in perpetuity. Winemakers and lovers readily leave their marks. Yes, there will be a few old initials carved on your own bark, but one must work hard so the holes do not overcome your own well-being. To protect your personal structure, walk away from anything inflicting little holes, for enough of them can take you down.

Harper woke from her dream feeling uneasy. That moment with her father seemed so real. She lost sense of time and place again. "What—where am I?" she cried out in panic, sitting up on the pallet and attempting to stand.

"Whoa there, Harpy. Please get back in bed. I brought you some mango and cassava." A young man presented her with a fresh *Musa* leaf brimming with beautiful orange fruit garnished with an orchid and a canteen of fresh rainwater.

"Wow, what ... I mean, um, I'm sorry. Oh, Mister ... um, Logan, is it?"

Mike looked out of his element, reminding Harper of a middle school boy alone with his first date. "How are you feeling?" he stammered.

She felt his discomfort, but in her weakened state she'd lost her usual guarded nature around men she didn't know well. She accepted his offering. "You know, Monte told me you wanted to take care of me. Why would he say that?"

Mike looked away, fidgeting with his pocket knife.

"Why, Mike, I won't bite. I just wanted to say thank you for being here, and for this beautiful dinner, um, breakfast ... what time is it?"

"Your recovery time is all that matters. Please eat up. You need your strength."

Her appetite suddenly back, she devoured the fruit and drank deeply from the canteen. "Mike, what on earth possessed you to be in this jungle with us, with me?"

She was slipping back into unconsciousness, falling back into her leaf-stuffed pillow, her eyes at half-mast.

"I had a wife in Brazzaville. Jeez, I've never talked to anyone about this before." Mike dropped into a sitting position on the forest floor next to Harper's pallet. "She was very beautiful."

Harper was fast asleep, tossing half-conscious on her leaf bed. Mike looked at her face and took in her helpless condition. He hadn't watched over another person in years.

"She was very beautiful," he whispered again. "She left her upper-middle class family to come to Africa. She could not stand the children's suffering. Neither could I. We lived quite happily in Kananga. She was teaching school children and I worked for a local diamond and mineral mine."

His face darkened as he wrung his hands.

"Then they came. The Mayi-Mayi saw her, pregnant with our child. They saw that she was teaching the children, even the girls. They waited until nighttime, after they had drugged up, and came for her. I was off at the mine. They could not stand future Mayi-Mayi opponents being educated for something better, so they slaughtered her. They slaughtered her and my baby, like animals."

He stopped. His knees were spread with his head hung between them. Time passed. Mike had no idea how much time, but the light dimmed and someone brought in a candle.

"*Abe baakon na sei ensa* is not necessarily true." Harper's voice was clear and her pretty face glowed by candlelight.

"Huh? What the hell does that mean?" Mike said, startled to find her suddenly awake.

"'One bad palm tree spoils the wine.' The local wine here is made from various palm trees. It is said that if one plant is past its prime, the whole lot is ruined." Harper spoke gently, obviously aware of Mike's pain.

"What do you mean? And how do you know this language?" His face turned hard and his voice was harsh.

"Gee whiz, Mike. I wondered why you view your fellow human as a threat. Now I know. I am sorry you have suffered so. I mean ... I can't imagine what you must ... well, I'm sorry."

"Why? You didn't do anything." His tone and expression softened.

"No, I didn't. But that doesn't make it any less painful for you."

She was starting to fade again. "Mike?"

He looked at her and smiled, showing slightly jagged teeth and soft eyes. "Yes, Harper?"

She looked up at him. "Ezekiel told me that fear could be my friend."

"Who?"

"One time someone told me… I don't remember who. Was it Ezekiel?" She was losing consciousness again.

He reached over to wipe the sweat off her forehead.

"Fear," she said softly but still coherently. "A very strange thing. It makes you do things without knowing why you are doing them."

"What do you mean?" He tried to hold on to her for just another minute.

"Someone once described me as fearless. When I am with other people, to them it seems like I'm not afraid of anything …." She tossed her head on the makeshift pillow. "But in reality …" She was barely audible now, her eyes at half-mast. "I'm afraid of everything." She drifted back into feverish sleep.

He looked at her, not knowing what to think. The pain of his loss was too much to bear under any circumstances. She'd obviously heard more than he had intended for her—or anyone—to know about him. And yet … the simple act of taking care of another human being stirred long buried emotions. Relief from bitterness, definitely—but something more.

Mike Logan couldn't define the feeling, but he liked it.

CHAPTER 25

The team sat in a circle around the campfire, mopping up the juices of alligator steaks with plantain fufu. Harper remained unconscious in her tent. A few feet away from the camp, a branch snapped. Mike put his hand on the hilt of the machete.

Quiet as rodents in the dark, they came. The first one stood a foot away from one of the tents, his black skin on his almost-naked body barely visible under the cover of night. Only his tribal jewelry shone in the firelight. He said nothing. Other men came and stood on either side of him, also in silence.

Hermann froze and whispered, "Do not move. Stay exactly where you are." His eyes never left the dark shadow of the first intruder.

The guide spoke to the tribesmen in what he thought would be their native language. The leader was unresponsive, as if he didn't understand. Hermann tried a different dialect. Again, no response. The leader lost patience and motioned to the other men, who silently moved in. A man stood at the back of each team member, making a human barricade while others ransacked the camp.

"Do not move." Hermann spoke again, voice low and tense. "Not one inch. Let them take what they want and they will go. Do not move."

Dave, Hermann, Mike and Chris squatted on the ground with their knees raised and their elbows resting on them. Sid remained in the semi-reclined pose he'd adopted after the meal. Claire kept her head down, her hair tucked under her hat.

One of the tribesmen picked up a canteen and put the strap over his head. It shone in the firelight. He laughed and showed his peers.

Another man spotted the aluminum pot by the fire pit and stuffed it by the handle into his rope belt. Sid made a move to sit up and defend the team's supplies.

"Mr. Lembowsky, if you make any aggressive action, they will kill you." Hermann's low voice offered no room for negotiation.

The tribesmen saw Sid sink back down and laughed. One of them picked up Dave's backpack. Another peered into an unoccupied tent. They edged close to Claire's medical pack.

"Hermann, do something," Dave said urgently while smiling at the natives. "We can't let them get the medical supplies. We need to create a diversion."

Sid couldn't contain himself any longer. "Why don't you just fucking shoot them?" His voice was harsh and loud.

"Lembowsky, shut up!" Dave said from behind clenched teeth, still wearing the false smile. "Stay put and they'll take what they want and leave. We can't shoot them all. They would kill us in an instant."

One of the tribesmen reached for the pack containing the GPS. Sid snapped. "Get your filthy hands off that, you dickhead!" He jumped up and wrestled with the native over the pack.

A collective spitting sound came from the men standing around the circle. Sid's eyes widened and his face froze. He stopped fighting and fell to the ground, face first, clutching the pack.

The tribesmen laughed heartily when Sid's body plopped onto the forest floor. They resumed rummaging anything they could lay their hands on from the camp. One of the men, eyeballing Claire's hat, reached to grab it.

At that moment, Harper emerged from the tent.

Her strawberry gold hair flowed around her shoulders, shining in the glow of the fire. She wore a white tank top and gauze drawstring trousers creating a surreal luminescence. The firelight danced in her blue and yellow eyes, making her look slightly demonic.

The natives stopped in their tracks. The mostly-naked men dropped to their knees and looked at the leader, obviously not knowing what to do. The black man looked up at her and started chanting.

Harper was still far from well, but the full force of her mental faculties had returned. She saw what was going on and instantly became a commanding stature worthy of a goddess.

They looked at her in awe, the tribesmen and the team. Suddenly the ground began to shake, slightly at first and then growing into a full-on rumble. The tents collapsed to the ground and the burning logs in the fire pit scattered. Branches fell. The ground shook so hard every man and woman, black and white, scrambled to stay upright.

The natives ran from the campsite, grabbing whatever they could carry before crashing through the forest. Then, the ground stopped shaking, leaving an uncanny silence.

The team could barely see each other in the scattered embers of the fire.

Sid still lay prone on the forest floor where he'd fallen. "Oh, my God!" Claire cried out when she reached him. Mike rushed to help her while Dave and Hermann got the fire going.

"Do not touch him!" Claire screamed at Mike. "He has likely been hit with poison darts. They could be tipped with red arrow frog poison that can infect you subdermally if you touch them. Get me a flashlight and my medical kit!"

"Jesus Christ! What the hell was that?" Dave said as he kicked the smoldering logs with the toe of his boot back into the fire pit.

"We must be close," Hermann said. "There are volcanoes on the eastern rim. One must have blown. Excellent timing!" He walked over to Harper and patted her shoulder. "That was fantastic! How did you do that?"

Harper was disoriented but an adrenalin rush had given her energy. "OK, does anyone want to tell me what the hell is going on?"

Mike responded with uncharacteristic agitation. "We had uninvited guests, something erupted, Lembowsky's dead, and all our shit is gone. Am I missing something?"

"I think the GPS is still here," Chris said, ever the optimist. "Claire, I believe Sid had hold of it when he went down. Is he OK?" He knelt next to Claire on the leaf-strewn forest floor where Sid still lay motionless.

"Does anyone still have a backpack with a pair of pliers?" Claire finished moving the branches and leaves that fell on Lembowsky. "The only way to remove these darts is with some kind of tool. We need to pull them out and dispose of them safely.

"Is he going to be all right, Claire?" The panic in Chris's voice was obvious.

Claire examined Sid with a flashlight while Mike pulled out the poisonous darts with the pliers on his Leatherman tool. "I am afraid he is in cardiac arrest." Claire's face was distraught. "Barring a miracle, there is nothing I can do here without a defibrillator."

"Well, Claire, we can try." Chris knelt on the jungle floor with her and began to perform CPR while Claire gave Sid mouth-to-mouth.

Once again, the ground began to shake. This time, it felt different, less of a rumble and more of a drum-beat.

Sid opened his eyes and sat up.

The thundering noise got louder, like a huge machine bearing straight down on them.

"What the hell? Another volcanic eruption?" Dave asked.

"This is different." Mike cocked his head toward the sound. "It's lower and coming from another direction."

He had to shout over the ever-increasing noise. "Hey, Hermann, is there anything in this jungle that stampedes?"

"Only forest elephants," Hermann yelled. He began to scramble up a vine-covered tree. Dave took his cue and grabbed Claire.

She hesitated for a second only to see the outline of a few small elephants silhouetted by the spotty firelight, headed in her direction. "But what about Sid?"

"Run!" Mike screamed to the group. He tackled Harper, threw her on the ground next to a log and covered her with his body.

Claire and Dave tried to help Sid to stand, but his legs were still wobbly. "Here, take this. I can make it. Get out of here." Sid handed Dave the backpack containing the GPS.

The elephants reached the edge of the camp, running fast and hard. Chris dove into a rock outcropping while Dave tossed Sid's pack to Claire, yelling at her to climb a tree. The roots of a vine were like steps for her and she scrambled up easily.

Dave shouted for Sid but his voice was lost over the heavy feet of stampeding elephants. He grabbed a heavy vine and shimmied up a tree, barely in time. The elephants were stomping through the camp, trampling everything in their path including the fire. The night turned pitch black and the animals kept coming.

Harper saw only darkness as she lay on the ground next to the log, Mike's body heavy on top of hers. The elephants ran past so closely she was certain one of the gigantic feet would crush her. She cowered in terror, the deafening rumble going on for hours.

She kept telling herself, *Don't lose hope*, but hope was in short supply.

CHAPTER 26

Finally, there was silence. Black, empty silence.

Dave spoke tentatively. "Is everyone okay? Anybody out there?"

"I'm okay, Dave. Does anyone have a torch?" Claire said from her perch among the branches.

"I'm OK, too. I'm here in the rocks. Harp? Mike? Sid?" Chris's voice was shaky.

"I am here, although I have no clue how to get down." Hermann's slight accent made him easy for Dave to identify.

"OK, that's four of you. Mike, Harp, where the hell are you?"

Harper was still on the ground where Mike had thrown her, her back slammed against the dirt. Mike lay on top of her, his nose touching hers. "Well, it seems our positions have changed, Mr. Logan." Mike could hear the smile in Harper's voice. "I know it is you; you have a distinctive aroma."

"Oh, really. I guess anyone gets a 'distinctive aroma' in the jungle after a while." His tone returned the smile.

"Harper! Mike!" Dave sounded frantic.

"We're here! We're OK!" The two of them shouted.

"Thank God. Sid? Sid?" Dave climbed down the vine and landed on solid ground. "Does anyone have any kind of light, a match or anything?"

Claire fished in Sid's pack. "Got it." She snapped on the flashlight and looked for faces. Dave was right in front of her, Hermann in a tree to her immediate right. "Chris, where are you?"

"Over here."

She aimed the torch and saw him waving with a fragile smile on his boyish face. Claire directed the flashlight in the general area where she had heard Mike's voice. Two blushing faces emerged from behind a log.

"Well, it seems you two fared well."

They both smiled sheepishly.

"Where is Sid? Claire, may I please have the flashlight?" Dave took the light and shined the beam over what was left of the campsite. Sid's broken glasses poked out of the mud. "Oh, God."

There was nothing anyone could do for Sid Lembowsky except dig a grave. The tribesmen made off with their hand shovel, so they used tree branches to scrape a hole in the soil. "Be sure to dig the hole deep; animals will smell the body and..." Dave instructed.

The remaining team members did as they were told, each wrapped in their own feelings of sorrow. Sid hadn't been the most likeable person but no one deserved to die on this mission, especially not under the feet of a rampaging herd of elephants. As they pushed sticks into the earth, rain poured down, adding to the atmosphere of gloom and despair.

The deluge let up before sunrise, allowing the group only about four hours of soggy sleep after burying Sid.

"OK, let's recap," Chris said, wringing out his shirt. "Our navigator is dead. The natives took our equipment and worshipped our little botanist here. A volcano erupted and there was an elephant stampede, anything else?" His slender body shivered in spite of the humidity.

"Well, just the one other thing." Mike held up a flattened canteen. "What drinking vessels the natives left us, the elephants trampled. In the jungle, nothing means anything without clean water. Without it, we will die in a couple of days."

"There are streams all over the place." Chris put his shirt back on.

"As you well know, Chris, there are more bacteria in a drop of jungle water than in all your lab's Petri dishes combined. The chief took one of our boiling pots and the other one is flatter than a ten-year-old girl. We will have to rely on rainwater."

Mike lifted the canvas of one of the smashed tents. "What will we put rainwater in? Are we going to stand in a downpour with our mouths open?"

Claire picked up scattered items from her medical kit, salvaging what she could from the debris left by the rampaging elephants.

Sergeant Dave Murano jumped into leadership mode. "Hermann, are there any coconuts around here? Any kind of large nut with a solid hull?" Dave peered into the trees, squinting.

"There are small coconuts, but I don't think they'll hold much."

"OK, folks, fan out. Bring back anything that can hold water. We need to be ready for the next rain," Dave ordered.

They took off with enthusiasm, but returned disappointed, with only a few unripe coconuts. Only Mike was grinning, emerging from the jungle carrying a small armadillo-like creature. He threw it on a rock and began to filet the animal.

"Is that breakfast, Mike?" Claire asked.

"Just a bonus. Hermann, can you make fufu from clay?" Mike held up the bowl-shaped shell of the animal.

"Excellent thinking, Mike! We will plug up the joints in the shell and use it as a drinking vessel!" Hermann kicked up leaf litter to evaluate the clay content of the soil.

"It will take some time to fill that up, I'm afraid." Claire tried not to let her panic show, knowing well the effects of dehydration on the human body.

"We'll see. In the meantime, let's eat." Mike put the carcass on a spit he carved from small palm shoots.

"If we could pry open this canteen without piercing it, maybe we could get some use from it, too." Dave examined the flattened canteen. "Great, people, let's get creative. Gather what we have left. I mean everything salvageable; we never know what may be useful. Chris, have you checked your equipment?"

"Yes sir, it is working perfectly. Has anyone checked the GPS? Does anyone know how to use it?"

Dave fingered the GPS equipment. "I'd been watching Sid, and I think I've got it. It should take me a few minutes to figure out how to call Pharmco to come and get us. Harper, do you have any idea how close we are?

"Well, here is the scenario," she said. "The plant we are looking for has rhizomes requiring sandy, well-drained soil. It will either be by a river with a large bank or in a high meadow. If the meadow is surrounded by any sort of canyon or cliffs, the geological contents of those cliffs must be igneous, not sedimentary. The eroded byproducts of igneous rocks would be a sandy porous soil, not clay or loam. Judging by our increasing elevation for the last few days, my bet is it will be a high meadow. Also, the growing habit of *Podophyllum* dictates that the plant lives in almost full sun, so a relatively large clearing is in order. The size of the plant material will be the dead giveaway. Rhizomes sprawl.

"One of the largest living things on earth is the *Aspen*. There is a grove of them in Colorado that covers over twenty-eight hundred acres. Since each tree is connected by an underground rhizome, it is considered a single organism.

"The plant we are seeking, if it exists, will cover a large area. I believe the flower will be white since its pollinators are either nocturnal or crepuscular, meaning they do their work at night, dawn or dusk. I don't know its exact reproductive cycle, which dictates its flowering dates. It may not even be in flower now, in which case we look for a large area of a single green, low-growing material. If we are extremely lucky and not dehydrated or dead, we may stumble across a large sunny meadow covered with small white flowers. In my mind's eye, it looks like snow."

Mike stared at her. "Wow, not just a pretty face."

"Good. So we have a plan," Dave said in his take-charge manner. "We can collect rainwater, we still have a machete, a Leatherman, some contents of the medical kit, the GPS, and everyone except Mike has managed to preserve their personal GPS locators.

"We also have some water purification tablets and Chris's chemistry set. Other miscellaneous items include Mike's armadillo bowl, the trampled tent canvases, one smashed canteen and our ingenuity."

"Mike, do we have a good supply of tools for igniting a fire?"

"You got it, Sarge. We have waterproof matches, which I keep on my person. We have a flint in case those are lost or damaged, and dammit, I can always rub two sticks together." Mike held up some small twigs in a cross, mimicking a caveman's stance.

"Excellent! Well then, let's get on our way." Dave stuffed the leftover supplies into a battered backpack. He slung it over his shoulder while examining the GPS equipment. "This way."

"Excuse me, Dave," Claire said. "Shouldn't we have some kind of … ceremony for … you know …." She tilted her head toward the fresh grave.

The team gathered at Sid's burial site and stood in awkward silence.

"Right. Dear Lord … anyone?" Dave looked around the group for help. "Mike, Chris, Harper, Claire, Hermann?"

Mike looked at the ground and shuffled his feet. The rest of the team followed his lead. Dave eyeballed the group. "Anyone?"

Mike couldn't help himself. "I'm sorry, the guy was a dick."

The rest of the group nodded in agreement. Before they knew it, they were laughing, breaking the 24 hour spell of sorrow and hopelessness.

"Well then," Claire spoke up in her pragmatic British way. "Dear Lord, bless this mess."

"Amen."

CHAPTER 27

Harper recovered rapidly and was able to keep up with the rest of the group. She suffered with occasional bouts of dizziness but overall felt fine both physically and emotionally. Either the heat wasn't too bad, or she was getting used to it. The perpetually annoying small flies, the *mfanifa*, dissipated as the foliage opened to the sky.

"According to the GPS and our current rate of travel, we will approach the targeted coordinates in the next day or so," Dave said. "Let's stop for a minute and see if we can collect some of this drizzle in the armadillo shell."

The other team members looked at each other with doubt. How could they collect and drink this fog-like mist? They'd had nothing to drink since the previous evening. As they entered a small clearing the rain began to fall in earnest and their frowns turned into smiles.

Mike had the armadillo-ish exoskeleton strapped to his back. Hermann's clay fufu had been pressed into every joint and area with the potential to leak. Mike cut three large *Musa* leaves and devised a sling for the shell in the most open area of the clearing, setting the 'bowl' in the middle. He took more of the broad, water-tight leaves and fashioned a funnel on top, stabilizing it by tying grasses to the shell.

"Very clever, Mr. Logan." Harper admired his handiwork. "Not just another pretty face."

He glared at her for a second before grumbling.

The large surface area of the leaf collar funneled a volume of water into the shell in a short time. Harper could almost taste the sweet, fresh liquid. So thirsty, so thirsty ....

The rain tapered off and the armadillo shell bowl was almost full. "Harper, since you are not entirely well, would you like the first swig?" Dave picked up the shell and handed it to her. "And not a single leak! Mike, you're a genius."

Harper cradled the shell and held it to her mouth.

Chris yelled "Stop!" and pushed the bowl out of her hands and onto the ground, spilling its precious contents.

"What the hell? Are you out of your mind?" Mike had one hand in a fist and the other gripping Chris's collar.

"Wait! Wait! I ... there was a drop of rainwater on my lab. I smelled rotten eggs. I ran a quick test. The water in that bowl contains a low grade of sulfuric acid." Chris stood cowering before Mike's angry posture.

Claire took the lab and studied the readout. "Sulfuric acid, even at a low grade, can eat away your esophagus, your stomach and your intestines. You would basically bleed to death internally. Since we have not had any fluids in almost eighteen hours, the effects would have been horrific." She looked at Chris. "Why Dr. Housdorf, I believed that you just saved our lives."

"Sulfuric acid? That means there actually was an eruption of a very active volcano nearby," Harper said. "It must have ejected a sulfur cloud into the air and mixed with the moisture in the atmosphere." Harper sniffed at a puddle in a rotted log. "Do you think the eruption caused the elephants to stampede?"

"Oh, yeah, the elephants. I almost forgot about them." Mike let go of Chris's collar, still in a foul mood. "And it caused the tribesmen to split."

Hermann smiled at Harper. "No, no. I think the dazzling beauty of Miss Harper scared them away."

Harper looked away, blushing.

"So there was a volcanic eruption. What does that mean?" Dave asked.

No one had an answer.

"How about the water purification tablets?" Harper suggested. What the chimpanzees didn't steal, the natives didn't take and the elephants didn't destroy, was stuffed in one remaining backpack.

"Claire, can you give me a count of the water purification tablets?" Dave said. "We might have to resort to them for now."

"Sid's final goodwill effort was falling on that pack and handing it to us before the elephants could trample it. Give me a second to find them."

Chris stepped in. "They won't do anything for a high acid content. They're made mostly of chlorine, designed as an antibiotic agent only. In fact, the addition of chlorine to the acid will introduce a mixture of sulfuric acid and hydrochloric acid. Even worse."

"Great. So how long before all the sulfur is gone from the atmosphere?" Dave's throat felt dry.

Harper still had on her scientist's hat. "I am not a geologist but I did study some post-eruption scenarios. Depending on the size of the gas cloud, in cubic feet that is, the wind and weather fronts, and the amount of precipitation, we could see an acceptable acid content in a couple of days or so."

The rest of the team cried in dismay, "A couple of days?"

"OK, OK, let's settle down," Dave said. "Chris, any suggestions?"

"Well, if we come across an underground spring, the water purification tablets would work." Chris tried to sound hopeful.

"We can also search for ripe, full coconuts and bulk up on our fruits." Mike was no longer angry. "We can also drink our pee."

A collective "yuck" arose from the group.

Harper came to Mike's defense, "What? The astronauts do it!"

CHAPTER 28

The dehydrated group trudged on in silence. The elevation gain leveled out some, but the heat was increasing. The team felt the air's acidic content in their lungs, slowing their progress. The only good thing about the acrid atmosphere was the reduced fly population.

They reached a large opening in the jungle which spit them out of the dense forest and onto a riverbank. The shores were broad and sandy and they saw a large expanse of sky. In this openness and light, Harper felt like she'd thrown off a heavy cloak.

The team stared east at the still-smoking cone of the volcano. Red lava streamed in gullies down the side. The bright hues of black mountain against azure sky, lacy white clouds and deep red of lava, were breathtaking.

A shallow pool in the river at their feet beckoned. "Water, water everywhere, and not a drop to drink." Harper contemplated dunking her head to cool off.

Claire shouted a warning. "Don't get any water in your eyes, I know it's tempting. But don't."

As Harper bent to the pool, she smelled rotten eggs and took Claire at her word.

"Shit, I could really use a bath." Harper tried not to look when Mike took off his shirt.

"I'll say." Harper teased. She urged to splash him, but didn't risk a drop in anyone's eyes.

Just then, a gunshot cracked in the jungle.

Dave jerked down to a stoop. "OK, people, let's move."

He motioned to them to crouch and pointed across the river. The water was wide but shallow. Holding their essential electronics above the water level, they made a swift and silent crossing. They dove into the jungle on the other side just as a Jeep filled with young black men waving rifles emerged from the trees.

"Mayi-Mayi." Hermann whispered as they hid themselves under the brush.

The Jeep crossed the river and was engulfed by the jungle about fifty feet from where the team lay hidden, where they stayed still until instructed to do otherwise.

Dave waited for ten minutes. He gave Mike the silent signal to get up and scout the area. Mike stealthily moved throughout the brush and then on the riverbank, holding his machete at the ready. All clear.

"They're gone. What was that? I thought there were no roads here, not to mention Jeeps or guns. What the hell is going on, Hermann?" Mike demanded.

"I don't know! This is the first time I have ever heard of the Mayi-Mayi anywhere near this area. Perhaps there is a new mine around here." Hermann sounded genuinely perplexed.

Dave whispered to his team. "OK, people. This changes our strategy. Harper, you mentioned the plant could be by a sandy river. Any promising signs?"

"No, Dave. This bank looks freshly cut by erosion. If this was the plant's habitat, the entire colony would have eroded downstream. But I really did not see any of *Podophyllum's* community members either. I don't think it was here."

Dave used the GPS to verify their location. "We are close, less than a day. We'll get to Harper's snow meadow, Chris will do the analysis, Pharmco will get us out in a matter of hours. We're almost there, gang. However, our MO must change. We travel in silence and pay very close attention. Harper and Claire, the Mayi-Mayi won't be so, shall we say, superstitious as to leave you alone. Do not leave our sight under any circumstances. Do you understand?"

"Do you understand?" Mike stepped face-to-face with Harper.

"Yes, mother." Sarcasm was normal for her in scary situations, but she could tell Mike didn't appreciate her attitude.

Dave took the fatherly tone a parent uses to stop bickering siblings. "Fine. Let's get some lunch and give those assholes a big head start. No fire tonight for obvious reasons, so let's gather all foodstuffs we can to make it through the day. Chris, by the looks of the sky, the sulfur cloud switched directions. Do you think we could use the next rainfall? Or perhaps the river?"

"I don't think we can use the river, at least not for another day or so. But as long as the wind doesn't shift, we should be able to drink from the shell at the next rainfall." Chris was wearing his little boy expression.

At the mention of rain, everyone looked up. Except for the cloud of gaseous vapor above the volcano, the sky was an expanse of blue. Not a rain cloud in sight.

The team walked in silence for hours, stopping only to check their coordinates or test the ripest coconuts for milk. They had better luck gathering fruit, sucking sweet liquid from it to slake their thirst. With more sunlight, edible plants were readily available, the fruit larger, riper and lower to the ground. They easily picked plantains, cassava, mangos, kola nuts, and even kahawa, the native equivalent of coffee.

"Wow, coffee! Gee, if I only had some water, or maybe some cream and sugar." Harper pictured a Starbucks sign hanging in the brush.

"A cup might be nice," Claire said.

The group chuckled.

Then, another gunshot in the brush. They dropped to the ground and wriggled toward a thicket. They lay flat, surrounded by dense foliage. A centipede slithered across Mike's arm. There was nothing he could do but ignore it.

Next, angry and aggressive yelling. Harper raised her head. She had a narrow view of a small village.

The leader of the Mayi-Mayi pointed a gun at a teenage boy. A woman and a girl stood beside him, his mother and perhaps his sister. The man with the gun harassed the boy, who shook his head and yelled back. The gunman motioned to his deputy, who pointed his gun at the mother and daughter. The other man grinned and jabbed the gun into the mother's belly. The leader indicated the women and yelled again at the boy. The boy resisted.

The second man threw the woman on the ground and called two other men. Harper watched in helpless terror as the men grabbed her legs while the first man took down his pants. The teenage boy screamed as the butt of the leader's rifle bashed him in the side of the head. Another man dragged the boy's limp body somewhere out of Harper's line of sight.

Harper wanted to cover her eyes, but could not. She counted six men who raped the woman. They now turned their attention to the young girl. She tried to run but they caught up with her. While the men were busy with the girl, the leader laughed loudly and took a large swig of something from a grimy plastic bottle. He wiped his mouth with his shirtsleeve and attached what looked like a bayonet onto his rifle.

Harper tried to stand when she figured out his plan. Claire held her tightly, forcing her to stay hidden. The Mayi-Mayi leader raped the woman with the sharp object. Blood spilled everywhere. The woman lost consciousness, her body falling limp. As the men left, the young girl, clothes torn and covered with mud, ran to her mother, screaming.

Harper put her head in her hands and cried silently. Claire had viewed only some of the terrible scene. She put her arm over Harper's back, knowing any attempt at comfort was futile.

CHAPTER 29

They waited silently in the brush, with a colony of ants crawling over them, until the Mayi-Mayi finally left and the terrified villagers retreated into their huts.

Harper still wept. The men waited patiently, not sure what she had witnessed, but knowing it was something terrible. When the team resumed travel, there was no laughter or banter as they grimly put one foot in front of the other.

The sunlight faded and they stopped to camp an hour later. Dave approved a fire against his better judgment. Hermann scouted a rocky mountain outcropping with a lookout. They built a small fire against the rocks and took great care to stay low and out of sight.

Mike trapped two rabbits while Hermann found a small bush used locally as a source of salad greens. Chris located a salt bed by the riverbank, regarded as a windfall for later. For now, they did not risk eating salt until they found a reliable water source.

The men were dehydrated but were more concerned with the psychological state of the women. No one spoke.

There were no tents, no creature comforts of any kind. Instead of a soft leaf-litter palette, they fashioned crude bedding out of the canvas from the ruined tents. That thin layer of rough cloth was all that separated them from the black stone of the mountainside.

Chris had first watch.

Harper couldn't sleep. She rose and walked to the lookout point. "Mind if I join you?" Without waiting for an answer, Harper sat next to Chris on the ledge.

The moon was full and for once they could see the night sky. The moonlight shone on the volcano and the surrounding area and in the distance the winding river glistened with diamond prisms.

"Beautiful isn't it?" Chris said, entranced.

Harper didn't speak for a while. "I really don't know what to think anymore. The Buddhist religion dictates that 'when one of us suffers, all of us suffer.' I can't embrace beauty knowing that people can be so cruel to each other. No way."

"Harp, I am so sorry for what happened today, whatever it was. If it will make you feel better, I really would like to hear about it."

"You really are sweet, Chris. Tell me something. What possessed you, obviously a talented chemist, to come to this hell on Earth?" Harper's tone was despondent.

"Harper, I don't know what to say. I think the human condition, something you obviously saw the worst side of today, is not in a very good place. Human emotions are becoming so intense."

He looked at the moon, his brown eyes misty. "I believe as life on this planet gets tougher, the intensity of emotional responses will get worse, off the charts."

"I think what I saw today results from the absolute pinnacle of desperation, ignorance, and betrayal." Harper's voice was a solemn whisper.

"Betrayal is perhaps the most severe human circumstance, commanding the most severe retribution." Chris looked at his feet, pretending to notice a large hole in his shoe for the first time.

They sat in silence for several minutes.

Chris finally spoke. "I was the top chemical analyst at MIT for thirteen years. I won the *Scientific American* award for innovation in chemical processes two years in a row. I traveled the world speaking to fellow scientists on the newly developing field of nanotechnology in field labs, clueless that someday I would hold one in my hand. By the way, the equipment Pharmco gave me is one of a handful in the world. MIT doesn't even have one."

"So is that why you came?" Harper looked at him.

"Well, not exactly. Speaking of betrayal …." Chris stopped himself. He had no intention of speaking so openly, but somehow Harper's presence comforted him to unburden his soul. He was compelled to be honest with her from the beginning, although he did not know why. Later, he surmised she was the type of person who brought that out in everyone.

She did not prod him. He continued in spite of himself.

"I was passed over five times for promotions, three times for the head of the department, twice for a fellowship, each time to a staff member who was inept, ignorant, arrogant, or a kiss ass.

"Not only was I, I mean, am I, the most qualified for any and all of those positions, I had a well-respected fellow chemist in my corner. He stood up for me, championed my cause, and helped me to present my case. We were … um … very close." He ran his fingers over the small pebbles covering the rocky slope.

She looked at him in the moonlight, his innocent face exhibiting obvious pain.

"He betrayed me. The entire time that we were, um, friends, he was talking about me behind my back. He covered up his own mistakes by blaming me. He set me up every time for the fall. The coup de grace was when I walked in on him recently with the dean." Chris's head dropped between his knees.

"Oh, God, Chris. I am so sorry. That is just plain wrong. I am so sorry." She put her arm around his shoulder. Her empathy connected her own pain to his. "Love's fucked up."

He looked at her with a teary smile, surprised that she had seen inside of him and discovered the true nature of the betrayal. "Yeah, love is fucked up."

They both laughed in spite of themselves.

CHAPTER 30

Harper woke with a stiff neck under a brilliant moon. Her arm was asleep and she propped herself up to stretch. She saw Claire collecting her medical gear.

"Going somewhere?" Harper whispered.

Claire put her index finger to her lips.

"You are not going anywhere without me." Harper looked around to see if anyone was watching them. Dave, Hermann, and Mike were asleep. Chris's head was slumped between his knees once again. She could hear faint snoring.

Harper knew exactly where Claire was headed and nothing in the world could stop her from going along. The two women crept silently around the back of the campsite and descended the mountain down a steep path. The moonlight was as bright as the light of day and they could see the village fire in the distance.

"It was only an hour or so from that thicket to this camp. We can make it there, do our thing, and be back before anyone misses us," Claire whispered to Harper.

"What are we waiting for?"

An hour later, Harper and Claire crept around the perimeter of the village of primitive huts.

"This one." Harper pointed to a shanty near the scene of the gang rape. She heard the women inside crying a soft, heart-wrenching melody. "Yes, this is the one."

Harper and Claire entered the front opening of the dwelling. When the women inside saw the white women intruders, they did not call for help, knowing that the strangers meant them no harm.

Claire reached into her battered medical kit and removed an item bearing the international symbol of help. The native women recognized the Red Cross and stood aside, letting Claire remove the bloody sheets. Harper asked the women for water, first in French, then Swahili. One was the girl whom Harper had seen earlier in the day screaming next to the raped woman. The girl nodded in understanding and left.

When Claire wiped off enough blood to examine the woman, her face went ashen. She tried to smile at the women attending to the unconscious victim, but Harper saw the desperation and hopelessness in Claire's face.

"Harper, you are my surgical nurse. This will be the most primitive circumstance you or I will ever encounter, but we have to try."

"Yes, we have to try." Harper set her lips with resolve.

The surgery could only be described as gruesome. Claire used her fingers to find the lacerations and attempted to suture them blindly. The mutilated woman came to consciousness on several occasions only to pass out again in pain. There was no anesthetic. The surrounding native women were strong and kept their attention ready in case they were needed. Harper asked for more cloths and water for the surgery and asked them to pray to their gods. When one of the women brought both Harper and the doctor a gourd filled with fresh water, they drank gratefully. They'd been so wrapped up in their mission they had forgotten their own extreme thirst.

Claire worked deftly for almost an hour. The woman was now resting. An old native woman placed ashes on the patient's head and gave her a honey colored liquid. She lowered her head in deference to Claire and began chanting over the victim's womb.

"I have done all I can, Harper." Claire stood up and washed her hands in a wooden bowl. "It is in God's hands now."

Harper and Claire stepped out of the hut. Directly in front of them stood five semi-naked men, each one carrying a spear.

"Uh oh. Now what?" Harper asked.

Claire threw up her hands in exhaustion. "I'm out of ideas."

Just then, the victim's daughter arrived and stood between the white women and the black men. The girl spoke in French. "My family's men will take you back to your camp."

She took Claire's hand and placed it on her heart. "Thank you," she whispered in Swahili. "Asante sana."

Claire did not need a translation.

The men gently herded Harper and Claire by the elbows and escorted them back into the jungle. They moved quickly through the brush, depositing the women at the base of the rocky hill.

The men bowed slightly and disappeared as if they had never existed.

"How did they know where we camped?" Harper whispered to Claire.

"I don't know. I guess we are the clueless ones."

The moon settled into a lower position but still showered the landscape with a brilliant glow. Harper and Claire easily climbed the rocks back to camp. Just before they came up and around to the back side of the camp, Harper stopped. She heard something—a sound only nature could make, sweet and musical.

"Claire, do you hear that?"

Claire paused and listened. "Is that what I think it is?"

Harper grinned, overcome with an emotion she thought she'd never feel again—hope. "A spring."

CHAPTER 31

"Where the hell have you been?" Mike scolded with fury. "Who the hell do you think you are? Indiana Jones?"

"Indiana Jane, if you please." Harper returned his anger with defiance. "Dr. Guthrie and I had work to do. We did it and returned safely ... what is your problem?"

"But you could have been killed, gotten lost, eaten by jaguars—anything! Shit! You scared the living daylights out of all of us!"

"Calm down there, Tarzan." She softened her tone. "We're OK." She took both his hands and held them down to her side. "We're OK."

"Jesus." He broke free from her hold and turned away. "Jesus."

Harper awoke the next morning as the first scattering of pink clouds kissed the top of the volcano. The steam and lava were gone, the formerly angry tiger now a kitten. Harper moved and felt something draped across her middle, trapping her. She turned her head to see that Mike had slept with his arm around her, undoubtedly to keep her from escaping again.

She smiled. *That's cute*, she said to herself. She lay back to relax for a moment longer before the day began. Suddenly she froze. About two feet from her, a huge white butterfly with orange and red spots landed on a rock, its wings slowly moving. Its wingspan was at least eleven inches.

"Wow." She knew there were more than nine hundred species of butterflies in sub-Saharan Africa, but never imagined she would be so close to such a rare specimen.

The beauty of the morning and the miracle of the butterfly overwhelmed her with astonishment, awe and reverence. She was too often wrapped up in herself and her intellect to just drink in the purity of nature without analyzing every scientific aspect. This moment, a frozen second of sheer wonder, took her totally by surprise. How much did she really need in life anyway? Right now, she had nothing. She was sleeping on hard stone, without any shelter, with near-strangers and an empty belly.

Yet, she had never felt more fulfilled. She was captivated by the warm memory of her father's words.

Fertilizers are tricky, you know. There are the big three: Nitrogen, phosphorous, and potassium. Nitrogen for greening, phosphorous for flowering and bud set, and potassium for root and stem structure. There are the micronutrients: calcium, sulfur, and manganese. Iron and some trace elements are also necessary.

The funny thing is that if a horticulturist applies fertilizer incorrectly, either in a concentration too high or with too many applications, the plant suffers what is called fertilizer 'burn.'

Amazingly, fertilizers are salts. Salts have a negative charge; the root nodes that are their targets have a positive charge. When applied in the proper ratio, one negative attracts to one positive. The necessary nutrient is then extracted from the salt and sent up into the plant material.

When the ratio is upset, the salts attach en masse to the root nodes, plugging them up, and the plant gets nothing. Not only that, salts 'burn' the roots just like when you put salt on a snail.

Too much of a good thing, I would say.

People's lives are just like that, Harper. When you are older, you will meet people with improper ratios. Some people will be incapable of their complete growth for lack of any nutrients.

Some people have been given too much to absorb so they end up with nothing—none of the proper nutrients going into their hearts.

I knew a woman once who had everything. In fact, she had so much of everything it made her mad because, even though she had so much, she was still the same miserable person as before.

You will meet those people, Harper, and nothing you do will make them happy. But you will also meet people who have barely anything and are the happiest on the planet.

Harper smiled to herself, feeling like one of those people.

Mike lifted his head so he could see her face, his arm still wrapped around her. "What are you smiling about?"

"Look." She nodded toward the giant butterfly still drying its wings on the rocks.

"Wow, look at that. It's big!" Just then, the butterfly took flight over their heads. The wingspan was so wide they felt a breeze on their faces as it passed.

"What? No fun scientific facts about butterflies?" Mike teased.

"Well, since you asked … the wings are covered with tiny scales. Thus the scientific name *Lepidoptera* from the ancient Greek word *lepis*, meaning scale, and *pteron*, meaning …."

"Sorry I asked."

"Well, Mr. Logan, cozy are we?" Claire smiled as she arched her back, stretching out what was assuredly an uncomfortable few hours of sleep.

Mike removed his arm from Harper's waist and stood. "I was making sure she stayed put for the rest of the night."

"Thank you, Mr. Logan." Harper also got up, rubbing her side.

"Oh, by the way, we discovered something of interest," Claire said with a sly grin. "Dr. Housdorf, bring your fab lab up here, please?" She made her way up the mountainside.

"Yes ma'am," Chris said dutifully.

Harper and Claire led the men to the spot where Harper had first heard the tinkle of running water. "Chris, would you run an analysis on this?" Harper showed the chemist the small spring with a flourish.

"Gladly, Miss Smith." He dipped the slide into the small puddle formed by the spring and inserted the specimen into the machine. He pressed several keys and entered data.

"Clean as a baby's bottom."

"What, exactly, does that mean Dr. Housdorf?" Dave's intense stare at the spring was only outweighed by his obvious desire for a drink.

"That means go for it." Chris said with his boyish smile.

"You mean … go for it?" Hermann was also fixated.

"Go for it."

CHAPTER 32

Euphoria swept over the team. They had fresh water at last. Dave checked the GPS and confirmed they'd come close to their destination. During a morning stroll around the campsite, Harper came across four large bird nests, yielding almost a dozen blue speckled eggs. She rubbed an oily palm hull on a broad flat rock and placed the makeshift stone skillet on the morning fire. She braided a thick palm husk into a circular form, soaked it in spring water and placed it on the heated flat rock. When Harper cracked the eggs onto the primitive frying pan, the palm husks cradled the eggs, which sizzled.

"Just like Denny's." Harper grinned at Mike triumphantly as the team gathered around the fire, drawn by the intoxicating aroma and sound of frying eggs.

"Oh, she can cook, too." He returned her smile.

"Well, some bacon and biscuits might be nice. Coffee, even."

"Would this fit your expectations, Mademoiselle?" Hermann held up a headless piglet, perhaps a pound of bacon.

"Wow that looks, err, delicious." Claire was primarily a vegetarian before this expedition, but currently ate whatever she could get.

"I snagged a couple of yams last night while we were out looking for you. I stumbled on them when I was running from the … I mean … tripped on a root." Chris produced five orange tubers. "We can make biscuits with these in the manner of fufu."

Hermann spoke up. "And I found some kahawa yesterday. With the armadillo shell, we can warm enough water to make African coffee. I even have a coconut. Maybe there is enough milk to make it creamy and sweet."

"And what are eggs without salt?" Chris displayed a leaf wrapped around a pinch of the sodium chloride he'd found on the riverbank the day before.

"This must be our lucky day!" Claire beamed, summing up the attitude of the team. They'd almost made it!

Claire and Harper also felt satisfied on that lovely morning knowing they had done something, no matter how feeble it may have been, to contribute to an otherwise hopeless situation. They didn't know if the woman survived the night, but they had done all they could.

"Do you think we could go check on her?" Harper whispered to Claire between bites of breakfast.

Claire put her hand up to her mouth and said softly, "They will never let us go without them, and once men get involved, there is sure to be a needlessly stupid outcome."

They smiled at each other in understanding.

"Now what are you two up to?" Dave said after a swig of African coffee. "Planning another escape?"

"No, sir. We promise to be good girls from here on out."

Harper stood erect and put up two fingers in a Girl Scout salute. Claire mimicked her.

"Very funny. OK, folks, let's finish breakfast and make tracks."

Mike emptied the contents of the last of the backpacks. With the scissors on his Leatherman, he cut out the plastic lining and carefully fashioned a pouch out of the plastic material. He tied the top with an elastic string that was attached to the pack's zipper, took the newly-made vessel to the spring and filled it up. With some heavy grasses, he made a braided sling.

Mike positioned the pouch over his shoulder. Very little of the life-giving water leaked.

"Okay, we're ready." He stood, machete in hand.

"Clever again, Mike." Dave said. "By the looks of things, we should be reaching the coordinates by mid-afternoon. We might be at the Nairobi Hilton tonight, folks!"

"Wouldn't that be something?" Chris said. His feelings of guilt over falling asleep during last night's watch were abating. He surprised Harper by giving her a small hug and mouthing the words "Thank you" while the rest of the team watched in curiosity.

"I'm just glad she's all right." He flashed a sheepish grin.

The team's enthusiasm swelled as they headed down the mountain, each one traveling with a light step. They kept a good pace, eager to reach their destination. They traveled in silence for two hours, the only sounds the jungle noises and a low whistling, one of Mike's endearing characteristics. He was especially fond of AC/DC's repertoire.

Despite the cheerful mood on the trail, Claire found the image of the village woman hard to shake. As painful as it was on occasion, she was fortunate to still embrace empathy and compassion as a doctor. It was incomprehensible to Claire that many modern physicians were so cold and clinical.

Harper thought about the woman as well, although from a different perspective. She imagined the boy was taken to work in the mines, to be groomed for future Mayi-Mayi dirty work. The boy had no hope. He had been lost. She felt a heavy wave of sadness for him. In a way, she hoped his mother had died so she wouldn't suffer his loss. This was the defining tragedy of Africa, the vicious circle the copilot mentioned back on the Pharmco jet.

"Harper, any clues?" Dave interrupted her thoughts as he punched up their location on the GPS once again. "The actual coordinates are about five miles from here. But those are approximate and we should be on the lookout for Harper's snowy meadow. Once we get to the actual coordinates, the target could be within a large radius."

"What is our elevation, Dave?" Harper tried to narrow down the radius.

Dave tapped a few more keys. A light flashed. "I don't know for sure, but we better get there soon. The battery warning light is on. We need this puppy to be fully operational to contact Pharmco. I am going to turn it off for now. Just keep going in this direction." Dave pointed straight ahead.

The foliage was so dense Mike used the machete to cut a path. A large snake slithered in front of them while a troop of small spider monkeys chattered overhead. The heat and humidity oppressed the team as *mfanifa* flies swarmed around their eyes, ears and mouths. Rain fell. The light mood of the morning turned dark.

"Surely we've gone more than five miles by now." Mike took off the makeshift water pouch and handed it to Harper.

Sweat, attracting the small black flies, poured off everyone's faces. Even Hermann looked uncomfortable.

Harper passed the pouch. "So, Hermann, where are you from?" His accent intrigued her since the day he joined the mission. The native dialect in the village the night before was distinct. She heard Monte's men speaking Swahili and another language she'd heard again in the village. They seemed related but not completely similar.

"I am from the Nord-Kivu Province, Mademoiselle. My family has lived in that province for many generations." Hermann took a large pull from the pouch, wiped his mouth, and spat into the brush.

"Tell me, Hermann, what was the language the natives in the village spoke yesterday?" Harper and Claire didn't share the details of the previous day's tragedy, agreeing between them there was no need to create more tension, and that men do not handle situations without solutions well.

"I believe they spoke Lingala—or at least a tribal version. Kongo/ Kituba and Tshiluba are mostly spoken in the west, although there are several hundred languages spoken in the DRC. I believe it is one of the problems in this country. There is much racial hatred."

"You mean blacks killing blacks?" Dave took the pouch.

"Yes, brothers killing brothers. It is a desperate time." Hermann looked away.

"And where did you learn to speak English so well?" Harper was intent on solving her puzzle. He used some French words, spoke Swahili well, but had something else … something different.

"My father was a general in the army. We moved around quite a bit when I was a child. I was schooled in the military housing."

Perhaps that was it. His accent, for lack of a better term, must be an amalgam of the various places he was raised.

"Hermann, why did you come with us? How did Pharmco find you?" By now, Harper knew information was a tenuous commodity in Africa and assumed he, like most locals, would be reticent to share.

Hermann's response met her expectations. "Well, Mademoiselle, I have served as guide on many missions. This is my job." He wiped the sweat off his forehead with a grimy bandana.

"Well, thank you for assisting us, Hermann." Claire put one hand on his shoulder and took the pouch from him with the other.

"Everyone had a drink?" Mike took the pouch and put what was left of the precious water back over his shoulder. "Let's go."

They traveled in single file through the thick forest. Harper instructed, "Keep an eye out for a sunny spot through the brush. Remember, we are looking for a large area of the same plant material."

Harper stooped to get a soil sample, dusting away the forest floor litter. She saw a small cat with a black spotted coat dart out of the brush. Hello kitty, she said to herself, thinking of the pet cats back home. Funny, she hadn't thought of California or her Big Sur cabin for days. Now that she held the picture of her former life in her mind, it seemed like a very lonely place.

"We are getting closer; I see sandy soil and two community members," she told the team. "Be alert."

"Yes, the world needs more 'lerts." Chris's attempt at humor was so feeble everyone chuckled out of pity.

The elevation gain increased as they trudged up a rocky slope. The foliage was getting thicker.

"Shouldn't we be on a flat area with less jungle? This seems like we are headed in the wrong direction." Chris was feeling claustrophobic, as was Harper.

They reached the top of the slope. The path forward was blocked by an outcropping of huge rocks, a fortress of black stone looming in front of them. There was no way around. The only option was scaling the boulders.

Mike evaluated the rocks for toeholds. "Shit. We have hit a dead end. Fucking now what?"

"Okay, let's not panic. Let me turn on the GPS and see where we are. Give me a second." Dave sat the system on a rocky ledge.

Following her intuition, Harper kneeled on the ground again to check the soil. She found a complete lack of clay components. The soil was extremely sandy, enabling her to dig with her bare fingers for about six inches. There she found it.

"Come here, you little bastard." Harper pulled the long organic material from the ground and broke off a twine-like piece.

"What is that, Harper?" Claire bent down closer. "Is that a root of something we're looking for?"

"No Claire, it isn't."

The team sighed in disappointment.

"It's a rhizome."

CHAPTER 33

Harper examined the long piece of plant material to determine the direction the shoot had come from. She got on all fours. "This way. Everyone ... dig!"

The entire team scrabbled through the dirt with whatever tool they could find, even their bare hands. Mike cut away the dense foliage above the ground while the team dug tirelessly below like crazed gophers. They stopped for a moment to catch their breaths. Only Harper remained focused on the task.

She laid chest-down on the soil, trying to see under the dense jungle. She shimmied under the brush, saluting a large frog on the way. Mike was right behind her, clearing big trunks and vines above her path.

She clutched the rhizome in her hand, pulling it up from the soil and following its direction. It snapped.

"Shit." She frantically sifted her fingers through the dirt and leaf litter to find the vital strand, but no luck.

"Can't we just go in the direction we were headed?" Mike was still above her.

"Funny thing about rhizomes, they can angle at the nodes. At intermittent intervals, they can shoot out tap roots from the meristematic tissue and redirect at right angles." She sat up and crossed her legs. She threw her hands up and slammed her head back into the soil in utter frustration, falling onto a soft tuft of moss. She looked up to where the sky should have been, only to see more thick foliage.

"Damn, I never thought I would say this, but I hate the color green." She closed her eyes, the back of her head still lying in the moss. She heard another frog croak and turned to see its bulging throat, like he was trying to tell her something. She was on his level and couldn't help smiling at the innocent creature.

"Jamba, Kermit. Quel est en haut?" She reached over to pet him. "I wish you could talk, my little wart-covered friend!"

The frog jumped away, taking one absent-minded look at his mossy perch. Harper saw a tiny shaft of light coming from under the brush. She wrinkled her nose and squinted.

Bright light. Curious.

"I see light!" She jumped to her knees, clawing through the brush. Mike was wiping sweat off his neck when he saw her tearing apart anything in her low-lying path.

"I'm right behind you, Harper." He swung the machete with full force, missing her head by just a few inches on several occasions.

She scratched and scraped, pushing away as much brush as she could.

And there it was. A clearing of about a third of an acre covered completely in white.

"Oh my God." Harper stood covered in mud, dirt under fingernails, leaf debris in her strawberry hair, and laughed.

Mike arrived next, shielding his eyes from the sudden glare. The rest of the team followed, one by one through the foliage tunnel Mike had chopped, and simply stared in awe.

The meadow. They found it at last!

CHAPTER 34

Oh my God, Harper repeated to herself.

Mike stood behind her, gazing at the snowy meadow. "Oh my God."

Claire and Chris burst into the clearing, their slim bodies squeezing into Mike's narrow tunnel side-by-side.

"Oh my God." Both doctors' eyes were as wide as their mouths.

Dave ducked his head under the foliage tunnel into a shower of sun on a field of white flowers. "Oh my God."

"Mon dieu!" Hermann was the last to make it through the narrow jungle passage.

The team stood still, not knowing what to do next, but aching to do something.

After several seconds, they looked at each other and burst into laughter, hugging, jumping up and down like children. Harper knew this was a moment few people ever get to experience. Most people never venture outside their own little boxes to achieve greatness.

She savored the moment, wanting to hold the feeling in her heart forever.

"OK people, let's not get ahead of ourselves." Sergeant Dave came back to reality. "Harper, could this be what we have been looking for?"

"Well, I'm not sure." She was on her knees examining one of the small white flowers.

"What? You're not sure?" Mike looked at Harper with raised eyebrows.

"Um, no, I'm not sure. Chris, would you mind?"

"Absolutely."

Chris knelt next to her with his field lab. She took out the Leatherman and, with the scissors, cut off one flower, careful to keep the blossom attached to the tool to not contaminate the specimen, and handed it to Chris.

He placed the specimen onto a slide and inserted the plant fragment into the field lab.

The team waited breathlessly, each with visions of the meal they'd order at the Nairobi Hilton that evening.

"Chris?" Harper impatiently stood in front of the chemist.

"Hold on, it's coming." The team moved in closer.

"No, I'm not getting much of a reading here. High concentration of phosphorous and some sugars." Chris shook his head. "It does have a highly developed pollen system."

Harper was on the ground, eye to eye with the plant. "Ok, perhaps the flower is too busy chemically to produce what we are looking for. Let's try the leaf and petiole."

She took the small scissors and gave Chris another specimen.

Something kept tugging at her. Something from the past ....

The miracle of every plant is the meristematic tissue. This is found at the nodes and contains the intricate ability to transform into any part necessary to the overall well-being and perpetuation of the species. The meristematic tissue can chemically alter itself into root, leaf, bud, shoot and petiole, anything.

Harper could see her father's eyes light up as he examined the central node of a hydrangea.

I think someday biologists will find that same type of meristematic tissue in a human being. It is inevitable.

What I am trying to tell you, child, is that everything you need, everything you could possibly require to help you achieve anything you want, be anything you want, is already deep inside of you.

"Everything I need ...." Harper said softly. She looked at Chris, who was shaking his head as he completed the analysis of the leaf.

"No—that's not it! It is in the meristematic tissue! That makes perfect sense! The tissue holds all the hormones and enzymes for the entire organism." She threw herself onto the ground, lunged toward the largest specimen and clipped the node.

She handed it to the chemist. The crew was silent as Chris sliced a sliver of the specimen and inserted it onto the slide. The battery power waned and the readout was agonizingly slow.

"Well?" Harper asked Chris.

"It's coming. There is a complex chemical composition in this sample. I see a very high nitriloside and thiocyanate component and an unusual ratio of beta-glycosidase."

"What the hell does that mean, Chris?" Mike looked anxiously at the doctor, swatting away a swarm of *mfanfifa*.

"It means, Mike…." Harper stood in front of the team with her shoulders erect and a large smile on her face. "It means we have found it."

"We found it?" Claire, Dave, Hermann, and Mike chimed in unison, each face bright with weary anticipation.

Harper looked at the team with great fondness.

"We found it."

Once again, the team laughed, hugged, and danced around the meadow in joyful abandon. Dave and Mike gave each other brotherly punches as Claire and Harper jumped like school girls. The sun and landscape echoed their mood, deep blue sky and black volcanic mountains cradling the meadow of white flowers, creating the perfect backdrop for their victory. In a flash, the horrors of the past week were nearly forgotten.

"OK, folks, let's get the hell out of here!" As usual, Dave was the first to regain authority.

"Hermann, help me get this GPS up and running so we can contact Pharmco." Dave turned on the machine and started memorizing their exact coordinates.

"Yes, sir!" Hermann eagerly reached for the radio attached to the system and began transmitting a message.

Harper gathered specimen samples of *Podophyllum* as well as the plant's surrounding community members. She searched the backpack for a container to preserve a soil sample but resorted to her pockets. She heard Hermann talking on the radio to their rescuers, laughing with the unseen party at the other end. The radio was apparently losing its battery charge as he kept talking louder and louder.

She wasn't worried; they each still had GPS chips on their persons. The rescue team would know where to find them and the meadow was plenty big enough for a chopper landing. She thought of her father again, how proud he would have been. She correlated meristematic tissue to her own life, knowing it would hold anything she needed, no matter what was thrown in her path in the future. She had taken a chance on something different. And succeeded.

Something different.

She looked at Hermann, listened to his words.

Something different.

Harper kept her eye on Hermann as she walked over to Mike and

Claire, who were still laughing heartily. They stood by the tunnel in the foliage carved by Mike's machete.

"Um, Mike?" The look on her face quickly put a damper on their good mood.

"What is it, Harp?" he touched her arm.

"Well, it's probably nothing." She looked over to the middle of the meadow where Chris, Dave and Hermann stood joking with one another. She caught Dave's eye. He was standing next to Hermann with the GPS. He saw something on her face that made him cross the meadow to join her, Mike and Claire.

"What's going on?" Dave asked when he reached them.

Harper kept her voice low and tried to keep a slight smile on her face. "I did not recognize the language Hermann was speaking over the radio."

"What do you mean? I was standing right there. It sounded like Swahili to me." Dave looked over to Hermann with an innocent smile.

"Maybe it was Lingala?" Claire asked.

"Do you remember what that crazy pilot said about the people from the east? That Pharmco would never hire them, that it was too risky. Isn't Uganda and Rwanda directly east of here? Didn't he say they would just as soon kill you as look at you?" Harper pretended to examine a *strelizia* flower.

"Yeah, what about it?" Dave sounded concerned.

"The language he spoke was not Swahili, or Lingala, or anything related." She looked at the small group. "I believe it was of Nilotic origin."

"So?" Mike said.

"They speak Nilotic languages in Uganda. The Ugandan militia supports the Mayi-Mayi. I heard about it on National Public Radio."

Dave looked at her sideways. "What are you saying, Harper?"

"I am saying if Pharmco wanted to rescue us, they would not be calling an organized crime gang. They would have their own choppers or at least some Congolese pilots who could be trusted."

They looked at each other, then at Chris and Hermann, still in the meadow.

"Listen." Claire said. "They're coming."

The thrum of choppers grew louder. Two gray helicopters with Russian writing on them, both smaller than Captain Gauld's clunker, dotted the sky.

Harper yelled over the increasing noise of the blades, "They must have been very close."

The first chopper touched down. Harper, Mike, Dave and Claire stayed where they were, not sure what was going to happen.

A large black man with a scar ripped across his face jumped out of the first helicopter before it touched the ground. He carried a semi-automatic rifle. He trotted over to Hermann and shook his hand. He asked something in an unknown dialect and looked at Chris, who still held the chemical field lab. Hermann pointed to it and nodded. The soldier also pointed at the lab and smiled. Chris seemed to understand and nodded his head with a grin, displaying his triumph.

The black man aimed the rifle at the field lab, and pulled the trigger. Chris screamed as a bullet entered his thigh and the lab fell to the ground. The man lifted the rifle and shot Chris in the forehead. Hermann laughed.

The man immediately moved the shotgun to the guide's head.

Hermann dropped as the bullet entered his brain. His last conscious expression was one of utter disbelief.

"Move it!" Dave pushed Harper into the narrow tunnel in front of him. Claire grabbed the backpack and scrambled right behind. Panting with terror and exhaustion, they arrived back at the big stone wall with no way out except the narrow path down the mountain.

"I will go back the way we came and distract them," Dave said.

At that very second, the young girl from the village slipped into view from behind a trailing *pothos* draping over the rocky barrier.

"Vous venez!" She motioned for Claire and Harper to duck under the ivy.

"Do what she says," Dave ordered. He nodded to Mike as they headed down the hill. Harper turned one last time and saw Mike pick off one of the guerillas.

Claire and Harper followed the girl down a dark shaft into the mountain, slowing to a stop when they lost the light from the entrance.

"We'll just sit tight until they leave." Harper turned to the girl. "Merci beaucoup, mon ami!" Even though the girl could not see the smile on her face, she heard it in her voice.

"Sorry, what the bloody hell just happened?" Claire asked.

"Shit, I don't know! Why did they kill Hermann and Chris?" Harper's heart sank at the thought of the sweet, gentle chemist. "Chris!"

"You do know what this means don't you?" Claire began rummaging through the backpack.

"No, what?"

"It means, my dearest Harper, that no one is coming to get us."

"Oh my God," Harper whispered, her stomach churning as reality sunk in. "No one is coming to get us."

CHAPTER 35

"Got it!" Claire pulled something out of the pack in the darkness. A click echoed through the cavern, followed by a beam of light. "The blessed torch! And it works!" She shined the light on both Harper and the native girl's face.

Their joy was short-lived as gunfire ricocheted off a side of the shaft. "What the hell?" Harper ducked and herded Claire and the girl further into the tunnel. As they frantically moved forward, Harper asked the girl in French how far down the tunnel went into the mountain. She could barely hear her response over the gunshots.

The girl scurried behind Claire and the flashlight, Harper right behind them in the dark, narrow cave. The native girl said in French, "The legend is the tunnel goes into the volcano and comes out the other side. No one has ever lived to tell if that is true. The volcano eats them before they ever come out."

They kept moving, desperately searching for a hiding place.

"Comment êtes-vous arrivé?" Harper needed answers.

The girl, sensing her fear and urgency, answered in rapid French. "I followed you. When I saw you were in trouble, I brought you to this cave. I tried to save you as you tried to save my mother."

An explosion boomed from the entrance of the tunnel. Rocks, dust and debris shot down the shaft, slamming into the women from behind. Harper, at the back of the trio, received the brunt of the force. She fell over the girl and Claire, trying to protect them from the heavy shrapnel.

The din of falling rubble finally stopped.

"Harper, Mademoiselle! Are you all right?" Claire scrambled to get up, helping the native girl dislodge small rocks from her face. She searched in the dark for the flashlight, digging it out of the debris. The torch was still on, although the light was fading. She picked it up and shined it on Harper.

She lay on the floor of the cave, covered in rubble.

The girl and the doctor carefully removed the rocks. There was a large gash across her forehead dripping blood into her eye. Her arms and back were also bloody. She did not move.

"Harper! Harper!" Claire tried to rouse her, fearing the worst. She checked Harper's pulse in her neck and wrist. She shined the flashlight into Harper's eye as she gingerly lifted the eyelid. Harper's pupil dilated.

"Thank God." Claire was not a religious woman but was truly grateful at that moment.

Harper slowly sat up, putting her hand to her forehead, wincing. Claire retrieved the first aid kit from the pack and administered to Harper's scrapes.

"Damn, is this the Nairobi Hilton?" Harper stood up, brushing dust and pebbles from her pants. "Not much on accoutrements, are they?"

Both the doctor and the girl smiled, the girl apparently understanding from Harper's tone of voice that she was making a weak attempt at humor.

"Very good, Harper and… what is your name, child?" Claire put her hand on the girl's arm.

"Comment vous appelez vous?" Harper asked.

"Shadea, Madame." Claire and Harper had not seen the girl smile before this moment. As tentative as it was, it was still a smile.

"Comment est votre mère?" Harper asked about the girl's mother.

Shadea stared at the light from the torch as it reflected off a pink quartz stripe on the cave wall. She looked back at Claire with a tear in her eye and shook her head.

Claire reached over and hugged her maternally. "I am so sorry, child." The girl wept in her arms.

Harper waited for the girl's sobs to quiet, then said, "Let's reassess our constantly changing situation." She knew it would take all her wits, scientific and otherwise, to get them out of this predicament.

"Let's sum up. Chris and Hermann are dead. The field lab has been destroyed. Dave is on the run with nothing except supplies he may have attached to his body. Thankfully, he distracted those men long enough to let us escape. And Mike, well, God only knows. I think I saw him kill the first man who came through from the meadow." Harper pressed the gauze a little harder onto her forehead.

"Why are they after us?" Claire dried the girl's eyes with her bandana.

Harper didn't respond. She studied her immediate surroundings. The tunnel was about five-feet tall and three-to-four-feet wide. She shined the light behind them only to see a solid wall of rock. She shined the light ahead of them and found a narrowing tunnel. She tried to quell her claustrophobia, shaking her head and body like a wet dog.

"It seems they want us gone and never heard from again. If, in fact, they are from the Ugandan militia and not from around here, they are unaware this tunnel has another end—at least, we hope it does—and they presume we will perish in here. They will spend the balance of their energy to hunt down and kill Dave and Mike."

"Well, I have every confidence in Dave and Mike. But why do they want us dead?"

Harper answered with another question. "Claire, did anyone know you were coming on this mission?"

"No, it all happened too fast. You?"

Harper looked thoughtful. "Me, too. And I know for a fact that no one would inquire after Chris if he didn't come home. Mike is a hired gun and a loner, and I am doubtful if Sid had any friends who would miss him in any event."

"What are you saying, Harper?" Claire was still holding the girl's hand.

"I am saying Pharmco brought us here to find the plant material and then eradicate us and the plant, with no one being the wiser." Harper's demeanor toughened. "I am saying they probably did the same thing to Dr. Merrill."

"Even if he didn't find the plant?"

"That's right. He knew too much."

"This doesn't make any sense," Claire said.

"Pharmco has no intention of anyone ever finding and processing the right variety of *Podophyllum*. My guess is they plan to eliminate the species forever."

"Good heavens! Why in the world would they want to do that?"

"Because cancer treatment is a one hundred billion dollar a year industry. Why would they want anything to interfere with profits like that?"

The women stood silently for a moment.

"Bastards." Claire scowled.

"Bastards." Harper agreed.

"Bastards!" Even though she didn't entirely understand, the native girl found resolve and stood to join her new team.

CHAPTER 36

The women forged on into the blackness, crawling through tight spaces as they moved from chamber to chamber. The flashlight flickered occasionally. Fortunately, they'd relied on fires to light their way through the night up until now, so the batteries might be OK.

Harper touched the outside of her pocket, reassuring herself the brass lighter Ursula gave her was still there. She hadn't used it but though it had been dunked in rivers and smashed against rocks, she hoped it still might work.

They wormed their way through a narrow passageway and entered a large cavern with an unusual odor. The flashlight revealed the source of the stink: a small pool with a greenish glow.

"Smells like petrol." Claire wrinkled her nose.

The flashlight blinked. It flickered on again, but Harper knew the light would fade out for good soon.

Petrol.

"I've got an idea." Harper aimed the waning flashlight at the ceiling. "Claire, do you still have the Leatherman?"

"Oui, Mademoiselle. I never let it leave my side. In fact, now that I have it, I think no girl should ever be without one."

Harper spoke to Shadea in French, telling her to gather small roots, anything that could be fashioned into a string or rope.

"Claire, take that tool and cut some of these hanging roots. We will need both thick ones and small ones. Let me give you a leg up."

Harper stripped off her khaki shirt and wrapped it around a stick she had found at the entrance of the cavern. Taking the twine-like roots that Shadea collected, she tied them around the shirt and the stick. She dipped the shirt into the pool and let it soak.

"Claire, while we still have some light, please fetch the matches. We will be ready with a torch when the flashlight finally gives up." She shined the light on her finished product, smiled with satisfaction, and stuck the crude torch into the back of her pants. The gasoline-like liquid burned slightly against her back but she ignored the slight pain.

"When we light this sucker, please be aware that my backside is coated with an extremely flammable substance. As a matter of fact, just for safety's sake, I think I will light the torch."

"Why Miss Harper, you are a clever girl." Claire smiled in admiration. "How in the world did you ever think of that?"

"Necessity really is the mother of invention." Harper returned the smile. "I don't suppose there is anything to eat or drink in that pack of yours. By the way, you are the clever girl for snagging that before our hasty departure."

"Thank you, but the answer is no. Mike had the water pouch and there hasn't been any food in this pack for days."

"Well, then, let's go." Harper gathered her resolve. She asked the native girl how long the tunnel might be so she could gauge the length of time needed for the torch, but the girl only shrugged.

"Well, let's make the best of it. We seem to be pretty safe in here. As long as we have light and oxygen, we'll be fine." Harper's role as leader made her forget all about her claustrophobia.

The three women silently climbed, slid and waded through various underground terrains. Occasionally they ran across a small subterranean stream, but they dared not drink from it, not without the water purification tablets.

The path was relatively clear. Dusty footprints let them know that other humans had attempted the same trip, though how long ago no one could say. The trio could only hope the path actually led to another exit.

They came to a very large cavern where the path huddled high against a wall. The trail was very narrow, each step almost impossible to see. With just the single flashlight, each of them had to wait until the light shone directly at her feet before she dared take the next step.

The native girl was clearly terrified. She clung to the cave walls, shuffling against the rock. Claire noticed it first.

"Harper, I think she is afraid of heights. Let's go a little slower."

"Claire, we have got to move. The flashlight is on its way out, and having been kicked out of Girl Scouts, I have no idea how long my shirt torch will burn."

"You were kicked out of Girl Scouts?" Claire said with a laugh.

The women held hands as they reached the end of the ledge, allowing a moment of rest on a flat rock at the top of the cavern.

"Yes, I was kicked out of Girl Scouts," Harper said while Claire continued to goad her.

"How on earth does one get ejected from Girl Scouts?"

"Well, the truth is, I didn't want a badge in cooking or sewing or art or archery." Harper pressed the bandage against her forehead. Whenever she stopped moving, the wound throbbed. "I wanted badges in the things the Boy Scouts did. You know, hunting, fishing, knife throwing. I got caught in the boy's camp and they threw me out."

The native girl regained her composure, even daring to peer over the rock to see if she could see the bottom of the cavern.

Harper remembered something she learned from the Boy Scouts. "Claire, let's throw something down to the bottom of the cave and see how deep it is." Harper liked the idea that the cave might be huge; it gave her the feeling of openness she desperately longed for.

"Good idea. Let me find a rock."

Harper said, "I have a better idea." She reached her hand into her bra and pulled out the small GPS device residing there since her pack had been delivered on the Pharmco corporate jet.

Claire saw the tracking device resting in Harper's hand. "Brilliant." She retrieved her GPS from her own undergarment and held it up.

They tossed the devices over the edge in unison. There was no sound for almost a minute, then, two faint thunks.

"OK! Let's move!" Harper directed the weak light to the narrow tunnel on the path ahead.

They lost track of time and direction. Harper thought they were headed consistently downward, which she reckoned was correct. They heard the scurry of sub-terrestrial rodents and their footsteps crunched on unidentified critters. Harper took the presences of these little animals as a good sign, there must be air shafts. She chose not to shine the light on the creatures.

Every time Harper got close to a claustrophobic meltdown, she distracted herself with brushing up on French. She spoke to Shadea about her family, her tribe, and her interests. The girl was shy but very sweet and Harper noticed her voice was a lovely combination of African Swahili gilded with a French lilt. Harper's mind was miles away when the girl started to cry.

"What happened? What did she say? Is she all right?" Claire stopped and shined the light on the girl's face.

"First of all, Claire … of all the Brits I know, you are the only one I have ever met who does not speak French." Harper was hungry and thirsty. She regretted snapping at Claire. "Shit, I'm sorry."

"You are absolutely correct, Harp. The truth is I do not speak a single language other than English, and I don't do that very well either." Claire stumbled over a root. "I just don't have the gift."

Harper knew she was right. It was a gift, one that had saved their lives.

"And thank God you have it, Harp. By the way, how did you ever suss out that Hermann was speaking Ugandan, did you say? And not Swahili?"

"Well, that is a good question. I knew the language Hermann spoke wasn't the same as Monte's men or the people in Shadea's village. I tried to distinguish a dialect to both of those languages to make it something from the Congo. Then something my father once said to me popped into my head. Something different. I stopped trying to add to a local language and went somewhere else. I heard a taped speech by Okot p'Bitek while I was in undergraduate school. Some of the speech was in his native language of Uganda, a language with a Nilotic base. I picked it up out of Hermann's radio transmission. I had heard that sound before."

"Bloody brilliant!" Claire was on her knees crawling through a narrow section of the tunnel. "You saved our lives, you know."

"Yeah, yeah, whatever." Harper didn't like the attention that came with being a hero. "Anyway, what I was trying to tell you is what Shadea told me in French." Harper smiled. "Claire, I'm just giving you some shit. Even if you did speak proper British French, I don't think you would understand much of what she is saying. It's convoluted by the native African dialect. Zaire was only taken by the French in the early twentieth century."

"Well, what did she say?"

Harper spoke to the girl to ask her if it was all right to convey her story. The girl seemed ashamed but nodded in acceptance.

"Claire, the woman, her mother, died. Her brother was taken to a Mayi-Mayi camp to be groomed for warfare and her father had to publically denounce his wife and daughter as whores. Her mother's dead body was burned in disgrace, thrown in with garbage. Shadea was forced to leave her village, where she lived all her life. She has been abandoned by her whole family. She has nowhere to live, nowhere to go."

Claire stopped. "What? It wasn't her fault! She was the victim!"

A single tear ran down Shadea's cheek.

The doctor shuddered. "Oh my God. I mean, sorry, what god would ever allow such a travesty?"

"Well, the good part is, kind of, that her dad stood up to support her. He loved his daughter and wanted her reputation to be restored."

"What do you mean 'kind of'?"

"They killed him for it. But at least she knows he loved her."

Harper looked at the girl and said something quietly in French with a sweet tone to her voice.

"Fucking bastards!" Claire said with uncharacteristic raw emotion.

"Precisely."

CHAPTER 37

"You know, of course, that the color black is the absence of light." Harper's only remaining defense mechanism against her mounting fear was analyzing everything to death.

"Oh?" Claire was hot and tired.

"Most people don't know that white is the combination of all colors. That is why stars shine as white."

"What? How could white be all colors combined?" Claire yawned involuntarily.

"If you were to shine a green, red, and blue light from a projector and merge them into one, the result would be pure white. Black is the complete lack of light.

"Take space, for example. The vacuum of open space is black while the full spectrum of elements in the galaxies reflects as white. Kind of makes you think about the whole god-devil thing, doesn't it?" Harper wiped her forehead. "Is it getting hot in here?"

"I think so, but I am menopausal. It's always hot." Claire dabbed her chest with a filthy bandana.

The native girl shook with fear. "Les dieux du volcan viennent pour nous!"

"Non, non. The volcano gods are on our side. Just like in Hawaii, Pele is a woman. She can shape the land, give it or take it away. She will take care of us."

The flashlight flickered one last time then faded to black. No amount of shaking, coaxing or cursing would convince the device to provide more light. The women were surrounded by complete darkness. Harper enlisted her photographic memory to visualize the path forward. She reached out for Shadea's hand and told her to do the same with Claire.

"Claire, please give me the matches." Harper's voice remained calm.

"Oui, Mademoiselle." Claire took the small package of waterproof matches from her breast pocket and reached over the native girl to hand them to Harper.

PURSUIT

A strange sound made the trio stop in their tracks. At first it was a slight 'swooshing,' then a flapping. Most disconcerting was a high-pitched screech echoing in the vast darkness. The native girl screamed.

They came in the complete darkness—hundreds of them.

They flew at the women's faces, clawed at their hair. They bit every exposed part of the women's bodies. Their numbers were so great they felt like a heavy blanket. Harper tried to position herself on top of the other women to protect them against the onslaught, but could not. The sheer volume of the flying mammals was overwhelming, pushing the team's faces into the guano that lay on the cave's floor.

The noise echoed, deafening the women. Harper tried to remember her zoology to distract herself from the reality of the situation.

They are bats. Thousands of them, mind you, but just bats. Unless they are rabid, they can't really hurt you. Well, unless they smother you.

That was it. *Don't let them smother us and we will be fine.* She buried her face in her undershirt and grabbed the other women by the arms. Rising to their knees and working together, they managed to shake off a substantial amount of the bats.

A deafening sound erupted from the next chamber. It turned into a blast, knocking the women back to the guano-slick floor.

The bats evacuated immediately.

"Jesus!" Harper rose slowly, wiping bat guano from her chin. "What is the deal with this continent? Can't anyone relax for even a minute?"

They were hit with an overwhelming blast of hot air.

"Les dieux du volcan!" The native girl threw herself to the ground, prostrate in worship.

A strong sulfur smell came in with the heat into their chamber. Harper spotted a faint red glow in the next chamber.

"Nous permettre d'aller!" Harper grabbed Shadea's hand in the blackness and lead her toward the source of the red glow. Claire followed by holding onto the girl's primitive dress.

"Harp, are you sure you know what you're doing?" Claire asked as the heat beat against her face.

"I am not sure of anything, Claire. Give me the matches."

"Jesus! The bats knocked them out of my hands! They are here somewhere. Damn, I can't see anything! Oh God, Harp, I am so sorry!" Claire started to cry.

"OK, OK! Let's not get our knickers in a twist. I have an idea." Harper

– 145 –

took the gasoline-soaked torch out of the back of her pants. Her hands were so coated with bat guano that the torch kept slipping from her grasp.

Bat guano. Hmmm. High concentrations of potassium nitrate and phosphorous.

She placed the torch on the ground and rolled it in the guano, completely covering the soaked shirt while Claire and Shadea tried to clean themselves off in the dark.

"OK, girls, here's the plan. Take off whatever you can spare and tie it around your nose and mouth and hands." Harper repeated the instructions in French. "Since we have no light, and I do not know the chemical composition of the gases here when mixed with butane, I think it unwise to try the lighter. I assume the red glow and heat we feel from the next chamber is from a small interior volcanic eruption. The eruption is probably what scared the bats away. We will proceed through that chamber as quickly as possible and light the torch with the molten lava."

"Are you always calm in situations like this?" Claire asked, her voice shaky.

"I'm almost always cool when the going gets tough," Harper replied. "But when we're out of danger, just watch—that's when I'll meltdown."

They edged to the portal of the next chamber and discovered a small cavern with a bubbling red pool. A narrow pathway on the left skirted the lava bed.

"Here we go. Keep your nose and mouth covered no matter what. We are going to get the next chamber fast. Watch your feet, cover your knees and hands. The ground may be very hot."

Harper repeated herself in French. She couldn't remember seeing shoes on the native girl's feet.

They crawled through the portal, Harper first. She dipped the torch in the lava, not knowing what to expect. Her hypothesis was that the potassium nitrate and phosphorous would make the torch glow brighter and last longer. She was not sure how the other elements in the guano would react.

The torch flared, then burned even and white, filling the small chamber with light as bright as the sun. Harper could easily follow the path to find the chamber's exit.

There wasn't one.

CHAPTER 38

"Shit!" Harper turned around. "Go back!"

The women followed her instructions only to discover the bats had reappeared, blocking the portal back to the room they'd come from.

Harper rotated herself back to the lava chamber.

"There must be a way out. This chamber would be entirely filled with smoke and fumes if there weren't." She took the torch and aimed it at the floor. Nothing. Solid rock.

Always remember to look up. She heard her father say it. She held the torch up. She could not see the chamber ceiling, but she did spot a small ledge about ten feet above the floor of the cavern. It seemed to lead to some sort of opening. She couldn't tell for sure if it really was a way out, or just the shadow of desperation and wishful thinking.

It took one look at the sheer panic on Claire's and Shadea's faces for Harper to act quickly.

"Claire! Give me a leg up!" Harper placed a foot on Claire's cupped hands and pulled herself up onto the small ledge. The heat and fumes were even stronger higher up in the chamber. She held the torch above her. The flame flickered.

"Excellent." She shouted below, "Claire, can you lift me any higher?" She heard the doctor grunt as she boosted her just enough to put the torch into a small tunnel to see inside. It was covered with webs. She placed the torch deeper inside to burn off the surrounding materials. She felt a cool breeze on her face.

"Here! Up here!" Harper jumped down and handed Claire the torch.

"You first, Claire." She put her hands together and gave the doctor a leg up. Claire scrambled onto the ledge and held out her hand for the girl. Shadea, overcome by a combination of terror and toxic fumes, was losing consciousness. Harper pushed her from behind as Claire pulled her up.

Harper was now in the chamber with no torch and no one to give her a boost. The noxious gases were starting to make her feel dizzy.

Don't panic now.

She called to Claire. "The Leatherman!"

Claire threw it to Harper. It slipped through her shaking fingers as her legs started to wobble. Claire held the torch over the ledge so Harper could see the gleaming metal of the Leatherman blade lying on the ground. She picked it up and dug into the side of the cave, making toe-holds for herself. She gathered all of her remaining strength and shim-mied up the wall. At that very moment, the bubbling pool of lava erupted. Fire licked at the bottom of the ledge.

"Move!" Claire was on all fours in front with the torch, burning the dense webs blocking the tunnel. The girl followed, moving blindly. Heat seared Harper's back and feet. The intensity was so great she thought she had lost her shoes. Perhaps the soles had burned off.

Then she remembered the African girl's feet. She didn't remember seeing any shoes.

The women crawled clumsily. The native girl between Claire and Harper could barely move, still semi-conscious. The tunnel was not more than three feet wide and tall and covered in slime. Claire did an excellent job burning off the dangling, webby material with the torch.

Tired, hungry and dehydrated, the women functioned purely on sur-vival instincts. The only thing keeping them going was the breath of fresh air coming from the forward direction. They reached a small space where they could sit upright. The room was less than four feet wide, but it gave the women a chance to catch their breaths. Harper took the torch and waved it around the room, burning up the cottony webs.

Shadea sat up against the wall, her eyes half closed. Harper aimed the torch in her direction and saw her face. "Claire, this is not good. Look at her."

Claire moved over to check the girl's vitals. Harper leaned against the wall, holding the torch for the physician. She was surprised she didn't feel claustrophobic, perhaps fear of small spaces was the least of her worries. She closed her eyes for a second to catch her breath and reboot her courage.

"Harper, can I have a little more light, please?" Claire was on her knees looking at the girl's pupils. Harper held the torch closer. As she did, she got a glimpse of something red. She lowered the torch to the floor of the small cave.

"Claire."

"Can I please have more light?"

"Claire."

"What?" Her tone was impatient.

"Look." Harper pointed to the girl's feet. The barefoot soles had burned completely off and the flesh was a pulpy mass of blood and dirt.

"Oh my God."

Harper thought she would faint. She snapped out of the lightheaded feeling as Claire took charge, diving into the first aid kit.

What was it Monte said? "Each one of you will be a hero at times, so you must each act as a hero at all times, as you just don't know which time will be yours."

Claire was the hero now. She deftly wrapped the girl's feet in alcohol-soaked gauze after rubbing petroleum jelly on the wounds so the dressing wouldn't pull off her remaining skin. She put three Tylenol tablets down the girl's throat and wiped Shadea's sweating brow with her own bandana.

"Is she going to be all right?" Harper was lost in admiration of Claire's skills.

She always hoped that someday she could do something to help others, like Claire was doing now. That was why she was in this godforsaken place. That she was never going to save the world now, that the glorious mission had all been a sham, came flooding back into her consciousness. Betrayal seemed to be the recurring theme of her life.

"Fuck. Let's get out of here." Harper looked at the girl, who seemed to be back in her body.

Harper asked in French, "Can you continue?" Harper's empathy came through to the girl. Shadea smiled weakly. "Oui."

The fact that she showed concern at all came as a surprise to Harper. She rarely allowed herself to indulge in emotions. Too vulnerable.

They resumed crawling on all fours, Harper in front burning away the cobwebs. The air was fresher and the little team picked up the pace. Harper looked ahead and thought she saw daylight in the far distance.

"I think I see something!" She turned around to smile at Shadea and Claire, shining the torch to see their faces.

"What is that?" Something on the native girl's face was moving.

Harper directed the torch to Claire. Similar objects were crawling on the doctor's face. Her pale British complexion made it possible for Harper to identify the intruders.

"Spiders!" Harper looked at her arms and saw hundreds, perhaps thousands, of tiny black spiders crawling all over her.

"Get them off of me!" Claire screamed like a teenager at a horror movie.

"Let's go!" Harper started to swat away the creatures while she lurched into a high speed crawl. Shadea and Claire continued to scream, fear lending speed to their arms and legs.

As they came closer to the light, they saw a hint of green. They rushed toward the opening in the tunnel, brushing off arachnids.

Harper pushed through the foliage curtain and fell out into a small clearing in the jungle. Shadea and Claire tumbled out behind her, still screaming. They stood up and looked at each other. They were still covered in small black spiders. The tiny insects were invading their clothes and hair, most likely as scared as they were.

"Take off your clothes!" Harper commanded. "Décoller vos vêtements!

All three tore away at what was left of their garments, shaking their hair vigorously. They helped each other pick off the spiders from their backs, finally getting rid of every last one.

The girl dropped to her knees as her feet gave out. Harper and Claire examined her and saw that the bandages were holding and the girl was all right considering this nightmare.

Claire and Harper looked at each other stark naked and laughed. They laughed like crazy women and danced in a circle. They had made it. Against all odds—they had made it.

That's when Harper noticed the tribesmen standing at the edge of the clearing.

CHAPTER 39

The men silently moved toward the women. There were seven of them, most wearing nothing but beads and tattoos.

Claire and Harper stood rigid, naked, in jungle boots. Their unbound hair framed their scratched and bloodied faces. Harper's large strawberry curls made her look like a rabid witch.

One of the men, apparently the leader, looked down at Shadea and said something in a language Harper vaguely recognized. He pointed to the girl's bandaged and bloody feet and motioned to two of the men. One of the men took off a cape-like garment and laid it down on the ground. Two of the other men picked up the native girl and placed her on the cape.

Harper lunged forward in a knee-jerk reaction.

"Harper, stop!" Claire screamed.

Four of the men jumped to grab both Harper and Claire, forcing their wrists to their backs. The native leader yelled something at them, but Harper had no idea what he said.

The other two men picked up the cape and carried the injured girl.

Claire and Harper were pushed together, their hands tied with leather thongs.

The group moved into the jungle, Shadea gently carried on the hammock-like cape. Claire and Harper, joined at the wrist, were prodded forward by the men behind them.

As they trudged on, Harper saw they were at the base of the volcano and that it was approaching dusk. She felt lightheaded from the lack of food and water.

Dusk. What day is this? How long were we in that tunnel? Was it only this morning I woke to see that beautiful butterfly? No, it couldn't have been. It is true time really does stand still in this place.

She recalled her father's notion that perhaps time really is nothing but an illusion, not to mention, "completely irrelevant."

They reached a small village and Shadea was taken to a hut. Harper and Claire stood in the middle of the clearing while the leader gave his instructions. They were led to a palm tree and tied to the trunk, back to back. The men left.

"What in the hell is going on here? If they are going to kill us, let's get it over with. If not, I could really use a drink." Harper tried to be brave, but her reservoir of courage was going dry. She stopped short when she heard a familiar voice.

"Well, well, well. What do we have here?" The voice belonged to Mike Logan, emerging from the brush with a monitor lizard draped over his shoulder.

"Harper. Claire." He grinned and threw the animal to the ground. "I can't tell you how nice, and I mean really nice, it is to see you both." He walked around the tree, slowly surveying the scenery.

Harper was never so acutely aware of her nakedness. Not only naked, but naked and tied to a tree with another naked woman and being ogled by Mike Logan. The only defense she had left was sarcasm.

"Mr. Logan. How lovely to see you." She feigned a smile. "Would you mind terribly cutting these ropes? We have been through a difficult ordeal and really could use some attention."

"Oh, I'll give you some attention all right." Mike licked his lips.

"Mr. Logan!" Claire shouted, her tone making it clear he'd better behave in a civilized manner.

"Oh, right. Let me get that for you." He cut the leather thongs with one slice of his long hunting knife.

Harper used her hand to sooth her bruised wrist.

"Are you OK?" He looked at her wrist and the bloody gash across her forehead.

"Oh, I'm fucking fantastic!" She reached up and slapped him as hard as she could. "That's for what you were thinking!" She stood in front of him, nipples erect, as he put his hand to his face, soothing the results of her right cross.

"Indeed, Mr. Logan!" Claire stood next to Harper. Even with both of their bodies dirty, sweaty, and bloody it was obvious Mike found them amazingly attractive. "Now, go and get us some water before we perish right here." Claire scolded like he was a naughty child.

"Um, yes ma'am."

"MAP, Claire." Harper watched as Mike scurried away, trying to regain his dignity.

"MAP, Miss Harp?"

"Yes, Claire. I have this theory I call 'MAP.' Men Are Pigs. Mike just substantiated my hypothesis, once and for all."

"Indeed. Now let's get something to eat!"

Mike cut large banana leaves for Claire and Harper to cover themselves, like Eve's fig leaf. The tribe leader was assured they were not witches and they were given water and fruit, as well as a hut and a pouch of water for bathing.

Claire washed quickly and left to find Shadea and check on her condition.

Harper was alone in the hut, examining the cut on her forehead by candlelight in a bowl of murky water. It was almost dark. The hut was all thatch with a dirt floor. No door, just a loose covering over the one opening. There were four leaf pallets for sleeping and a low, makeshift table. This tribe was a hunter-gatherer group, well stocked and peaceful.

She heard a dull rap against the thatch.

"Harper? Are you all right? Can I come in?" Mike stood at the opening of the hut.

She checked that she was adequately covered by the toga-like wrap the village women gave her. She didn't want to bring out Mike's lascivious frat boy personality again.

She approached the opening. "What do you want, Logan?"

"I want to say I'm sorry. I was just having a little fun. It's not every day that a man finds himself in, well, such a situation."

He flashed that smile for a second, then thought better of it and rearranged his face into something more sincere.

"Hmm. I guess the fact that you are a man makes it impossible for you to act otherwise." She whispered under her breath 'MAP.' He didn't hear her.

"Do you have any idea what we have been through?" She still hadn't had her anticipated meltdown. She wondered why. She felt safe now; it was okay to relax and let her hair down. She wondered if she had lost the ability to feel any emotion at all.

"How did you find me, I mean us?" Harper asked. "How did you know out of all the villages in Africa, this is where we'd end up?"

"Well, I knew where you entered the tunnel. I circled back after the choppers left and saw that the entrance had been blown to bits. I've heard the legend that the tunnel went all the way through the volcano, although I didn't believe it. Still, I thought it was worth a try."

"You hiked all the way around the volcano just in case we might have been able to get through the tunnel?"

He nodded and looked at her in the candlelight. He saw the thoughts travel across her face and sensed the scared child hidden deep behind her brave facade.

"Harper," he said, as he sat down on one of the leaf pallets, "come here." He motioned for her to sit next to him.

Harper heard the native women singing in the village, the crackle of the central fire and the people laughing. She thought about the men in the meadow killing her friend Chris in cold blood, the darkness of the tunnel, the bats in her hair, the stink of the toxic fumes steaming from the lava. She thought about Shadea and her life, her courage, her feet. She thought about how the weight of the world seemed always to be on her shoulders.

She sat next to Mike.

And then she cried.

CHAPTER 40

The feast was amazing, so much local food and drink that, after days of semi-starvation, Harper's stomach groaned with excess. The native men danced, a ritual meant to appease the fertility gods. They had large wooden clubs attached to their penises and shimmied while the women clapped and laughed.

Shadea was brought out to the fire on a pallet and Harper was thrilled to learn she had been taken in as one of the tribe's own. She did not know if this tribe knew or cared about her undeserved past, but Harper was hopeful.

Claire happily attended to the medical needs of the tribe. She had delivered a baby earlier in the evening. Harper smiled knowing that her friend, first and foremost a physician, needed more than anything to know her skills were wanted and appreciated. In short, she was having the time of her life.

Harper drifted into a dreamy state, enthralled by the music and dance, sedated by the fermented drink offered by the tribal leader. He ordered beads and feathers woven into her hair. The native women dressed her and Claire in colored trinkets. The lady adventurers who actually survived the trek through the volcanic tunnel were the talk of the village.

Harper was enchanted by the purity, the innocence of the tribe. Children danced in naked abandon, sharing the lack of inhibitions with their parents. She looked across the circle of the fire to see someone staring at her, returning her smile, appreciating the same wonders.

Her heart swelled as she felt the connection. The connection she had been desperately trying to squelch since it first surfaced.

Mike made the journey around the circle. The music was loud, the dancing frenetic. He stood in front of her and offered his hand. She looked up and took it. He led her to the dance.

Then he led her into the hut.

CHAPTER 41

Claire chirped at the first light of morning. "Bloody brilliant! I have cured two cases of malaria, amputated a gangrenous toe, and sutured a slash from a leopard's claw." The doctor beamed as she began to wash her face in a bowl of brackish water.

Harper leaned up on one elbow. "Incredible! You are the bomb!"

"The bomb? What in bloody hell does that mean?" Claire stopped, dirty water dripping from her chin. She looked over to the pallet where Harper had been sleeping. Claire's jaw dropped in amazement.

"It means that you are an awesome force to be reckoned with." Mike leaned up on his elbow directly behind Harper, his bare chest exposed.

Claire smiled knowingly. "Oh, I see." She grabbed for the primitive toga that had served as clothing for Harper the previous night and wiped her face and hands. "Well, Mike, you had a nice evening then?"

Harper turned around to look at him. "Yes, Mr. Logan, how was it?"

He smiled at her as if she was the only other person in the hut. "Bloody brilliant!"

Harper returned his smile.

"Okay, well, I guess I can take a hint. Why should I sleep now?" Claire grinned and ducked out of the hut.

Mike rose and began shaving his beard with his hunting knife.

"So yesterday, when we were in the tunnel, did you ever give up and think we were dead?" She was admiring the view of his naked backside.

"Never." He turned around as he pressed Harper's toga against a bleeding nick on his chin. "Can you please look at my face when we're talking?"

"Oh, sorry." Harper blushed as she looked away.

Mike continued. "I have seen you in action. I knew if there was a way to make it, you would."

"Really?" She lay back down, enjoying the warmth between her thighs.

He saw her naked body and the look on her face.

"Yes, really."

Noon arrived with the sound of small children playing in the village. "Oh, I almost forgot." He sleepily kissed her forehead. "I have a surprise for you."

She opened her eyes and saw what was left of her original jungle couture, her khaki pants and her white tank top, clean and lying across the low table.

"My clothes! That's so sweet! Thank you!"

"Oh, I didn't do that. Claire must have made the arrangements. Apparently it wouldn't do for a young lady such as you to walk around without appropriate apparel or, God forbid, without any apparel at all. I, however, would prefer it."

Harper used her fingers as a hairbrush, spreading large strawberry curls around her shoulders, enjoying the effect her beauty had on Mike. For a moment he just stared, then finally stuttered, "No, I have a different surprise for you. I'll show you."

She pretended to examine the large hole burned in the bottom of her boot. She looked up to him, throwing her long hair back as she smiled. "Show me."

He gently pressed her onto the straw bed.

CHAPTER 42

They enjoyed a light, delicious lunch together, smiling like love-struck teenagers. Claire sat with Shadea and the tribe's shaman, learning how to communicate, making some success with hand gestures and comical body language. The native people laughed with gentle good humor.

Claire finally asked the question she and Harper had been avoiding since they arrived at the village. "Mike, do you have any idea what happened to Dave?"

Harper looked down. She felt guilty for being so happy, knowing that Dave had undoubtedly either been shot by the guerillas or lost in the jungle and devoured by some large predator.

"Claire, I'm sorry. I have not seen him or heard any of the tribal people talk of him." He sensed Harper's sadness and put his arm around her. "I'm sorry."

Claire bowed her head.

"But I would never underestimate Dave Murano. He is one hell of a soldier. And look, you girls made it." He put his finger under Harper's chin, raising her face to meet his. "And I'm so glad you did."

"So what does this mean? It's just the three of us. We have no passports, no money, and no way of getting home." Harper was jarred into reality, the glow of intimacy quickly vanishing.

"As I said, I have a surprise for you, for you both. I heard a rumor in the village and I think we should go check it out. Claire, Harp, come with me."

Mike waved to the tribal chief and spoke to him in a Bantu dialect.

"Why Mr. Logan, you have been holding out on us. You do speak the language, don't you? Why haven't you shown us that card?' Claire teased.

"Yes, Mr. Logan, why haven't you shown us that card?" Harper pulled away from him as her suspicious nature took over.

"Well, maybe I thought you should have all the glory. After all, I had the machete, the pistol, and I happen to like being in the background."

Harper relaxed, recognizing their mutual dislike of unwanted attention.

"Let's go." He motioned to a trail leading into the jungle. "Just follow the path, ladies."

They passed a group of baboons bathing in a small stream. The narrow trail followed the creek, leading up a small incline to a clearing. A tree house stood next to a large stone outcropping. A waterfall spilled over the rocks. Orchids and bromeliads covered the surrounding rocks, partnering with trees and ferns. A paddlewheel dipped into the waterfall, flowing fresh water to the interior of the house.

"Wow, it looks just like my favorite place at Disneyland when I was a little girl, The Swiss Family Treehouse," Harper said.

Mike approached a bell hanging on a hand carved totem and gave it a firm tug.

Harper stepped in front of Mike and Claire, not knowing what to expect, but strangely compelled to move forward and place herself front and center.

"Who is it? What do you want?" a gruff voice replied to the bell.

Harper cocked her head and crumpled her eyebrows. Something was familiar. Something was ....

"Dr. Merrill!"

The man stood on a plank in front of the tree house and put his hand over his brow to shade the light as the strawberry-haired girl ran toward the house.

"Stop right there! Who is it? What do you want? Why have you come here?" He climbed down the primitive ladder. "Stop! Or she will eat you!"

Harper obeyed just as a large jaguar pounced, pushing her to the ground.

"Sheila! Off!"

The large spotted cat froze at the man's voice. Harper was pinned to the jungle floor by a large paw. The cat gave her a friendly look and licked her face with a huge, sand-papered tongue.

The jaguar backed away quietly when the large man drew near. He helped Harper up from the ground, only to have her throw herself into his arms.

"Dr. Merrill! Oh my God! You're OK!" She sobbed into his chest.

"Miss Smith?" He reached down and pulled up her face with his hands. "Harper Morgan Smith?"

Mike Logan shook his head. "Damn, how is it that everybody knows all those names!"

CHAPTER 43

D r. Merrill was a tall, barrel-chested man in his late fifties with a big mustache and deep brown hair streaked with gray. The wrinkles at the sides of his eyes and mouth indicated a hearty soul with the love of life and laughter. Reading glasses hung on a leather cord around his neck. He wore a tie-dyed sarong, a grass hat sporting a peacock feather, and a fan strapped to his forehead, spinning away cheerfully. A small spider monkey perched on his shoulder.

He looked at Harper with sheer, open-mouthed, wide-eyed astonishment.

"What the hell are you doing here?" He took her elbow and led her toward the tree house. "Who are these people?"

"Oh, I'm terribly sorry. This is Dr. Claire Guthrie. She is the medical doctor on our mission." Harper presented Claire to her mentor who was enthralled by her whiskey eyes and shapely silhouette. He took her hand and kissed it, holding it firmly as he led her to the ladder.

"Oh, and I'm Mike." Logan held out his hand. Dr. Merrill was too preoccupied with Claire to even notice. Logan recovered his dignity by using the hand to smooth out his hair.

"Shall we have tea, Dr. Guthrie?" Dr. Merrill sent her up the ladder first, jumping on behind her, his smiling face positioned at the perfect angle to watch her curvy hips ascend the ladder.

The four of them emerged through a wooden floor into a hexagonal room. The monkey jumped up to a perch to munch on plantains. A wooden plank table with stools covered in woven plant materials stood in the center, holding a bowl of fresh fruit. On one side of the room, a rivulet of water spilled over a rock, dropping into an oblong bowl and draining to an unseen location below. The room had traditional walls roughly halfway up and open to the air above, with mesh surrounding the open spaces.

"Jane!" Dr. Merrill yelled in Swahili. "Jane, where are you?"

Claire and Harper looked at each other and grinned. "Jane?"

"Yes, well, her name is Janikula. She is an orphan from a local village. She cooks and cleans and you know, takes care of things around here." Dr. Merrill called for her again. "Jane!"

A small black face emerged from a porthole in the side of the room. She smiled sweetly and scurried in to attend to his wishes.

Merrill addressed the girl in her native tongue. "Jane, get some tea for us, please." He then turned his attention to the doctor. "Honey and milk, Dr. Guthrie?" His voice was as warm and sugary as the drink he offered.

"Oh, yes, please!" Claire returned Dr. Merrill's smile.

The native girl was uncomfortable by the exchange and called for the monkey, who jumped on her shoulder.

"OK, Harper. Start from the beginning," Dr. Merrill said. "Pharmco is likely involved and since I am still trying to figure out what those assholes are up to, I don't want you to leave out a single thing." He said something in Swahili to the servant girl. She nodded, sneered at Claire, and left.

Harper started with the email at her cabin in Big Sur. She took him through the flight on the Pharmco corporate jet and described how she hid her contract by stuffing the magazine in the manila folder and giving the original document to Ursula.

This part of the story was brand-new to Mike. "Wish I'd thought of that!" he laughed, sending a look of admiration to Harper.

"Old Vandervere must have shit when he pulled out the magazine instead of the contract!" Harper agreed with a wide grin.

"Harp, you still don't get it do you?" Dr. Merrill remained solemn, refusing to join with the laughter. "Pharmco has no intention of fulfilling your contract."

He looked at her in earnest. "No one ever even looked in that envelope. I'm sure all the so-called contracts went directly into the shredder."

She stared at him in disbelief, her heart plummeting to her feet. Was she really that naïve? Could she have been duped so thoroughly? She usually had such a keen sense for dishonesty. Betrayed again! How long is that going to be the recurring theme of her life?

"Don't feel badly, Harp. We were all taken in." Claire put her arm around Harper's shoulder as the servant girl entered the room with the tea, the monkey with her. He jumped off her shoulder into Dr. Merrill's lap. He welcomed the primate with a crunchy treat.

"Let's get past this now, please," he said. "We must figure out our next move."

Harper continued her saga. She described Monte Jones and Dave's near drowning. She relived her fever and the tribesmen, the elephant stampede, the death of Sid Lembowsky, the volcanic eruption. She described Mike's cleverness in fashioning the armadillo shell to gather water and showered him with looks of praise. The tiny waterfall at the side of the room trickled softly while Mike returned the admiring gaze.

She talked on until day turned to dusk, telling the story of the Mayi-Mayi in the village, the rape of the woman and her daughter, and the abduction of the teenage boy. Dr. Merrill shook his head and grimaced.

"Those fucking bastards," Dr. Merrill said, standing to look out at a distant field in the waning sunlight. "The only reason the local Mayi gang don't turn me in is that I supply them with kilo upon kilo of cannabis."

Sensing his despair over the Mayi-Mayi problem, Harper moved on to the good part of her tale, the part she knew would bring a smile to his face.

"We got close to the coordinates you gave Pharmco and started looking. Thanks to your notes and everything you taught me, I was able to extrapolate the soil content and community members of *Podophyllum peltatum*. With the help of a frog and a fluke, we found it."

Dr. Merrill had been cleaning the monkey's fingernails with a pocket-knife. He stopped abruptly and looked up at her in the candlelight. "You found it?" He raised his eyebrows.

"Yes, Dr. Merrill… we found it." Harper smiled at him, their botanical connection locked.

"Oh my God," whispered Merrill. "You mean you tested the enzyme ratios, the auxin components?"

"Yes. The chemical analysis was conclusive."

He hesitated. "And where was the appropriate formula?" His eyes were wide with anticipation.

"Just where you taught me to look."

"The meristematic tissue?"

"The meristematic tissue."

They jumped up and hugged each other, laughing.

Claire and Mike had no idea what they were talking about but enjoyed the moment of triumph.

The servant girl arrived to announce dinner.

"Oh thank you, Jane!" Claire beamed graciously at the girl, who acted embarrassed by her earlier disdain of the Englishwoman. Dr. Merrill also thanked the girl and kissed her on the forehead. She smiled in appreciation.

"OK, folks, let's eat," Merrill said with a gesture toward the heavily-laden table. "I hope you don't mind that I am a vegetarian. My animal family here would not appreciate my ingesting one of their friends."

"Mind? Are you joking?" Claire gave Dr. Merrill a look of genuine appreciation.

The meal was the best since the team arrived in Africa. Crusted baked yams with goat cheese, a mixture of greens, forest mushrooms and kola nuts, millet and sorghum bread with fresh butter and cassava jam, and an egg frittata covered with a brown spicy sauce. A cold pitcher of palm wine accompanied the feast.

"Wow, this is fantastic!" Mike said between mouthfuls.

"I am so glad you like it, Mister … sorry, I don't think I caught your name." Dr. Merrill acted as if he had just noticed Mike in the room for the first time.

"Dr. Merrill, this is the guy I have been telling you about all day! Mr. Logan! You know, Mike!" Harper put her hand on Mike's arm.

"Oh, yes, well of course." Dr. Merrill said, not in the least bit embarrassed. He returned his attention to his glass of *Pombo*.

Harper continued her tale between courses: the tunnel, the petrol pool, the bats, the lava, Shadea's feet, the spiders. She shook off her claustrophobia as she relived the horrors of the trek through the volcanic mountain. The only part she left out was her and Claire being tied to the palm tree, naked.

Mike couldn't resist filling in that bit for Dr. Merrill. The two laughed, sharing a moment of manly mirth.

After the laughter died down, Dr. Merrill got serious. "This is what we'll do." He stood up and paced the room. "I will go to the surrounding villages in the morning and find out what is going on. Pharmco has most likely offered the Mayi-Mayi, the Ugandan militia and every bounty hunter in the Congo basin, possibly the entire country, a price on your heads. Even though they think you perished in the cave, they are much too thorough to let it rest with that."

Harper, Claire and Mike looked at each other in despair. They had already been through so much together—now it looked like their troubles were just beginning.

CHAPTER 44

"Mr. Logan, stay here with Miss Smith and Dr. Guthrie and protect them," Dr. Merrill instructed. "Jane will take care of your needs and I will show you how the house works in the morning. I will travel in disguise so as not to tip anyone off."

"What if someone comes here?" Harper had reached the end of her tolerance when it came to danger. Mike instinctively checked his machete.

"The locals won't come up here because of my relationship with the ghost," Dr. Merrill said. "No one will come."

"The ghost?" Harper and Claire said simultaneously.

"Oh, it's nothing. Tonight, we rest. Mr. Logan, I do not wish our young Miss Smith to sleep alone. Would you mind staying with her in the guest room?"

"I think I can manage that, Dr. Merrill." Mike smiled boyishly.

"Dr. Guthrie, you will sleep in my bed."

"I beg your pardon, sir!" Even in the dim candlelight, everyone saw Claire blush.

Merrill smiled. "I will sleep in the hammock by the garden."

Claire relaxed.

"I will need to keep Sheila and Kiku company."

"Oh yes, the leopard." Harper rubbed her cheek, feeling the intensity of the hot, rough tongue. Kiku, the spider monkey, jumped over to her and mimicked the rubbing motion.

"How did you get a pet leopard?"

"I rescued her from a poacher's trap when she was just a few months old. She has never left my side." He looked out to the garden where the large spotted cat lounged on a flat rock, her tail swaying to the rhythm of the waterfall.

"An amazing creature. I would trust her with my life." He looked at her with affection.

"Dr. Claire will fit in here," Merrill continued. "There are always British doctors in and out of the Congo with *Médecins Sans Frontières*. There is also an office in Kinshasa for Conservation International and their people are always about. She won't stand out as much, especially if you become separated. They will be looking for Americans, I think."

Merrill turned to Harper. "You, my dear, are a different story. There is no such thing as a girl like you not standing out. Hell, you stood out at the university!" He studied her from head to toe with fatherly pride.

She had no idea what he was talking about.

"Getting you out of here will be a difficult task." Merrill shook his head. "A very difficult task." He looked at her again, his brow furrowed. "Most difficult."

A rope ladder dangling overhead the main room led Harper and Mike to the guest bedroom. The line ran along a big branch of the tree to a plank on a top level of the tree house. In the dark, a high-pitched voice spoke in Swahili. *"Jambo, habari gani."*

Harper startled in surprise, wondering if she was simply hearing things, or if the wine with dinner contained something hallucinogenic. She lifted the candle and spied a white cockatoo with a yellow crest cocking its head in her direction. *"Jambo, jambo!"* the bird said again. Harper smiled. *"Nzuri!* I'm fine, and hello to you, too!" She liked this place.

At the end of the ladder stood another portal, similar to the small one in the main room. The girl opened it to let Harper and Mike enter. Harper held up the small candle and ducked inside.

The room was also hexagonal but had walls all the way up to the ceiling. A large rope hammock, big enough for two and covered with cocoa-bean-hull pillows and soft blankets, occupied the center of the room. Orchids decorated the enchanting cabin.

Jane followed them in with a larger candle, set it on a table, and opened the upper part of the walls with a pulley system. Harper and Mike saw through the mesh covering to the torch-lit waterfall and gardens below them.

A flat rock dripped water into a copper bowl at the side of the room. Two hollowed-out coconut hulls, for drinking, had been placed by the tiny waterfall.

Jane gave the couple a rough-hewn fabric for towels and pointed to coconut soap in a small kola nut hull. She gestured to a small platform at the back of the room with a hole in the middle. A small grass curtain separated the plank and the bedroom. Harper thought, *The privy!*

"Wow, better than the Nairobi Hilton!" Harper smiled at Mike.

He looked at her shining hair in the candlelight. "I can't imagine a better hotel anywhere in the world."

Harper turned to thank the girl with a hug of gratitude and said, "*Lala salama Janikula, asante sana,*" goodnight and thank you in Swahili. The girl stepped through the portal and left.

Mike took off his machete and placed it next to the hammock. He had a thoughtful look on his face. "What do you think he meant by showing us how the house 'worked'?" he said, as he pulled his shirt over his head.

"What do you think he meant by his relationship with the 'ghost'?" Her shirt was also coming off over her head. Mike reached over to help her. There was a small pile of clothes at the foot of the hammock in a matter of seconds.

"All I care about right now is you." He took her chin in his hand and lifted her lips to his. He gazed into her eyes in the candlelight. They brightly danced with blue and yellow specks.

She kissed him and they fell into the hammock as pillows and orchids covered their entwined bodies.

CHAPTER 45

The white cockatoo screeching, "Hello, Jambo!" heralded the arrival of dawn.

"Well, hello there." Harper smiled at the bird perched on the end of the hammock.

"Harper? Mr. Logan?" A deep voice bellowed from below. "Time to rise and shine!"

Mike's head was lying next to Harper's on a soft pillow, a faint but discernible grin on his face.

"Wake up, sleepy head. Didn't you hear your orders? Time to rise and shine." Harper moved a wispy curl from his temple.

"Oh, I already have achieved the rise part, now it's your turn to glow." He stroked her hair.

"You mean shine, don't you? My turn to shine?" She tossed her strawberry curls and attempted to clamber out of the hammock gracefully.

"You have been shining all your life, Harpy. I think that it's now safe to say that a glow is all over your face." He propped up his head with a muscled arm.

"Shameless flatterer." She finally wriggled her big toe free from a small knot of the hammock and tumbled onto the planks.

"I am the same as I ever have been," Harper said, picking herself up off the floor with mustered dignity. "A smart, safe, and well-disciplined person." She held up her chin and dressed herself.

"Speaking of safe, how do I know you don't have AIDS?" she questioned him with a calculating look. "A big percentage of this population has it, you know."

She turned away, hiding her face.

He recognized the shield. He never realized until this moment his own armor was just as obvious, just as debilitating.

"Do you really think I would risk your life for a little sex?" He immediately regretted his choice of words.

"Is that what this is? A little sex?" She zipped up her khaki pants and quickly exited the portal. She scurried down the rope ladder with a scowl on her face.

"Jesus. Women." Mike said to himself as he dressed, securing his machete for action.

"Harper! How lovely to see you! What a glorious day!" Dr. Merrill greeted Harper when she arrived in the main room. He already had his disguise in place, reminding Harper of Dr. Livingstone, complete with pith helmet and monocle.

"Um, good morning." She tried not to laugh.

"Well then, when Mr. Logan comes down, we will proceed with your instructions. I may be gone for a day or two, depending on what I find out. You two will have to hold down the fort, as it were."

Claire appeared from the jungle, petting the small monkey on her shoulder.

"Dr. Merrill," she approached him as Kiku jumped from her shoulder to his. "If it is all right, I would appreciate it if you could take me as far as the village so I may attend to my patients."

"And how did we sleep, my lovely doctor?" He towered over her tiny figure.

"Splendid! Your bed is lovely. Thank you." Her neck bent at a forty-five degree angle to look up into his face and her feet unconsciously rose to her toes.

"I would be honored to escort you to the village. After hearing Shadea's story, I am also anxious to see how she is getting on." Dr. Merrill took Claire's hand and tucked it into his elbow, patting it attentively.

Mike jumped down from the second level, bypassing the ladder. He came to the group with all business written on his face.

"All right, then, now that we have assembled, let's take a tour of the compound," Dr. Merrill said. "It is imperative that everything run smoothly, for reasons you will soon find out ... Jane!"

He petted Sheila the leopard with affection as he waited for the girl to join the group.

They walked up the rocky outcropping, skirting the waterfall. Merrill and Jane headed the procession, the native girl stepping in front of Claire at the last moment. Claire let her pass with a polite smile, feeling oddly guilty for intruding. Harper followed Claire while Mike trailed. He picked a bright purple *oncidium* orchid and handed it to Harper as they climbed up the rocks. She took it and, without any acknowledgement, handed it to Claire. The doctor smiled and put it behind her ear as she joyfully bounded up the rocks like a little nanny goat.

Mike got the message and retreated to the back of the group.

"This system runs my little house." Dr. Merrill exuded pride, tempered with humility.

On a flat rock, water spilled into a heavy wooden tray. The tray had several exits from which the water could flow in equal amounts. The first exit led to a hollowed-out log sending the water into a flat box with no top. A green mossy substance filled the container.

"The water flow is separated into three streams. As you can see there are three trays, each with a different biofiltering ingredient," Dr. Merrill said.

"The first tray is an algae variety I have been propagating for this purpose. It filters out larger biotics and small animals or insects. The second tray is filled with a charcoal-mineral mix which deletes heavy metals. The third tray is filled with other aquatic plant material which further oxygenates the water and, frankly, makes it taste great."

Dr. Merrill viewed the system with unabashed pride.

"The most highly biofiltered water goes into the house in the form of the domestic 'tap' water for drinking. The second most filtered water is directed to bathing and the washing of clothes." He gestured toward the clean and tidy shirt, jacket and trousers in his Doctor Livingstone get-up. "The third stream goes to my crops. It is imperative that e. coli, or any other contaminant, does not infiltrate any of my edible or sustainable crops."

Dr. Merrill stood with arms outstretched like Moses in front of the Red Sea as he displayed his botanical domain.

"Speaking of which, I devised a human waste treatment system that not only makes every living space on this compound fit for sanitary habitation, it is completely separated from any and all possibilities of biotic contamination. The waste is treated organically with friendly bacteria and fed into a small creek flowing into an underground filtration system. Layers of natural percolation purify the water before it gets into any underground water source used by humans or drains into any aquatic system." Merrill smiled to himself.

"I can produce enough legumes, melons, tubers and corn to sustain a village of fifty people, as well as myself and Jane. As of yet, I can't persuade Sheila to become a vegetarian, although that could happen if she has sufficient protein enzyme and amino acid ratio, supplied by a legume/grain mixture. That formula is a sustainable *Gaia* concoction."

Dr. Merrill had reverted to the pre-professorial intern that Harper had only heard about in university lore. For a second, she visualized him as a young man, before the burden of academic politics had weighed in so heavily on his psyche.

"Dr. Merrill." Harper stood next to him, not as his student but as a peer for the first time. "What you have here is amazing and we are honored to play even a small part. You have always been a visionary, but you have outdone yourself."

He gave her a fatherly hug.

Steam exuded from the top of the stone outcropping. "What's this?" Harper asked.

Dr. Merrill bounded over to the cluster of rocks. "My dear Harper, this is my little geothermal gift from the planet's interior. Humans have taken advantage of geothermals since the Paleolithic era. This land actually has everything humans need for a rich life. Sadly, the corruption of Africa's leaders squelches any sort of knowledge with respect to this gift. If the Kyoto treaty on carbon emissions is rewritten, Africa may get cheap loans and know-how to help install more geothermal power stations. However, I am dubious of that ever happening. But this powerhouse of mine heats up over 100 kiloliters per day and can be adjusted to any temperature."

He took Claire's hand and walked her over to three levers. "Dr. Guthrie, would you please lift this first lever?"

Claire raised the device with her right hand as Dr. Merrill placed her left hand under the spigot.

"Cool." Her British accent cooed.

"Now try this one." He placed her hand under the second stream of water.

"Warm, nice and warm."

"That is what we use for bathing. The algae filter cleans the water before it reaches spigot one and two so the cool water and the warm water may be used by humans and animals. We do not need purified water for the third lever."

"Why is that, Doc?" Mike was fascinated.

"Because the third lever has water laced with myriad minerals coming directly from the earth's mantle. The temperature is a steady 216.5 degrees. No living thing can survive in water so hot. That includes bacteria, including e. coli. We use this water for sanitization. You know, soaking dirty dishes and laundry and the like. And with this lever, we never need to waste precious fuel to boil water." Dr. Merrill paused to smile, obviously pleased at his inventiveness.

"God really has given man—oh pardon me, Mademoiselle, and woman—everything they need to survive quite happily with minimal strife." He had not realized he was still holding Claire's hand. Now he kissed the hand lightly. "All we need is a little education and ingenuity."

Jane huffed with anger and backed away from the group.

Dr. Merrill continued, "My crops are fed hydroponically through bamboo shoots with a fertilizer derived from, again, algae. As I once hypothesized in my class …"

Harper chimed in, "Yes, I remember!" She immediately regretted encroaching on his stage. "Oh, please continue, Professor."

"As I was saying, algae, phylums I have studied intensely, are in fact our sustainable answer to fuel, fertilizers, crop production and most human needs." Merrill walked over to one of his propagation trays and admired the contents.

"My observations that algae use quantum mechanics to photosynthesize will soon be solidified by science. This is what maximizes the fuel-to-output ratio."

"Very impressive, Dr. Merrill." Claire smiled coyly.

Merrill gazed at her for a long moment, finally tearing himself away to address Mike. "I will escort the lovely doctor to the village. Jane will attend to your needs. Sheila and Kiku will make sure that you and Harper are safe."

CHAPTER 46

"Dr. Guthrie, shall we?" Merrill offered his arm to the doctor in the garden of his tree house. Claire grabbed her newly stocked medical pack and placed her hand in the crook of his arm.

"Will you be all right, Harp?" Claire sensed the tension between her friend and the mercenary.

"Bloody fantastic." Harper kissed Dr. Merrill on the cheek and gave Claire a hug, wishing them both luck. "We will see you when you return and not to worry, we will make sure all is well here."

The doctors left the compound engaged in each other and their missions.

Harp headed to the algae ponds.

Kiku preened himself on Mike's shoulder and the leopard slunk around his feet, wrapping her tail around him, as he whispered into Jane's ear. Jane tried her best, but couldn't hide a smile.

Jane made an excuse about cleaning up the breakfast dishes and left the garden. Mike knelt to stroke Sheila. The big cat purred with obvious affection.

Harper sighed. She knew exactly how Sheila felt. Something about Mike Logan simply could not be resisted, neither by human nor feline females.

"It appears we are on our own today, Miss Smith." His swarthy smile was disarming.

Harper wore homemade goggles, gloves and an apron, intending to immerse herself in the world of science. "What do you want, Mike?" she said without looking at him.

Filtered sunlight streamed through the canopy as exotic birds trilled and chirped. Sparkling droplets trickled off waxy foliage into experimental algae ponds. Mike felt one with something, something he had not experienced since stroking his wife's pregnant belly.

"I want nothing, Harper." Mike was fully aware of her shield, a trait he struggled with as well. "I have everything I could possibly need right here."

She did not look away from her work, but his words opened up a soft spot deep inside.

"I'm sorry Mike." She pushed her makeshift goggles to the top of her head, tangling strands of her strawberry curls. The goggles left reddish circles around her eyes.

"You know ...." she stammered as she toyed with strands of algae.

"Yes, Harp, I do know."

Finally she looked at him. "It seems we are alone in this, um, Eden-like place." Harper unconsciously moved toward him.

"It seems that is the case." He embraced her as she gently placed her head against his chest. He stroked her hair.

She looked up and smiled. "It's just like Swiss Family Robinson."

His passion became obvious. "Not exactly."

CHAPTER 47

Harper awoke to pleasurable sounds and smells: the fragrance of jungle blossoms, the aroma of fresh coffee, the songs of exotic birds, the whisper of leaves in the breeze. Yet none delighted her more than Mike, snoring lightly at her side. Orchid blossoms covered them both, cascading from the sides of the hammock. The tiny waterfall babbled a cheerful greeting. Sheila groaned and stretched at the base of the tree house.

"Mike ... Mike," she whispered as she gently nudged him awake. "Mike ...."

A harsh voice from below shattered the morning peace. "I told you you would get your stuff when it was ready."

Harper jumped to the mesh window as Mike grabbed the machete.

Unfamiliar voices spoke in Swahili. "The crop is not ready!"

Dr. Merrill sounded uncharacteristically agitated. Harper heard Sheila growl.

Mike peered from the top floor of the tree house to see Merrill surrounded by African gangsters. He ducked below the half wall and pushed Harper to the floor. "We've got to get out of here."

"No, we have to help Dr. Merrill." Harper stood up.

Mike grabbed her pants. "They're after us, not him. Get dressed and get out of here."

Harper whispered as she edged one eye above the wall. "Shit."

"Exactly," echoed Mike.

She watched in helpless horror as the invaders pushed her beloved Doctor Merrill against a kola tree. The huge cat pounced on the marauders, her claws slicing jugulars. Shots rang out. Kiku screamed and Jane stood frozen in fear. She had a brief glimpse of Claire grabbing Jane from behind and pulling her into the dense brush.

"You need to go." Mike said decisively. "There." He pointed to the privy.

"There?" She stood in defiance.

He forced her feet first into the privy.

"But ...."

"Go. Now." He shoved her down the opening.

A blood-curdling cry came from the leopard.

Mike raced out the portal onto a large upper branch. He crossed the limb to a platform, placed the machete into the belt loop of his pants and grabbed a thick rope.

One of the gangsters, only a teenager, held a semi-automatic rifle barrel against Merrill's throat. The professor had an expression of sheer terror on his face. Sheila lay at his feet with blood spurting from her nose. The cat, using her last ounce of strength, reached up with one paw and gently stroked his leg in farewell.

Mike screamed like a banshee as he swung from the rope to the compound floor. The teenage gangster holding the rifle on Merrill turned his head in the direction of the unearthly sound. Mike's boot heel crushed his throat. Two quick punches disabled the other Mayi criminals. Kiku jumped onto another's face, biting and clawing.

Meanwhile, Harper careened down the waste tube. In an instant, which seemed like an eternity, she hit the bottom. An eight-inch layer of waste lined the bottom of the vat. She found no way out other than the way she came in. She heard the horrifying shots, grunts, punches and screams, caught glimpses of the desperate action through slits in the planks. Harper instinctively raised her hands to her cover her mouth to keep from screaming, but her hands were covered in excrement.

Then, silence. Harper trembled in panic, fearing the worst. She forced herself to sit as still as she could and stifled her sobs.

Then came the sound of a different kind of grunt. Something different, she thought. Leaf litter muffled confused scuffling noises. She heard the snaps of guns cocking, but no actual shots. Swahili swear words filled the air, but they conveyed only fear, not defiance. The low, guttural sound became louder, sounding to Harper like a primate.

Then, the clomp of retreating footsteps, the Mayi-Mayi apparently scattering without firing a shot. The Swahili voices wailed in panic. Harper thought she heard 'ghost' in Swahili but could not be sure due to multiple intonations and dialects.

Harper desperately wanted to call to Mike, Dr. Merrill, Jane, Claire, especially Claire, but willed herself to silence. Her terror gradually subsided and she regained her grip on logic and intellect. She felt a new strength running through her, although she couldn't say what it was or where it came from.

The growling noise continued to grow in volume. She heard another animal noise, unmistakably feline, weak yet serious, bent on vengeance.

A machete sliced furiously through the septic tank wall. Harper shrank back into the rear corner, scooping to fill both hands with its nasty contents. It wasn't much in the way of a weapon, but it was all she had to work with.

Mike froze when he spotted her, a mixture of relief and revulsion on his face. He smiled slightly and placed a hand over his nose.

"Well, well, Harpy, my girl," He reached for her hand. "Reveling in the same old shit?"

She grabbed his wrist, momentarily considering pulling him into her stinky situation but thought better of it. "Why, yes, Mr. Logan. It is just like spending the day with you."

He helped her stand, determined she was unhurt, and decided that cleaning her up would be a waste of time. He was about to make another wisecrack at her expense when his mood changed abruptly.

"Let's go!" He almost yanked her arm from its socket as he jerked her from the vat, pulling her to the creek that flowed from the exit valve. Heavy footsteps pounded behind them in pursuit. She focused on one foot in front of the other on the uneven surface of the creek bed. In her desperate rush to get away, she barely wondered why Mike chose to run in the creek instead of on solid ground.

Dogs barked and the weak feline growl got stronger. Harper glanced back long enough to see a bloodied yet resolute leopard swatting the canines away from the prostrate body of Dr. Merrill. The Mayi were backing away from something Harper could not see, their eyes reflecting awe and fear.

Mike grabbed her hand. "Go!" He forced her to run down the creek bed. "It won't be long before they follow us."

CHAPTER 48

Harper and Mike followed the creek down the ravine until they reached a small cove where the waterway split into three directions. Harper figured out Mike's logic for staying in the water: it would make it more difficult for the dogs to track them. She hoped the clinging septic tank odors might also put the dogs off the scent.

But she knew that eventually they would be found.

Mike's eyes combed the area for their next move. "This way." He grabbed her hand as they clambered up a rocky bed, shimmying up the moss-covered boulders until Harper thought her chest would explode.

Dogs barked in the distance. "Trying to outrun them will be suicide," Mike said. He pointed to a low, broad rock skirting the creek. "There."

"There, what?"

He didn't answer, just pushed her to the ground and rolled her under the rock, digging out enough to tuck themselves as far back as possible. He used a broken root to remove traces of their tracks in the wet sand. Harper, pinned between the back wall of the tiny cave and Mike, wondered why the rock wall was so smooth and spongy, then dismissed the thought, willing herself to stay still and silent.

Mike had his machete in his hand as the dogs trotted by. Footsteps sloshed in the creek, passing by their hiding place and moving on. Mike whispered to Harper, "Stay put. Do not move until I tell you to."

"But …." She winced as the soft wall behind her started to move.

Mike's expression was hard and stern as he strained to hear the location and direction of the Mayi-Mayi. "But what, Harper?" he snarled in a whisper.

The large anaconda, so cozy with Harper, slithered out into the creek directly in front of Mike, so close he could smell the sewage rubbed off from Harper's back onto newly-molted skin. She probably dislodged the reptile from its lair by upsetting its sensitive olfactory organs. He thought to himself, Good job, girl!

They stayed in the small cave for a short time. Mike feared the Mayi would double back once they realized they'd been duped. He pulled Harper out from under the rock and pointed above the creek to a steep rocky slope.

They scrambled up the boulders, slipping on mossy surfaces. When they reached the top, Mike lay flat and looked over the ravine below. He motioned for Harper to do the same. From their perch about one hundred feet high, they saw the dogs jumping and barking at the foot of the rocks below them. The men shaded their eyes and looked up. Harper and Mike pulled back. The dogs kept slipping on the slimy surfaces of the rocks, but the men were able to grab a foothold.

"Shit, they're coming after us!" Mike pulled the machete from his belt loop, ready for action. Harper moved away from the overlook in search of rocks large enough to stop the Mayi's advance.

Just as she placed the third rock onto her primitive arsenal, her ears perked from the same guttural, growling sound she'd first heard at Dr. Merrill's compound.

Mike, still peering over the ravine, whispered, "What the fuck is that?"

The dogs whined and the men froze in their tracks. Harper crawled to the edge of the cliff just in time to see a white gorilla with raised arms and bared teeth charging the men.

"The ghost," they whispered to each other.

They seized the opportunity and began to run.

After a laborious hour of chopping through brush and scrambling over branches, Mike motioned for a stop next to a waterfall. Gasping for breath, he cupped his hands under the water and splashed his face.

Harper merely fell to the ground in exhaustion.

"I have no idea where we are, Harp," he said, dropping his head into his hands. "We could be heading right back to their camp. Shit."

He was sweaty and filthy. Harper never saw a man so sincerely discouraged and distraught.

"Well, let's take a look at things," she said as she rose to a standing position by the waterfall.

"What things?"

"We escaped from Dr. Merrill's compound from the waste stream of the septic tank, right?"

Mike flashed a faint smile. "Oh, yeah. And by the way, you still stink!"

"Very funny, asshole." She laughed, knowing her stench had most likely saved their lives.

"Well, Dr. Merrill is a pretty smart cookie. He would have built the septic tank and the creek carrying the waste in the farthest corner of the compound." She put her hand to her chin and grimaced as she found traces of sewage.

"And?" Mike removed his shirt and began rinsing out sweat and dirt in the running water.

She shifted her focus away from Mike's bare chest and back to her theory. "That would be the leeward side. You know, so the smell would be blown away from the compound instead of into it."

"Go on." He sounded intrigued.

"And, he would make sure the contaminants could not flow back in to any human water supply. So, since most of the population lives in the west and we are so far in the east …."

He stopped her. "Right. So we were heading almost due east when we left the camp." He studied the thick underside of the forest canopy. There was still no sky to be seen, no clue to the position of the sun. "The Congo River basin makes a big arc over the northwestern part of the country. We are most likely at the base of the mountains, which means the eastern arc of the river will be to our northeast. That being said, to get through those mountains will be difficult. Going to the northwest will be easier." He paused. "But they will expect that."

She rummaged in the soil to find some edible roots, washed them in the trickle and handed one to Mike as she bit into the other.

"I think our best bet is to make it to the river basin and hitchhike on some kind of transportation headed for Kinshasa," he said after chewing and swallowing. "We can contact the American Consulate there and they can get us out of here."

"How far do you think we are from anywhere?" Harper finished her snack and attempted to clean the remaining sewage from her body and clothing.

Mike stood up and stretched. "Let's travel a few more hours this evening, collecting anything we can eat or drink. We'll find a safe place to camp, preferably above the forest floor. No fires."

He looked at the large hole in his boot. "I have no idea how far we are from anything, much less where we are going."

"Well, then, let's get started."

CHAPTER 49

Three days later, they saw a bit of blue peeking through the dense jungle. Mike and Harper cheered, for a moment forgetting their exhaustion, hunger and fear. As the brush became less dense, the patches of sky grew larger. Harper and Mike spilled out of the jungle onto a white sandy beach hugging a brownish-green river.

The ears of a hippopotamus, ridiculously tiny for such an animal, Harper thought, twitched in the water. Dozens of aquatic birds took flight at the arrival of two humans. The bright sunlight intensified the hues of the gorgeous scenery. Harper practically kissed the sandy shoreline.

Mike strode into the shallows of the river and decapitated several fish with his machete. "Our ban on fires is lifted." He skewered the fish, setting the bounty on a large, waxy leaf. "Collect what you can for fuel. Tonight we eat."

The ambience became almost festive. Harper gathered vegetarian delicacies while Mike added a few small animals to the barbeque. They prepared an early evening fire to be less obvious in the dark. They camped just inside the brush and slept soundly in each other's arms.

Harper woke with a start just as the first rays of dawn broke through the forest.

"Mike, wake up."

He looked at her with one sleepy eye. "What?"

"I hear something. It sounds like, like …."

Mike bolted upright as they both whispered, "A plane!"

They stumbled toward the beach and crouched behind shrubs. A large, battered cargo plane with Russian writing on the sides sat directly on the opposite side of the river. "It doesn't look like a military aircraft. It's too old," Mike said. He stood to get a better look. "I see crates and some workers. And the plane is facing west. It's headed to Kananga!"

"So what should we do?" Harper stood to join him. She calculated the width of the river as two large crocodiles slithered into the water from the other side.

"It's at least a half mile across the river from here," Mike said. "Let's go downstream and see if we can find a narrower crossing. We'll have better luck avoiding crocs in more rapid currents." He wiped his forehead with the back of his hand. "How good a swimmer are you?"

"Pretty good. I suppose it depends on how rapid the currents are."

Mike grabbed the machete. "Good. We'll make a raft. It doesn't have to be too sturdy, just get us to the other side. You cover up any remains of our camp and I'll head downstream and collect materials." He kissed her on the forehead. "Be quick about it. We don't know how long the Russian clunker will be staying."

"I'll be right behind you." She covered the spent campfire with sand and erased foot and body prints from the previous evening's lodgings. A six-inch Goliath beetle ambled into the area scavenging for food scraps. The scientist in her stopped to marvel at its huge brown and white striped shell. After evaluating the position of its mouth, she saw that it would not bite her. She picked it up, amazed at the weight of the insect.

"Bye-bye, Mr. Goliath, and happy hunting," she said softly. "I shan't be seeing you again. I'm going home!"

She skipped like a girl as she returned to the shoreline. Beads of sweat glistened in the sunlight on Mike's shirtless back as he wielded the machete against tree branches to make the raft. Harper instinctively stripped chameadora husks and pothos tendrils for twine. Within an hour, they had assembled a crude raft and prepared for launch.

The spot downstream Mike chose for crossing was only about 50 yards from shore to opposite shore, but an island in the middle caused the river to churn vigorously on either side. The noise of the rapids made it impossible to speak in anything less than a shout. "We'll cross here!" Mike yelled. "The current will pull us severely to the west so be prepared!"

"Be prepared for what?" Harper hollered back.

"How the crap should I know?" He shoved Harper onto the raft, stuck a makeshift pole into the sand and pushed off.

The wild current swiftly sent them into a mad swirl, forcing them to lie on their bellies, paddling with their hands and pushing off of large rocks with their feet.

"The island!" Mike shouted.

"What?"

"Head toward the island. Let's land there and reassess."

The raft lost a chunk when it dashed against a large rock. A family of fresh water otters laughed at them. Harper and Mike crawled onto the island, gasping for breath. Mike hauled up what was left of the raft onto the tiny beach.

"That did not go well, did it?" Harper said.

"Shit, I've had better luck at the track." He lay on his back on the sand, laughing.

"Now what?" Harper peered over the rocks in the center of the island at the plane. The propellers began to spin.

"Mike, we have got to go … the plane is leaving!"

"Dammit! OK, we are going to have to swim for it. When you get to the other side, run as fast as you can to the plane in as much cover as you can find and get on it! There should be an opening in the rear for cargo. They should be finished loading the cargo and will only be using the cockpit entry. Hide yourself and do not come out until they have safely landed." He kissed her hard on the lips and dove into the river.

"But … shit! What? Are you kidding me?" She tried to stifle tears but salty drops slid down her cheeks anyway. "OK, here goes nothing." She jumped into the river, bobbling and flailing aimlessly.

After six or seven dunkings under the rapids, Harper felt like giving up. The river had a mind of its own and it seemed she was not part of its plan. She stopped paddling and let the rushing water take her wherever it wanted. *Pretend you're a kayak*, she thought to herself as she attempted to surf the waves.

She came up for air to see a smiling face with sharp yellow teeth nose-to-nose with her. She knew him. The southern sea otter was friendly to everyone from Big Sur to Marin. She hoped his African cousin would prove to be equally helpful.

"Hi there!" She followed the mammal's movements and let him swim her toward the shore. He escorted her to safety before he flipped his tail back into the rapids.

Mike and Harper flopped onto the beach at about the same time, both looking like drowned cats.

"Hey," he whispered as loudly as he dared.

Harper was face-down in the sand, not moving.

"HEY!"

He rose to his feet against his better judgment. When she finally lifted her head, river water poured from her mouth and half of her face was covered in sand.

"Fucking, what? 'Hey,' your ass. Thanks for leaving me there." She flipped her hair back and started to get up.

"OK, sorry I left you." He said in a grunting whisper just barely loud enough to be heard over the rapids. "I had to check out the 'sitch'."

The plane's propellers approached full throttle. "Let's go, girl. The 'sitch' is leaving without us. And I mean NOW!"

They sprinted to a bush with clothes dripping and shoes squishing, crept into the cargo loading area and slipped into the rear of the plane. The cavernous space was filled with pallets and crates. Mike and Harper hid themselves between some unmarked wooden cases.

"I think we're going to be OK now, Harp." He wrapped his arm around her shoulder as they nestled in a small crevice amidst the cargo. "The worst is over."

For the second time in what seemed like weeks, Harper was filled with hope.

CHAPTER 50

As the plane reached cruising altitude, the roar of the engines and the slight rocking motion sent Harper into a semi-conscious, dreamlike state. She felt her father looking her in the eye, a rare occurrence.

When an organism is under stress, extraneous factors can and will take advantage of that stress. Take the plant that does not have enough water and/or nutrients, or for that matter, support. All issues of pests, disease, auto-immune deficiencies and less than optimum growth result from lack of support.

She awoke and reviewed her current circumstances. Perhaps the lack of parental support gave her the strength to survive her ordeal in Africa. If she'd been coddled as a child, as she desperately wished, she might never have made it this far alive.

Mike's head rested on a pallet as his hand held a tight grip on the machete. She watched him drift off with his eyes half open.

To Harper, the plane floated in the substrata. She was afraid to be too hopeful, but she couldn't help it. By this time tonight, she could be bedding down in a real, honest-to-God hotel. She was overcome with a sense of peace and gratitude as she placed her head on Mike's chest and prepared to nap, hoping to encounter her father again in her dreams.

Mike made a startled grunting sound, jolting Harper back to reality.

She awoke to see a black boy of about ten shoving a rifle into Mike's face.

He's just a child, Harper thought. Surely he means us no harm.

"Jambo, Jambo rafiki!" She gave the boy a friendly, maternal smile.

He responded by slamming the butt of the gun to the side of her head.

Harper didn't know how much time had passed when she finally returned to consciousness. All she knew was she and Mike had been bound at both their wrists and feet. The boy faced them, the rifle sitting across his knees.

Harper said, *"Unakwenda wapi sasa?"* Swahili for "Where are we going?"

The aircraft began to descend.

The boy did not answer except for a toothless grin. He got up and headed toward the cockpit. Harper twisted her body around enough to see an old man at the plane's controls. He picked up the radio. Mike writhed at her side, trying to loosen himself from the tight ropes.

Harper tried to release her bonds. "What luck to encounter the world's greatest Boy Scout knot expert."

"No shit! If only I could reach my machete. I couldn't get out of these if I were Houdini!"

Mike glanced at the cockpit where the old man continued to jabber into the radio. "We have got to get to him so he doesn't warn whoever is at the other end of this flight."

The boy returned, rifle in hand. Harper smiled as she spoke. "How do you propose to do that, Mr. Logan?"

Mike also smiled at the boy. "Shit, I have no fucking clue."

CHAPTER 51

His uniform was immaculately pressed and decorated. His perfect smile was adorned with the occasional solid gold tooth. Although short, his stature was erect and confident. He addressed them in French. "*Bienvenue Monsieur et Mademoiselle*; we are honored that you have come to join us."

The glare off his medals in the evening sun made Harper and Mike wince.

"My name is Colonel N'jardu and I am in command here."

Mike stood defiantly. The twenty or so men surrounding the Colonel cocked their rifles.

Harper figured she'd better do something to diffuse the tension of the meeting. She returned the military man's greeting in a northern French dialect. "Bon jour, Colonel! We have been separated from our humanitarian mission and would very much appreciate assistance in returning to our group."

Mike couldn't pick up every word but realized she was speaking French with a Celtic accent. He looked at Harper and gave her a nod of understanding.

"What be ye saying to the lovely young man, lass?" Mike said.

"Wheel me love, I was just askin' him to return us to our flock." With a flick of her shoulder, she moved her strawberry hair to the front of her chest.

"I speak English well, sir and madam." The Colonel looked at Harper and Mike sideways. "I am sorry that you have been misplaced from your group. Perhaps I have heard of your mission. Where are you from?"

Harper and Mike spoke simultaneously. "Scotland." "Ireland."

Harper gave Mike a look that clearly said, "Shut up and let me do the talking."

"We're bein' from both Scotland and The Emerald Isle. Me 'usband don't' be likin' it too much when he is reminded we come from different clans, sometimes warrin' nations."

"Aye, 'tis true." Mike looked down at her. "But truth be told, I'll be lovin' her anyway."

"I see." The Colonel sneered. He spoke to one of the men next to him in a native dialect. The man nodded and sliced the knotted ropes from Harper's and Mike's wrists with a razor-sharp hand knife, missing their hands by millimeters. "Please forgive the crude treatment by our countrymen, but these are dangerous times."

"Oh blimey, no worries lad!" Mike rubbed his wrists. "It seems that things are always dangerous around this bonnie lass!" Harper and Mike exchanged looks of triumph. *It's working—we make a great team!*

They were rewarded with another bop on their noggins, awakening only after who-knows-how-long to rub large knots on their heads.

Harper was the first to speak. "OK, this is just becoming annoying."

She could feel the egg coming up on her forehead. A purple and yellow lump was rising on the back of Mike's skull. He looked at her, wincing. "Fucking now what?"

As their vision cleared, the pair surveyed their surroundings. They were unshackled and lying on the dirt floor of a six by six concrete cell with a narrow, barred door. No windows, no chairs, no beds, and no facilities.

"Well, Harpy, I am not sure how you do it, but every minute with you goes from bad to worse."

"Gee, thanks, back at'cha. Now what?"

"Well, there is something I've never told you about that might come in handy."

"Like what? You have telekinetic powers?"

"I've got money sewn into my shorts, pay from my last mercenary job." He peered through the bars. "Let's see who might be up for a bribe."

Harper put her finger to her lips. "Remember, we are missionaries from Scotland, or Ireland, or whatever."

"Oh yeah, right." He adjusted his accent. "Aye, laddies! Won't ye be comin' 'ere?"

She could not stifle her laugh and gave him a thumbs-up.

A large black man approached the cell. "What do you want?" His voice was such an intense baritone even the floor seemed to reverberate.

Harper sensed Mike's hair bristle and jumped up to intervene. "Me husband and I would like to speak with our Consulate, this bein' a huge mistake and all."

The large man nodded and motioned for an unseen person to come to the cell.

Harper grinned cockily. "See, just a little communication and we can get this all straightened out." Mike retuned her sarcastic thumbs up.

Two uniformed men opened the narrow cell door. Mike and Harper poised themselves to run the second they were released. The men flashed rotten-toothed grins as they motioned for Harper and Mike to exit. Harper looked at Mike and kissed him on the cheek. He grinned and held out his hand. "Ladies first."

Harper returned his look. "Why thank you, Mr. Logan."

A split second after Mike saw one of the men cover Harper's mouth with a cloth, a sharp rap on his skull made him lose consciousness for the third time that day.

CHAPTER 52

The man woke up to the taste of blood dripping from the side of his mouth. He looked around with a barely functioning eye to find himself tied to a chair in a stark room.

A voice he couldn't identify came from a hidden speaker. "Dr. Vandervere, we do not tolerate failure."

"But we can be sure that they are dead. No one survives the Mayi-Mayi." Vandervere didn't even convince himself, let alone his audience.

"Your only mission was to find the material, then eradicate both the species and the people who found it. There are four bodies missing, not to mention Merrill."

"But, sir, I hired the most ruthless killers in Africa."

"And yet, members of the team are unaccounted for."

Vandervere became aware of the wires connected to his temples.

As the lights flickered, Vandervere flashed back to his days hunting wild game, his favorite dominatrix, and his father with the black leather belt in his hand.

CHAPTER 53

Mike regained consciousness in a slump with a sore neck and a welt on his cheek. His first thought was for Harper and what might be happening to her. He felt unsettled by a conflicting surge of emotions, the need to maintain the cool, calm stance of the mercenary at war with his increasing affection for the young botanist.

He rose on shaky legs to assess the situation. He couldn't see anyone, but heard the voices of two men he assumed were guards. They spoke in the Nilotic language Harper had pointed out, even though he felt sure they were in or near Kananga. That meant the men were not locals and most likely hired for this job and this job only.

Mike let out a sigh of relief. Harper's captors must know her value to Pharmco. They hadn't abducted her to sell her as another run-of-the-mill sex slave.

The large man sported a smarmy smile. "Well then, what do we be havin' here, my love?"

Harper looked right through the man as the drug took over more of her mind.

"This one be mine for the night." His large hand caressed her strawberry hair. "*Salongo, alinga mosala!*"

The crowd roared.

Harper's ears perked at the familiar voice, but she was physically unable to do or say anything.

The large man picked her up and flung her over his shoulder like a sack of barley and headed into the back rooms.

The crowd roared even louder as she passed out.

Harper came to with a wet cloth on her forehead. The large man sat on the bed next to her as her focus sharpened.

"Oh my God." She could barely speak, but a meek smile came to her face. "Monte."

"Yes, my little sparrow." His broad face beamed at her. "It is very fortunate I happened to be in this place this evening. It is also very fortunate they have no idea who you are, and that you have a bounty on your head, or you would be in an even worse situation. As it is, even your run-of-the-mill sadomasochist would have paid handsomely for your company."

"Why do I feel so horrible? What kind of drug have they given me? Or have I just lost my mind?"

"It does not matter now," Monte said. "Quaaludes are easy to overcome once you recognize the symptoms. They do not exist in the Americas now, but anthranilic acid is very easy to come by here. It mixes well with Viagra."

He handed her a dirty cup filled with something resembling muddy coffee and said, "We need to get you out of here. Where is Logan?"

Harper choked back sobs, knowing that her emotions would be a toxic combination with an anxiolytic drug like Quaaludes. "We were captured by some military guy and taken to a jail cell. I can only imagine where he is now." The tears spilled from her eyes despite her best efforts.

"Even a fool would see that you are in love with him." Monte bellowed and looked at her with fatherly tenderness. She had longed all her life to receive such a look. Even in her drugged condition, she marveled at how it had come from such a person in such a place.

Monte picked up a two-way radio and began to speak. Harper wasn't able to place the dialect. Normally, she would be distressed at this failure of her talent, but somehow tonight it didn't matter. She felt safe in the large hands of Monte Jones.

Gunshots fired in the distance as Mike attempted to escape the small cell using every trick learned from his extensive mercenary experience. He mentally took inventory of the weapons in his pitiful arsenal: Harper's brass lighter, his military belt buckle, his hands, a menacing expression on his face. That was it.

Then he remembered the twenty thousand dollars sewn into his shorts. Money that would surely get him killed.

"Mistah Logan." Two brawny men whom Mike assumed were guards smiled large, gold-toothed smiles.

"Now what?" Mike growled.

The men laughed heartily. "We have been sent by Mr. Monte Jones to rescue your sorry ass, mon." They used a soldering iron to melt the primitive bars, creating a small opening at the base. Mike crawled through.

"Where is Harper?" He demanded as soon as he stood on the side of freedom.

"We be takin' you to her. She will be needin' some rescuin', mon. *Salongo, alinga mosala!*"

"Bring it on," Mike said firmly. Somehow, Harper was no longer the fringe benefit. She had become the prize.

CHAPTER 54

L oud footsteps echoed in the hallway.

"Your boyfriend better show up soon." Monte paced in the small, grimy room. "And you had better get your wits together ...."

Angry voices joined the footsteps on the other side of the door.

Monte lumbered toward the bed and started making guttural noises. When Harper gave him a puzzled look, he jerked a thumb to the door. Even though still drugged, she caught on and began moaning in the spirit of ecstasy.

The voices outside turned into raucous laughter. The footsteps moved on to the next door. Harper couldn't figure out what they were looking for, but put her faith in Monte to deal with the situation.

Monte checked the base of the door to make sure there were no shadows, then faced the wall. "Take off your clothes," he ordered.

"What?" Was Monte not trustable after all?

"Take off those hooker clothes. Now!" Monte rummaged through his backpack.

This time, she did not waver. The drug was wearing off and she picked up the urgency in Monte's voice.

"Put this on. Wash off the paint they put on your face and tie up your hair. NOW!"

Harper didn't hesitate. She grabbed the baggy khakis, shirt, bandana and hat he threw at her and put them on, stepping back into her own personality. With a grimy towel, she wiped off the garish makeup. The only item she kept from her unseemly wardrobe was a pretty reed necklace. By the time she finished, her senses had completely returned.

Monte looked at his watch. "Go to the window. Do you see anything?" Monte kept his gaze fixed firmly at the light at the bottom of the door, checking for shadowed footsteps.

Harper tucked her hair under the bandana, knotted it, and plopped the hat on top. She peeked out the small window in the back of the brothel. It was a mere rectangular opening, no glass, just a pair of iron bars roughly fifteen feet from the ground. All she saw was a busy city street. "What am I supposed to be looking for?"

A moment later, the roar of a motorbike's engine overwhelmed the dull vibration of the traffic. A black man with a determined look sat in the driver's seat and a crazed white passenger called her name.

Monte raced to the window. "You must go now."

"What?"

Monte lifted his heel in a karate kick and punched out the bars. "NOW!"

Harper watched in confusion and astonishment as Monte took an earthenware jug from the table beside the bed and slammed it against the back of his own head with a sickening crack. *What was he doing? Does he really expect me to jump through that little window?*

The Mayi hit men who had been lurking outside burst through the door. No way out except the window. Harper swallowed her fear and jumped.

Remember, my little lotus, 'fear' is a four letter word.

Her father's words echoed in her mind as she hurtled herself over the window ledge and out to ... well, she had no idea what or where, but she knew staying in that room would be certain death—or worse.

Time stood still as she hovered in mid-air. She heard no traffic noises, no shouts, no rush of wind. Only her father's voice.

There are just a couple of other toxic words in the human language, words that have no existence in the natural world, as they have no meaning.

They are very powerful words and if you add them together, they can, and will, destroy mankind.

His face floated in front of her. *What are those words, Father?*

Guilt and regret. Her father had looked at the ground as he covered something in the soil with his shoe. *Guilt makes people feel badly and regret makes people do stupid things.*

Or maybe it is the other way around, but I am sure it is both. I guarantee you that plants, animals, ecosystems, anything in nature, as well as 'Gaia,'—living or not—does not subscribe to fear, guilt, or regret. Those emotions are selfish. They do not serve the survival of any species.

In that cathartic split second she came to terms with her own fear, guilt and regret.

The magic moment vanished as quickly as it had come. Harper landed in a man's lap as the Triumph motorcycle passed under the window. Strong arms wrapped themselves around her and held her tightly. *Another man holding me captive,* she thought, wondering how she would get away this time.

Harper pulled the brim of her hat up to look at this latest captor. Mike's smile beamed back at her. Both laughed in amazement while the driver looked back at them with a huge grin.

Just as the driver turned to face the road, a bullet slammed into his eyeball.

The bike lurched forward. Mike pushed the dead man into the dirt, leaped into the driver's seat, and thrust the motorcycle in a 90-degree turn.

"Are you OK?" he screamed to Harper at fifty kilometers an hour. The motorcycle careened down a residential path, barely missing several large trees.

"*Salinga, alongo mosala!*" Harper bellowed.

He smiled to himself, but only for a second. The Mayi were right behind them.

CHAPTER 55

The tall, bald man with the silver tooth had been tied to the same log in the same hut for what seemed like weeks. The village elders and shamans argued about his fate. Ever since the large white man wandered into the village, nearly unconscious from dengue fever, nothing had been the same. Some incidents were downright odd, in the opinion of the tribal elders.

Volcanic ash covered much of the canopy above the village. The rains disappeared. The silver back gorillas were acting strangely, moving their families to new areas, places they'd never before inhabited.

Even worse, Dr. Merrill was missing. His compound was deserted except for Kiki the monkey, who sat on his master's desk day and night, refusing to move until he returned.

But to the villagers, the worst possible thing was the death of the leopard.

It all started when one of the village girls was about to deliver a child. Two of the hunting party set out to bring Dr. Merrill back to the village. There was always a ceremonial feast in Dr. Merrill's honor, as the man helped the villagers with medical emergencies and gave them useful advice on farming. When the scouts arrived to find the tree house abandoned and Sheila's carcass splayed across a log, they wrapped the leopard in banana leaves and carried her back to the village. The tribe's people wept and gave her a funeral fit for royalty.

The locals had stayed in their huts ever since.

Then the bald white man arrived, delirious and weak with fever.

As far as the shamans were concerned, it meant only one thing. The Mayi warriors were getting close. There were rumors they had come to a village not too far away, raped the women, and took the young boys and men as unwilling recruits in their wars.

The elders had no plan for dealing with the Mayi on that inevitable day when they would invade their village. They had no weapons other than sticks and rocks to fend off the Mayi's arsenal of automatic rifles. It was just a matter of time.

The bald man with the silver tooth survived the dengue fever and while recovering, managed to extract a few tentative smiles from some of the women and children who came to give him food and water.

He had a friendly face and it served him well now.

He also knew it was only a matter of time before the rapists and butchers came to this peaceful village and he must do something soon. Very soon.

He understood some Swahili but was also aware that more than two-hundred fifty distinct languages were used on the Continent. This made communication next-to-impossible and contributed to the in-fighting and many civil wars plaguing the troubled land. This particular village used a Bantu language he was not familiar with. The only conversation he managed was with one teenage girl who spoke some French.

On the first morning when he felt well enough to sit up and speak for an extended time, he asked the girl to bring in the men, all the men—the elders, the shamans and the warriors—and translate.

If anything could be done to save this village, he knew it was up to him—Sergeant Dave Murano.

CHAPTER 56

The Triumph zoomed in and out of traffic on a main road, Harper's arms circled around Mike's waist, her chest and head pressed firmly against his back.

Mike had no idea where he was going or what he should do next, other than flee. All he possessed, besides the motorcycle, was that money sewn into his shorts. But to use American dollars to buy food or gasoline would tip off the pursuers for sure. As for attempting to bribe an official to get them across the border ... well, he might as well sign his death warrant.

All he knew was he and Harper had prices on their heads and the local authorities would not only be of no help, but were probably in league with the Pharmco bounty hunters.

He didn't see or hear anyone on their heels, but he knew the pursuers were closing in. Time to do something unexpected.

A dump truck lumbered west off the main road. Mike turned sharply and followed. Harper concentrated on clinging to Mike and keeping herself upright on the back of the motorcycle.

Sunset was drawing close, but Mike did not turn on the motorcycle's headlight in the growing gloom. He just tailed the dump truck up close. The truck had a ladder down the back and a double rear axle, shielding the motorcycle. He could only hope his pursuers did not see them turn off the main road. He also hoped Harper would be able to climb up the ladder onto the truck.

Bright headlights turned dusk into daylight as a Jeep screeched behind them. The gangsters were back.

The light illuminated a possible escape Mike otherwise might have missed, a dirt trail rising up a hill parallel with the road. He abruptly turned up the trail and gunned the throttle. Harper closed her eyes and clutched Mike with all her strength.

"Harp! Do you have a shoelace?" he said with his jaw clenched.

"What?"

"A shoelace."

"What for?"

"So I can light it on fire."

Why was he thinking about starting a fire at a time like this? "I have a reed necklace. Would that work?"

"Excellent. Take it off and twist it like a wick." He was going slower now, keeping pace with the dump truck on the lower, parallel road.

"OK, here." She removed the necklace and handed it to him.

Mike unscrewed the motorcycle's gas cap. "When I say jump, jump."

"You're kidding me right? Jump where?"

"Where do you think? The garbage truck."

"Seriously?"

"Just do it." He inserted the reed necklace into the gas tank, leaving a small tail dangling outside. He flicked the lighter that Harper had received from Ursula so long ago and held it to the wick.

"NOW!"

They jumped down into the back of the garbage-filled truck as the gas tank of the Triumph exploded.

Mike peered over the rear of the truck bed to see the Jeep turn up the hill. Perfect. Just like he planned, he'd distracted the pursuers with loud noise and fire.

He and Harper were safe for the moment in the back of a smelly, slow-moving dump truck. But he knew better than to relax.

They'd be back, and sooner rather than later.

CHAPTER 57

Six men stood in a circle around Sergeant Dave Murano. His wrists were still tied, but he tried to look as powerful and imposing as he could. He smiled at the men, showing his silver tooth.

One of the elders called to someone outside the hut. The French-speaking teenaged translator entered. Her eyes appropriately lowered and she waited for instructions.

The men spoke among themselves and then said something directed to him. The girl repeated in French, "What do you know about the Mayi-Mayi?"

Dave looked them in the eyes, one by one, and conveyed disgust through his expression. "They will come and either kill your male infants or steal your young boys for warfare, most likely both."

The translator quietly repeated what Dave said.

The village men looked at each other without surprise. They had heard the rumors.

"Then they will rape your women, even the pregnant women." Dave lowered his eyes, feeling shame for the crimes of the male sex. The girl continued to translate in the Bantu hybrid.

The elders held blank expressions. This was not news to them. Nothing was said for several minutes as the elders and shamans mulled over their options. The senior shaman spoke and the girl translated. "What do you plan to do about it?"

Dave looked up and smiled. This was the first glimmer of hope, the first sign the tribesmen would accept him as an ally instead of an omen of bad tidings. One of the elders said something to a young man guarding the door of the hut. He left his post and untied the ropes binding Dave's wrists. Dave rubbed his hands and straightened his back. He faced his former captors and looked them in the eyes.

He spoke in English. "Let's kick their asses!"

No translation was necessary.

CHAPTER 58

Harper and Mike bounced painfully in the back of the stinky truck. It was dark with no moon. The only thing Harper could see was Mike peering over the back and sides of the truck, trying to assess the location of their pursuers.

The dump truck lumbered along a rutted gravel road. Harper spotted headlights following them in the distance—not a good sign.

"Time to move on," Mike said.

"Already?" She had almost reached the end of her will to live. If she was going to die anyway, well, just get on with it. Better than this never-ending ordeal of hunger, thirst, filth and terror.

Just then, a thought came to her: the entire continent of Africa had succumbed to this same primitive lack of civility. There was nothing to lose.

And another thing—if she died, her mother would collect on her life insurance policy. Harper knew full well her mother would spend the windfall on useless crap in a pathetic attempt to increase her social status. The last thing her mother would use the money for was the betterment of the planet.

That thought helped Harper pull herself back together. Damned if she would die now and let her mother waste what, at this point, was her very well-earned reward!

To the right of the dump truck, the trail where the Triumph had exploded continued. To the left was a steep cliff with large trees covered in thick vines from top to bottom.

Mike looked at the cliff and the trees with great intensity. Harper realized he was planning to jump out of the truck in the direction of the precipice, and he would expect her to follow.

CHAPTER 59

Claire finished making a poultice of cacao and mixed tubers, then rubbed it on Richard's neck.

"That should do it." Claire delighted at Richard Merrill's smile. He stroked her forearm with affection before she pulled it away.

"Ground Wasps are nasty little buggers, aren't they?" Claire said, while reassembling the less high tech but more practical version of her medical kit.

"Indeed, Claire." He sat up to look out over the perch where they camped. With Richard's botanical knowledge and Claire's medicinal and nutritional skill, they were a natural team for life on the run, living off the land. Richard tried to keep his spirits up, knowing full well that until the Mayi-Mayi were contained in some way, he would never be able to return to his beloved tree house compound, his research, his highly satisfying way of life.

He inwardly mourned for Janikula, Kiki, and his highly hybridized algae, but mostly for Sheila. He had never felt a connection of that magnitude with another being. It seemed to him the spirits of man and leopard had some kind of relationship in a previous existence. It was uncanny. He felt a similar bond with Claire.

Unused to letting a man take the lead, Claire found to her delight that deferring to Richard's knowledge and experience gave her an unexpected freedom. She thought he was one of the few men she'd ever encountered who was her equal on every level, and marveled at the twists of fate that brought the two of them together.

So it was on that morning in the middle of the vast jungle, she said something she had never uttered in her previous life. "What do you think we should do, Richard?"

CHAPTER 60

With his hands free, Dave more effectively described his plan to the villagers.

First, he asked some questions though he was certain he knew the answers. He spoke to the men directly, the teenage girl staying to help with translation only occasionally.

Men speak a common language in war.

Dave asked if they had guns.

Heads shook. No.

"How many men are able to fight?"

About thirty.

"What about spears, blow darts, slings, or anything else of use against a handful of men with AK-47s?"

The faces staring back at him went blank.

Quietly, the young man guarding the door approached Dave and handed him a small leather pouch. Dave opened it, discovered powder, wet his finger and dipped it inside.

His signature silver-toothed smile beamed. The chemical formula dated back to the fourteenth century: sulfur, charcoal and potassium nitrate, all abundant on the Dark Continent. A real weapon at last!

The village men looked puzzled before a common expression came over each one of their faces. It was the same look of admiration Dave received from his father when he was a teenager and was elected captain of the varsity football team. He felt a surge of confidence and hope.

Dave put his hands together double fisted, and made a deep rumbling noise. Once he was sure that he had everyone's attention, he let his hands go, fingers splayed, mimicking an explosion.

"BOOM!"

Every man grunted, answering in the language of war.

CHAPTER 61

The garbage truck lurched and rumbled along the dirt road. The noise and lack of natural light made it next-to-impossible for Mike to put a coherent escape plan together. Harper huddled in one corner atop the filthy load, nearing the end of her strength and sanity.

It was then he realized he was committing the worst possible error in survival: he was not thinking like the enemy.

If he were the pursuer, he would have immediately ascertained that the explosion of the bike was a diversion and the prey had more than likely scrambled into the dump truck. Only two options remained: stay on the truck until it reached the landfill, or jump off.

Mike put himself into the shoes of the pursuer. The jungle was vast and dense, and there was no moon. He'd need to either bring in portable flood lights and search dogs, or wait until morning.

Somehow, he figured that between the resources of the Mayi-Mayi, the Pharmco bounty hunters and local law enforcement, they'd easily bring in dogs and searchlights.

Again he peered over the side toward the jungle. The truck's headlights shone on the west side of the road as it made sharp turns. Mike saw one-hundred-foot trees covered with vines. The tree branches arched over the road at intervals, and their trunks clung to the steep slopes of the cliff.

The searchlights on the pursuers' Jeep swept side-to-side on the road as the vehicle gained on the dump truck.

Mike thought to himself, if we never touch the ground, dogs cannot track us.

"Harper, wake up," he said. "We are going where you have always wanted to be."

She could only imagine his smile in the deep, moonless dark and said nothing, just got on all fours and crawled behind him to the west side of the truck.

"When I say now, jump up on to the tree above you. It is only a foot or so. Use the vines like a ladder. Move as fast as you can to the opposite side of the tree so you are out of sight."

He repeated the instructions, louder so she could hear over the diesel engine's noise.

The truck driver heard their voices and slowed to look in the rear view mirror just as Mike and Harper leaped up to latch onto the overhanging vines.

Must have smoked too much ganja, the driver told himself. Still, he made a mental note of the approximate time and place, just in case those guys following in the Jeep asked for information—and offered more weed as payment.

"Harp," Mike said in a low whisper after the loud truck had passed. "Are you OK?"

"Are you fucking nuts?"

Good, he thought. She's fine. "Use the vines to help you move along the trees. Get as far out of sight from the road as possible. Wrap yourself in these large elephant-ear looking leaves."

"*Schindapsys-pothos*, you idiot," she murmured to herself. She shimmied along the trunk over the dirt road to an elbow in the tree, coming to settle about thirty feet from the road. She positioned herself flat against the trunk and wrapped vines around her arms and legs. She took the giant *pothos* leaf, at least as tall as she was and three times as wide, and bent the petiole so the leaf shielded her entirely from the road.

She hoped Mike was as successful in hiding himself.

She heard the Jeep's engine pass on the dirt road below them. A weak spotlight flashed just below her. She instinctively stayed still, turning her head away from the light. Still, she couldn't avoid a glimpse of the ground, so very far away from her little nest on the tree branch. She told herself not to think about it.

The Jeep and the floodlight were gone for at least ten minutes before she heard Mike call for her.

"Yes, I'm here," she answered his strained whisper.

"Good. Stay put."

"How long?"

"Until I tell you it's safe to go. If you can secure yourself well enough and you are sure you are invisible, try to get a little sleep."

"You know, that sounds pretty good. I think I can do that." She nestled in a little tighter. Mike had been right—this is where she always wanted to be. She felt right at home tangled in the tree. It was surprisingly comfortable as long as she didn't think about how high she was from the ground. Or about the tree ants scurrying across her back.

"I will try to forget I am starving and ready to die of thirst," Harp murmured just before drifting off.

"Dying of thirst is the least of our worries. Trust me on that one."

CHAPTER 62

The older boys in the tribe carried sacks of black rocks and yellow chalk to a pit where Dave stood. Some of the youths ground the rock and chalk into powder, while the women of the tribe crafted a loosely woven reed cloth. The strongest men dug a huge hole in the center of the village while others carted away the debris.

The entire population of the village except for the very young and very old worked toward a single, common goal with cheerfulness and determination. There was very little conversation with the exception of chattering children.

Dave smiled as he surveyed the scene, thinking of his own children. He quickly turned his thoughts away from hurtful memories after wondering briefly if his loss was fueling this current project. For whatever reason, he truly wanted to help these people.

One of the elders studied Dave's face and saw the transformation from joy to sorrow to resolve. He smiled the universal message of compassion, and Dave understood.

They both realized that no matter what, people are all the same inside.
A bond was forged.

CHAPTER 63

A t dawn dogs whined in the rain as men followed with raised machine guns.

Harper awoke abruptly, still entwined in her root and vine cradle, and peered to the ground far below.

The men seemed to be checking for tracks and a place where the fugitives might have hit the leaf litter. After a few moments, they decided this was not the place where their prey had touched ground and moved on.

Mike allowed at least an hour to pass before he dared make a sound. "Harp?" he said in a loud whisper.

No answer.

"Harper! Are you OK?" He sounded frantic.

"Yeah, I'm OK. My arms are asleep and I just peed on myself, but I'm good. At least I'm alive and I managed to catch some rain water with my hands." She paused to slurp from her cupped hands. "Now what?"

"We descend." She could hear Mike rustle the huge leaves.

"OK, I'm on it." She climbed like a nimble monkey down the tree trunk, using the vines as stairs.

"The only problem here is that the rain will cover their tracks but will increase ours." Mike crouched to examine the ground.

"Oh, I'm so glad that is our only problem," she said with a sly smile.

"Okay, Miss Smart Ass, let's go." He kissed her on the forehead and took off in a southern direction. "Try to find something to eat that does not involve cooking."

"Like this?" Harper pulled two tubers from the wet soil.

"Sweet!" Mike took one and broke it open with a sharp rock, giving her the larger half.

"Where are we going?" Harper asked between bites, avoiding the tough, dirt-covered skin.

"They'll assume we'll head west. That means we will go south. If we are in the general vicinity of Kananga, we will encounter some villages to the south. I know it's a long shot but perhaps we can find some help in one of those villages."

"Or we can find the Mayi as well." She kept walking and eating, wiping her face with Monte Jones's bandana.

For the first time since they'd been separated in the jail cell many hours earlier, they had the opportunity to catch up. "Tell me, how was it that you landed in my arms from that window?" Mike asked.

"Monte Jones."

"Monte? How did he find you?"

"I'm not quite sure. I was dressed up like a prostitute and given drugs after they took me from the jail. The next thing I remember, Monte was pushing me out a little window." She touched a spadix on a bright red antherium. "Then I landed in your arms."

He threw his arms around her and caressed her rain-soaked hair with his large hands.

"And that is where you should always land."

Normally she would have responded with something smart and flippant. But after all she'd been through, all she could do was relax in his embrace and whisper, "Happy landings."

CHAPTER 64

The Jeep roared into the village in a cloud of dust in the late afternoon. Dave was just tying off the last sack when he heard the commotion in the center of the village.

The senior tribesman boldly walked up to the Jeep and asked the man with the hat what he wanted. The man laughed and gestured toward another man in the back seat. He aimed an AK-47 at the elder and pulled the trigger. The tribal leader collapsed in a bloody heap on the ground.

Dave heard the shots and gritted his teeth. He strode out from behind the huts and halted at the far end of the village.

"It's me you want. Leave these people alone." He stood defiantly, yelling at the Jeep.

Fifty yards stood between Dave and the Jeep. No villagers were visible.

The man in the hat grinned, flashing a gold tooth.

"Come here and talk to me like a man," Dave said. "Like a man, mon."

The man broke into laughter. He cocked his head to the right and squinted at Dave, then motioned for the driver to move in his direction. The Jeep began to drive across the center of the village.

The men in the Jeep held their machine guns at the ready. The people of the tribe emerged from their huts to watch. The Mayi were used to seeing local villagers run in terror from them. The stoicism of these people caught them off guard. They lowered their weapons just as the Jeep crossed the loosely woven tarps and plunged into the giant pit.

The villagers immediately had the pit surrounded, raining balls of gunpowder and fiery arrows. The men in the Jeep were able to fire only a few rounds into the air.

Just as Dave had promised, the explosion made a loud and satisfying "BOOM!"

CHAPTER 65

The south proved to be more arid than eastern Congo. Mike was adamant about no fires: the jungle was not as dense and any aircraft flying overhead at night would spot smoke or light in the uninhabited areas. Lack of food and water were swiftly becoming issues.

Harper's resolve was also at risk. Mike sensed she was losing her will to survive.

"Stay with me, girl. We can do this." He held her chin in his hand, tilting her face up to his. She loved it when he did that. She had wanted her father to validate her in that way. The moment passed and she re-attached herself to the present situation.

"You know, one of the main reasons the Neanderthals perished as hominids and Homo sapiens, also known as h. habilis, survived, was that the hominids found in the German Neander Valley were very picky about their diet." She spoke not to Mike but to a small scorpion.

Her complexion was sallow. Mike again worried about her health, both physically and emotionally.

"That being said," Harper continued, "they also needed about three hundred-fifty calories per day more than h. sapiens due to their build and lifestyle. About fifty-five thousand years ago, their inhabited climates changed drastically about every decade."

To Mike's great surprise, Harper grabbed the scorpion by the tail and skewered the body with a small stick. "That is a tremendous swing in a very short time. Only the fittest would have survived such events."

She quickly speared four more small scorpions and sparked the brass lighter, creating a tiny barbecue.

Mike smiled to himself. She was back in the game.

She talked as the arachnids roasted. "Actually, the human/Homo sapiens is hard-wired for the hunter-gatherer diet: meat, berries, indigenous vegetables, nuts, anything you would encounter in the natural habitat. No processed dairy, no wheat products, no sugars, nothing you wouldn't find in the wild. I have come to believe in the last few weeks, or however long we have been in this hell-slash-heaven, that if we would stick to our native diets, the ever-present threat of modern-day cancers would be abolished."

Harper finished her lecture while Mike listened with admiration. "As luck would have it, I also happen to belong to the Homo sapiens species."

After slogging through the wet and muddy jungle for two days, enduring searing heat and high humidity, Harper and Mike reached a village.

"This seems a little more civilized than what we are used to." Mike whispered as they crouched in the brush to survey the collection of huts.

"Wow, I used to think Big Sur was outside the realm of civilization."

A square building painted blue stood in the center of the village.

"That writing on the side of the wall—what does it say?" Mike asked.

"Who cares what it says?" Harper began to rise. "The language is the important thing."

"What do you think you're doing?" Mike reached up and grabbed the back of her shirt to pull her down.

"It is in Swahili ... and it's a bar." She broke away from his grasp.

"Get back here. You can't go in there!" Mike yanked her arm and forced her to a crouch. "First of all, we have not come this far for you to disobey me and get us both killed." Mike's voice was a stern whisper.

"I'm sorry, did you say 'disobey'?" She stood up with conviction. "Besides, I can't think of anything better right now than a stiff drink."

"Apparently you haven't read the sign all the way." Mike rose next to her. "If you look closely, I am pretty sure it says something like, 'No women allowed'."

Harper studied the sign again. *Shit, he was right, dammit.*

"So now what?" She plopped down in the brush like a pouting child.

"I go in and see what is going on and you stay here."

"Fine." Her face was turned away, her lower lip sticking out. "Have some pombi for me."

He couldn't help smiling. She was beautiful even when having a tantrum.

An engine roared overhead. Mike dropped to the ground and used his body to cover Harper's.

A helicopter. They looked at each other. A helicopter, a bar.

"It couldn't be." Mike whispered as he studied the chopper. "It's a different make, and yet ...."

The craft landed and the whirring blades came to a halt. The pilot practically fell out of the chopper door and headed straight for the blue building.

"Oh shit!" Harper put her hand over her mouth. "It's him! Captain Gauld!"

"Can we trust him?" Mike whispered. "He can get us out of here. But is he working for Pharmco?"

"What choice do we have?" Harper asked.

"It's a different chopper. It looks pretty beat up and judging by the way he is staggering to the bar, he probably has not retained gainful employment." Mike stood, dusted off his shorts and smoothed his disheveled hair.

"Be careful in there," Harper said.

"I'll just talk to him, that's all. I'll act as if I know nothing about the massacre in the meadow and I don't know where you are."

"I guess that's as good a plan as any."

"When you see that the coast is clear, you run across the clearing and get in the chopper. In any event, he will get you out of here no matter who he is working for. Hide yourself well and do not come out until I give you the signal. I'll get him to keep drinking."

"That shouldn't be hard." Harper smirked. "What if the cockpit is locked?"

"Does the dude look like he has the where-with-all to handle keys? I will buy him a drink," Mike said. "I will try to get him to take me in the chopper to his next destination. If he is working for Pharmco, I'll find out. Worst case scenario, I will take him out during the flight and you and I will fly to Kinshasa."

Harper looked up at him. "You can fly a helicopter?"

"Uh, sure," he replied after a moment's hesitation.

Harper was not so sure. "Well, just don't get him too drunk."

"I doubt that is even possible. Wish me luck." He reached down to kiss her cheek.

"Me, too." She returned the kiss and prepared to run.

CHAPTER 66

"Do you think we should make for the American or the British Embassy in Kinshasa?" Claire smashed willow bark with a makeshift mortar, not looking at Richard's face. She really did not want to go back to London or the bureaucracy of Doctors Without Borders. In fact, she really didn't want to do anything but be lost in the jungle with Richard.

Claire dug through her bag and wondered if Harper and Logan had survived. It made her queasy to think the slime hired by 'that wretched pharmaceutical company' had won. The thought took her back to the campsite where Sid Lembowsky perished, then to the meadow where Chris and Hermann were brutally murdered. But the cave was the most vivid in her memory. Harper exhibited incredible grace under pressure in that ordeal. Claire remembered with awe the leadership qualities the young woman did not even suspect she possessed.

"Oh, no," the lady doctor said to herself out loud, "she is fine."

"What did you say, darling?" Richard asked.

"I was just wondering about the others. Sergeant Murano, for example. He was, I mean is, of course, quite a resourceful chap and I will forever be grateful for his quick thinking in leading those brutal men away from us."

Richard wrapped his large hands around her tiny fingers. "If it was not so dangerous here, I would stay in the jungle with you forever. I will remember our precious hours at the compound and pray that someday we might find another place like it."

He looked into her whiskey eyes, "But I am afraid we will never be able to go back there."

Tears brimmed. "Never?"

"No, my beauty. Never." He gave her a tender smile.

"Bloody fucking hell." She kicked a pebble down the slope of the hill.

"My sentiments exactly."

"So where do we go from …." She stopped in mid-sentence. A large explosion boomed in the distance.

Richard shaded his eyes to look out over the valley from their rocky perch. A fiery blast was followed by a faint sound of human cheers.

"If my calculations are correct, that is the village of Kilembe. I am sure there is no electricity, no gas, nothing that could generate such an explosion in any of these tribal villages." Richard cocked his head to the right. "That means something is up."

"Something is definitely up and my gut instinct is, someone we know is involved," she agreed, adding, "If something blew up, people were injured. We must attend to the wounded." She was already on her feet collecting her pack.

"Well then, mi' lady, we shan't keep them waiting." He put on his pack and gestured his hand for her to lead the way.

"No mi' lord, we shan't." She stood on tiptoe to kiss him on the cheek and made a light step over a prickly shrub in the direction of the explosion.

CHAPTER 67

M ike slapped the pilot on the back. "Well, if it isn't Captain Gauld."
"Uh, hey, kumbaya, dude!" Gauld focused his bleary eyes, trying to place the newcomer in the bar, and failed. "Let me buy you a drink! We don't get many ex-pats way out here. What did you say your name was?" Gauld motioned to the bartender.

"Don't you remember, amigo? The Zipperco Christmas party?" Mike knew there was no way Gauld would remember anything that transpired during a company Christmas party.

The Captain looked at him fuzzily. "Oh, yeah! Hey, whazzup?"

He shoved a drink into Mike's hand. "Let's toast! I just got fired from that piece of shit company. I don't know about you, but I can't wait to get out of this Godforsaken place. I want to get back to my spread in Louisiana."

"Yeah? How would you get there? That pile of bolts and rubber-bands parked outside wouldn't even make it across the street, let alone all the way across the Atlantic."

"Well, I would get on a Boeing 747 and bail of course!" The pilot took a large swig from his drink. "I got everything I need in the way of papers except cash to buy the ticket."

"I have cash." Mike threw his head back to down the shot. "I just ain't got no passport. He looked at Gauld eye-to-eye. "I lost it in the jungle."

The pilot shot him a skeptical look. "Yeah, right, of course you did. And I lost my virginity when I got married."

They both laughed.

"Shiyatt, the only way to get out of here, if you have no passport, is through the American Embassy."

"Really, that's a coincidence!" Mike slapped him on the back. "That's just where I am headed!" Mike signaled to the bartender for another round.

"No shit!" Gauld drained his glass. "I think I was supposed to meet someone, some people maybe, here. That's why I came to this hole in the butt crack of the Congo. I don't see anyone here who looks like they are looking for me, so …."

His eyes were at half-mast. "You got cash, I got a chopper, let's fucking go!"

Gauld headed out the door as the bartender looked for payment.

Mike had no money on him except large American bills. He did not want to make any trouble, much less alert anyone that white men were in this remote village. He felt into his pockets and found the brass lighter. He threw it on the bar and headed toward the chopper to join the inebriated pilot.

The bartender looked at the beat-up lighter and stuffed it in his pocket. Any type of technology, no matter how primitive, was valuable tender.

"Thanks for coming with me, bro," Gauld said. "I just needed someone to talk me into it. There is nothing here for me now. What did you say your name was?" The pilot struggled into the cockpit while Mike looked for signs of Harper.

She peeked out from behind a coarse green military blanket and smiled.

"My name is Mike and I can't tell you how great it is to see you." Mike helped Captain Gauld with his seatbelt as the engine revved and the chopper blades began to rotate. In a moment, they were off the ground.

Harper's heart soared with the aircraft, even as she remembered the betrayal in the Russian cargo plane. She was pinning all of her hopes— her life itself—on a drunken pilot in a rickety clunker of a helicopter, but compared to what she'd been through, she figured the odds were clearly in her favor.

CHAPTER 68

Dave shook the hand of the senior village elder and hid his fears for the future. He knew the Mayi-Mayi would be back, whether or not they knew of the destruction of the Jeep and the men inside. He needed a defense plan against future attacks—and fast.

The young men of the village were using primitive shovels to fill in the giant pit in the center of the village and to get it covered up quickly. The last thing they needed was an overhead reconnaissance plane or helicopter spotting the wreckage and alerting the Mayi-Mayi. Dave directed the village women to spread leaf litter over the pit and erect the village's version of a market on the spot.

Richard and Claire crouched in the brush nearby and watched the operation.

"Why, Richard, that silver-toothed man is my friend, Sergeant Dave Murano. He is alive!" A broad smile came over Claire's small English face.

"Is he the one you've been telling me about, the leader from your team?" Richard felt a mixture of emotions—jealousy of another man's history with her and relief that another warrior stood by to protect her.

"Yes, and it appears he has helped these villagers. Let's go and say hello." Before he could stop her, she ran out into the middle of the village where her lost friend stood. She threw her arms around him.

"Shit," Richard muttered under his breath before emerging to follow her.

"Richard, this is one of our team members, Sergeant Dave Murano." She looked up at him and smiled. "Dave, I can't believe you are here ... and alive! How did you escape? Oh, and bloody hell, thank you for saving our lives!" She shuddered at the recollection of Shadea's burned feet and the heat of the lava chamber. Again, she thought of Harper and her heroism in the cave. Will I ever see her again? she wondered.

"Dave led those bastards away from us while Harper and I hid out in to the caves," Claire finished.

Richard reached over to shake the man's hand. "Yes, quite the hero I have heard."

Dave returned his handshake vigorously.

"I am Dr. Richard Merrill."

"Oh, Richard, I am terribly sorry." Claire blushed, obviously flustered. "This is Dr. Merrill. He was on the same quest before us and was lost in the jungle."

"Well, technically, I was lost from the grips of Pharmco. I knew exactly where I was."

"We can catch up later. Right now we have to formulate a plan to keep the Mayi from retaliating against this village." Dave was suddenly serious.

"What in the bloody hell happened here? We heard the explosion and saw the smoke. That's how we came to find you. We reckoned there would be injured to care for." Claire walked toward the acrid wisps still wafting from the half-filled pit.

The villagers were throwing water on the smoke, unaware that it was actually making the plume grow larger.

Dave jogged over to the elders and instructed them to throw dirt into the smoldering pit. He motioned for the young men to hurry their work. The longer the evidence was visible, the greater the chance the Mayi would figure out what happened to their band of terrorists.

"We set a trap for a Jeep full of Mayi-Mayi. They fell for it. They were not expecting any defensive moves from the country folk." Dave grabbed a palm husk and began to put his own back into the group effort. Richard and Claire grabbed tools and pitched in.

"Do you think they knew where their thugs were headed?" Claire asked as she wiped perspiration from her forehead and tossed another shovel full of dirt into the pit.

"I was watching them as they entered the village and no one was on a walkie-talkie," Dave said, swatting away small flies attracted to the sweat on his bald head. "But that does not mean no one knew where they were going back at their base camp. We can only hope they are not that well organized."

The villagers, young and old, men and women, all but the youngest children, worked feverishly to hide the charred remains of their enemy and the evidence of what they had done to them.

Dave watched the smallest children play hide and seek. He hoped to God he hadn't signed their death warrants.

CHAPTER 69

"So, how did you say you got here from Louisiana?" Mike yelled over the whup-whup of the chopper. No luxuries like an intercom on this ancient craft.

"Well, I got a great offer from this oil company to ... gee, you look kinda familiar. Have we met?" With his free hand, the pilot pulled his bag up from behind the seat.

"Really? Wow, that's so interesting." Mike continued to pump Gauld for information while keeping his eye on Harper. He figured she could not hear any of the conversation over the roar of the blades and engine.

"Do you do any side jobs?" Mike continued with his fishing expedition.

"That depends." The pilot took the last swig of whatever was in his pack. "Random people hire me to deliver or rescue folks to or from remote places in the DRC." He held the empty container up to the window to confirm its lack of content. "But I don't really know why anyone would come to this shit-hole. There was this one group ...."

Mike wanted to stop this train of thought, if in fact there was one. He thought Captain Gauld's train had left the station long ago.

"So now that you have been laid off from ... um, Zipperco," Mike said, choosing his words carefully. "Do you ever work for other people as well? I mean, besides side jobs?"

The pilot shook his empty flask again, just to be sure. "No. In fact, the only job since I was fired was to meet some person, or some people, they were not clear or maybe I'm not clear, at that bar where I met you."

The pilot stared at Mike. "Are you sure we haven't met someplace before?"

Mike ducked his left hand behind the seats and motioned for Harper to come forward.

"Well, Greg, I think we may have met." With his peripheral vision, Gauld saw a blur of strawberry hair swirl around the cockpit.

Harper bent to whisper in the pilot's ear. "Hi Captain. Long time no see."

Gauld stared at her and dropped the controls in complete shock. The chopper lost altitude a few hundred feet before the pilot regained his composure. Harper landed awkwardly in the pilot's lap.

"Hey, I remember you!" Greg smiled at her lasciviously. He looked at Mike and finally put it all together. "Yeah, yeah, you guys!"

He wiped his dry mouth with the back of his hand. "Where is everyone else?"

Gauld took in the sad, despairing looks on Mike's and Harper's faces. "Aw, shiyatt. Don't tell me."

Mike gave Gauld a brief run-down of the events since he'd dropped them off in the jungle.

"You're shittin' me, right?" The pilot said when Mike had finished.

"I am so not shittin' you."

"For cryin' out loud, let's get the fuck out of here!' Gauld yanked on the throttle.

The three broke into a spontaneous round of "God Bless America" as Gauld steered the chopper straight toward Kinshasa and the American Embassy.

CHAPTER 70

Dave, Claire, and Richard crouched in a hut with the tribal elders. Dave created a primitive blackboard by smoothing the dirt floor and holding a sharp stick. All they needed was a plan to defend the village, now and in the future.

As of that moment, he had nothing.

"Okay, this is where we are." Dave made a concentrated effort to smile with confidence. "They will come with guns. They will come in anger."

Dave looked at every man, overlooking Claire out of the respect for village culture. It did not offend her; she understood and lowered her eyes.

Dave stammered, looking for the right words in French.

"Dave, I mean Sergeant Murano, may I help?" Claire whispered to Dave, keeping her eyes down. "Why don't we call in that charming girl to help us communicate?"

Dave spelled out the situation, item by item, using sketches in the sand to augment the teenager's combination of French and Swahili.

"Excuse me, Dave," Claire spoke in a low, respectful voice in English. "I am quite sure they are aware of their liabilities." She smiled meekly. "Perhaps we should focus on our assets."

The villagers nodded and smiled in Claire's direction.

Dave looked blank. "I can't think of any." He smiled as he spoke in English, trying unsuccessfully to hide his lack of strategy.

Claire sat slightly straighter and spoke softly but assertively.

"In my country, when you are trying to defeat an adversary, there are several components to victory." Dave translated her words into French while wondering what she was leading up to.

The villagers looked at Claire in earnest as the teenage translator repeated in Swahili.

Claire did her best not to make it look like she was taking control. She realized that in this country, in these primitive villages, the good ideas must always appear to come from the men. Not that much different in so-called civilized nations, she thought to herself.

She forced herself to appear soft, feminine and timid. "I am not sure, but my father used to tell me, if you want to defeat an enemy, you must have the following components."

Dave translated to the teenage girl in French as she addressed the villagers in Swahili. The men leaned forward.

"First, you must have education. People must know what is going on. That way, they can be wary and future generations will not buy into evil." She looked around the hut for disagreement, but the men continued to cling to her every word.

"Secondly, there must be a plan and everyone must thoroughly understand their part in it."

The men nodded their heads in agreement.

"Thirdly, it is imperative that there is some sort of defense."

Again, nods of interest.

"Lastly, the most important thing must be a diversion."

Dave looked at her and stroked his fingers down what had become a substantial black beard. "*Une diversion.*"

"Oui, monsieur, education, a plan, a defense, and a diversion."

Dave's military training kicked in as his brain began to concoct a plan.

Richard didn't speak a word of French, but that didn't stop him from formulating a plan of his own.

CHAPTER 71

The chopper landed in an obscure section of the Kinshasa International Airport tarmac. Harper's sense of relief and safety was surpassed only by the camaraderie forged between the two passengers and pilot of the helicopter.

The blades slowed to a stop as Mike helped Harper out of the cabin. They fell into a joyful embrace.

"We made it!" Harper kissed him hard on the mouth. There were tears in her eyes. Her strawberry hair swirled about Mike's face.

"Thank God." He was not used to expressing gratitude to a higher power, but this time it seemed utterly appropriate. "We made it."

Greg Gauld completed his engine shut-off sequence and stepped outside the cockpit. "Nice to be in civilization." He looked around, "Kinda sorta." He reached in to grab his bag.

"Time for a drink. I know this little bar just down the road."

The pilot locked the cabin and saluted his passengers. Mike laughed and shook the pilot's hand. "Boy, you must know every bar in this, and possibly every other, country." A smile broke across Mike's dirty, stubbly face.

"Well, more bars in more places. That's my slogan!"

Harper giggled, a sound she hadn't made in a long time. "I think we should head right for the embassy, don't you?" She grinned at the pilot.

Gauld returned her smile. "Cool. I will catch up with you two. Go and get everything situated with the embassy. I already have a passport, so all I have to do is buy a ticket."

He stopped and dropped his duffel bag on the tarmac. "Hey, Logan, there is only one thing I forgot."

Mike kissed Harper's forehead and looked at the pilot. "What is that, Greg?"

"Could you spare me some cash? They will take US dollars here and I really could use a drink."

"Captain Gauld, I would be happy ... no, honored, to spot you a drink." He smiled at Harper and reached under his shorts. "In fact, I would be happy to spot you several drinks!" Mike ripped out the packet sewn into the lining of his pants and grabbed a hundred dollar bill.

Harper crinkled her forehead and turned sideways from the pilot. "Are you sure you want to give him that much?" she whispered to Mike. "We may never find him again with so much money. Not to mention, aren't we just encouraging him to go off on a bender?"

Mike glanced at the pilot, who only slightly staggered while adjusting his pants and moistening his grimy hand to smooth back his hair. "He'll be all right," Mike said reassuringly.

"Where do we find a cab?" Mike asked, thinking of someone else in the driver's seat for a change.

"Go past that aircraft and through the terminal. Cabs will be at the front and they all know the way to the U.S. Embassy. After I have a civilized drink, none of that palm wine shit, I will prep the chopper for sale. I need to unload it before we leave so I have some cash when I get home." He stuffed the bill in his shirt pocket.

"You're a good man, Logan. Thanks." Gauld saluted the couple and headed off the tarmac in the direction of the airport bar, then called, "Oh, and Logan, if I don't get enough for the chopper, can you spot me enough to buy a ticket back to Baton Rouge?"

"Shiyatt, I will buy you a fucking ticket to the moon." Mike hollered back. "We'll be back in a few hours, once we get our passport situation straightened out. So don't you go off with some young waitress."

"Oooh, some young waitress. That sounds pretty good." Gauld turned on his heel and made for a shack at the edge of the tarmac. "See ya, kids."

"See ya, Cap'n." They both waved.

"Well, Harpy, what do you say we get to a shower and a nice clean bed?" Mike herded her toward the airport gates.

"A shower." Her eyes dreamily lifted. "And a nice, clean bed."

His thoughts were already back on the straw mat in the village. As far as he was concerned, any bed would do, clean or not.

"But first, the embassy," Harper said firmly.

He sighed. "I suppose you're right. Business before pleasure."

The taxi to the embassy turned out to be an ancient, dilapidated Renault, but as far as Mike and Harper were concerned, no limousine was ever so luxurious. The vehicle chugged away from the N'djili Airport up the highway to Kinshasa. Although crowded and dirty, Harper found the city charming. Black faces offered broad, white smiles. Children played in the streets. Harper returned their smiles with a child-like appreciation for her own life, a sentiment she'd never felt before.

The cabby spoke Swahili and Harper cheerfully carried on an amicable conversation. She seemed expressive, personable, and even chatty to Mike. He had mostly seen her brain at work and found this social side of her most attractive. He liked a person who felt comfortable in her own skin. Even if that skin happened to be covered with the grime of a refugee.

The driver said, "American embassy, 310 Avenue de Aviateurs. Nous sommes ici."

Mike and Harper looked at each other and kissed with sheer relief and gratitude.

"I remember that the ambassador here is from Michigan. I think his name is Garvelink." Mike said. "He's supposed to be a good guy."

Mike paid the driver with an American fifty dollar bill. The man smiled a toothless grin. Harper gave him a warm hug and thanked him in Swahili, then French. The cabby noticeably blushed through his dark skin and bowed his head to her. He stuffed the fortune in his pocket, hailed a street vendor for cigarettes and retired to the front of the cab for a long-awaited smoke.

Mike and Harper could barely control their glee as they stepped onto the sidewalk in front of the embassy building. They were thirsty, starving, and filthy but also glowing.

They had made it at last!

CHAPTER 72

Richard searched the village perimeter with a long stick and a sharp eye. He wore tattered netting attached to the brim of his hat. Claire crept up behind him, looking into the trees and down at the ground, trying to figure out what he was looking for.

"Have you found anything?" Her whisper startled his concentration.

"Madame, I would appreciate any opportunity you might give me to solve this conundrum of our impending mission." He did not look at her, keeping his focus on the ground.

Claire slunk behind his shadow.

"Aha!" Richard poked the stick into a *Photinia* tree and lightly struck a branch.

Claire heard buzzing coupled with Richard's laughter.

"There they are, the little bastards. Carnivorous and highly aggressive."

Claire crouched behind Merrill in awe. Thousands of bees clung to a hive that reminded her of a papier mache medicine ball. Claire was not afraid of bees but had seen anaphylactic shock on more than several occasions. The symptoms were not only terrifying, they could easily be deadly. She began to understand what mischief Richard might be planning.

"Here is part of our defense mechanism," Richard said with a sly smile. "All we have to do is figure out a way to deliver the bomb."

"That's easy," she said. "I studied medieval history at university. What you need is a trebuchet."

"What?" He admired a large drone tickling the exposed part of his arm.

"You know, a trebuchet."

He cocked his head at her, shrugging his shoulders.

"You know, that thing that flings items from a far distance, landing on the enemy." She demonstrated with her arms and hands.

"You mean a catapult?" He laughed and attempted to kiss her forehead through the netting.

"Yes, that's it!" She smiled. "Using a catapult and as many beehives as we can muster, maybe we can use that as a component of our defense. Of course, that is only one component. We must have others, as well as a plan for the diversion."

"Well done mi' lady." He lowered his gaze to her whiskey eyes. "We are now on our way. I have a plan."

"The whole plan?' She looked up at him.

"The defense, the education, and the diversion. Yes, the whole plan."

"I knew you would," she said, lifting the net from his hat for a proper kiss.

CHAPTER 73

Mike and Harper, grinning like teenagers, put their feet onto the first step of the American Embassy.

Harper stopped short, suddenly grabbing Mike's elbow and breaking into a run. She didn't slow down until they were both hidden around a corner of the building.

"What?" Mike asked. "Something wrong?"

"Magnus." Harper whispered, peering around the corner.

"Magnus?

"You know, Magnus. That guy who came to pick me up in Big Sur. Vandervere's goon." Her whisper was in a frantic high pitch.

"I never met him," Mike said. He looked around the corner with one eye and saw nothing but the usual people walking up and down the steps to the embassy. Two men in business suits shook hands. "Is one of those guys Magnus?"

"Yes. The white guy in a suit." Her voice trembled.

"They're both white guys." Mike looked again around the corner. "And they are both wearing suits."

She dared to peek around the corner again and got a glimpse of the men walking away from each other, one heading toward the Avenue de Aviateurs and the other toward the embassy entrance. She backed around the corner. "That must be the ambassador."

"What? The skinny one who just entered the building? You think he's in league with Vandervere and Pharmco?"

She answered with another question. "Do you know why politicians get sent to these Godforsaken places to be the American ambassadors?"

"Uh ... because they want to help Americans abroad?" He kept his eye on the large man still outside, the one Harper thought was Magnus.

"Haven't you ever heard of Valerie Plame?" she demanded.

"What does she ...?"

"Her husband was assigned to some horrible post because of a political scandal his CIA wife had been involved in." She slid down the concrete wall of the embassy building to the ground. The narrow alleyway where they hid stank of urine, but she was beyond caring.

"Even here, it is all political." She looked up at Mike as he covertly watched Magnus, who stood on the sidewalk and lit a cigarette, unaware.

"It's over." Her head fell in to her hands.

He gazed down at her with compassion. They had been through so much together. "OK, let's not forget I have all this cash stashed in my clothes." He knelt down and picked her up by the elbows.

"We have come this far. We will get home, don't worry." He lifted her chin so their eyes met. "Don't worry."

She smiled tentatively, feeling only slightly reassured.

A shot rang out.

Mike looked around the corner of the building just in time to see Magnus lunging for them. He held a menacing Dutch Mauser carbine. The large Dutchman was talking into his lapel as he lumbered toward Mike and Harper.

"It's time to go." Mike yanked Harper's arm and dashed toward the same cab they arrived in. The newly-rich driver sat on the front bumper chatting and laughing with the locals. He held a clump of keys in one hand.

Mike jumped into the driver's seat while Harper ducked into the passenger compartment and crouched on the floor. Mike hot-wired the cab and honked the horn so the crowd parted. Shouting an apology to the astounded cabby, he stomped the gas pedal to the floor. He hoped there was enough fuel to get them to the airport, and that Captain Gauld would be sober enough to fly them somewhere, anywhere but here.

Magnus jumped into a black Mercedes 600C and took off in pursuit of the Renault sedan. The cab sped through the downtown area. Mike was fully aware he might not outrun the 600C Luxury Sedan, but he should be able to out-maneuver the heavy, chauffeur-driven limo. The embassy was right on the Congo River. Even a Mercedes could not navigate a river.

CHAPTER 74

The young black man tugged on the hand-woven hemp rope.

"It works!" Dave knew it would, but was still boyishly proud when it did.

Dave spoke to the tribe in French. "When the boy sees them coming from his hidden lookout, he will pull the rope. We will hear the warning bell and load the trebuchets." His primary goal was that no one be hurt during the defensive action. Darts and spears would require the traditionally-peaceful tribe members to show themselves, making them much too easy a target for machine guns. The attack must be stealthy.

Richard approached the sergeant. "There is no way we will have enough time to get the hives and load the catapults between the time the boy rings the bell and they arrive in the center of the village. It is lucky enough this village has only one point of entry, the same spot the previous Mayi marauders entered. The other three sides are completely locked in by the jungle. But we are going to need a whole lot more than luck."

"You're right," Dave said. "That moment is when we will need the diversion." The two men kicked leaf litter with their shoes, not quite sure of the answer. It should have been easy—only it wasn't.

Richard spoke softly to Claire. "That part was the only thing I was missing."

She smiled. "Oh bloody hell, you knew all along I was going to do it."

"What on earth are you talking about?" He smiled slyly.

She stood up straight, making herself as imposing as possible. "I will do it."

Dave looked at her. "No way. No fucking way." He turned to Richard. "Do you have any idea what they will do to her?"

"My dearest Sergeant Murano, how do you think you would fare in hand-to-hand combat with this beautiful little hellcat?" Richard gave Claire an admiring glance.

She stood as tall as an NBA All-Star. "Don't worry about me. I can handle them."

Richard kissed her on the mouth.

"Have it your way," Dave said. "But I am not just giving them this little present without back-up."

CHAPTER 75

Mike maneuvered the stolen cab through the crowded and filthy neighborhood streets. It was impossible to travel at more than a frustrating crawl without crushing the hordes of people in the roadway. Worse, once he was able create a wedge through the teeming masses, the Mercedes was able to follow with ease. Mike tried to compensate by making as many unexpected turns as possible.

He knew the Mercedes would easily overtake the beat-up Renault once they hit the main highway to the airport. The little cab did not stand a chance.

Mike sniffed the air ... water.

"We are going by water," he said to Harper, who remained curled in a fetal position on the floor of the car. "Get yourself ready to roll out into the river." He had to yell to be heard over the sound of the cab's whining flywheel.

He pulled the steering wheel to a sharp right, his arm muscles taut with the effort.

"OK, I'm ready." She managed a slight smile.

"That's my girl." He hooked a sharp left into an alley barely wide enough to drive through and stepped on the gas. He had no idea where he was, but knew if he kept the cab headed in a more-or-less northern direction, eventually he'd reach water. Through the cab's grimy windshield, Mike spotted the docks lining the side of the river. So far, luck had been on his side. He hoped fate would continue to deal him a winning hand.

The cab sped across the docks, tossing several deckhands into the drink. The Mercedes stayed close behind, but the larger, heavier vehicle was at a disadvantage when it came to twisting and turning in small spaces.

"OK, when I say go, open the door and roll out into the water. Wait for further instructions. Got it?" He did not mean to bark orders, but the situation offered no room for error.

She nodded. When he saw her check the door to make sure it was unlocked, he knew she understood.

He stood on the gas pedal and set his trajectory while scoping the marina for a suitable getaway vehicle. The N'dajili Airport was inland and he planned to locate a marker on the river for ships dealing in airline cargo. His mind worked out the details as the cab took off from the dock at a forty-five degree angle at sixty miles an hour.

He glanced in the side mirror to see the Mercedes screech to a halt with the front left wheel hanging off the end of the dock. Magnus jumped out, shooting at the flying cab.

Harper raised herself to her knees and placed her hand on the door handle, her nerves quivering with tension, adrenalin racing.

The river flowed about forty feet below them. Mike knew it was imperative that they time the jump with precision—far enough away not to be hit by the cab, yet close enough to not be hit by bullets.

At ten feet, he gave the order. "Go!"

CHAPTER 76

"OK, we have the warning system, the hives, and our gorgeous little diversion," Dave said. "What else?"

"What are your thoughts?" The eldest shaman spoke in French, addressing Dave with the highest respect. They had come a long way from the day Dave staggered into the village delirious with fever and imprisoned in one of the huts.

"We cannot risk any warrior's exposure, so the attack must come from an invisible source." Dave stroked his chin. "How about sabotage?"

The elders and shamans of the village were obviously familiar with the French term. They smiled toothless grins. Dave, Claire and Richard nodded to each other.

"I think we've got it," Claire summed up the feeling of the group.

Every man returned her smile.

CHAPTER 77

The cab landed with a hard splash in the Congo River. Mike and Harper bobbed in the petrol-laced water, gasping for air, right in the path of a slow-moving barge returning to the docks.

"Harp," he whispered urgently, "grab hold of the back side of that barge."

She treaded water, her nose and mouth barely able to take in air. She couldn't hear a word but saw him gesture toward the barge. She had no clue why Mike wanted to return to the marina, but kicked her legs and thrust her arms through the murky water to follow him. She'd never given over her trust so completely to another human being, but she figured after all they'd been through Mike had earned it.

The barge was situated at an angle so anyone watching from the docks could not see the bedraggled figures of Mike and Harper clinging to the back. A sturdy motorboat cut through the water, obviously in pursuit of them, while Magnus and his driver headed upstream in the Mercedes, their guns positioned from the open windows.

Harper and Mike clung to the bumpers of the slow-moving barge as it headed downstream, directly back to the docks.

CHAPTER 78

It wasn't the first time Captain Gauld had been slapped by a girl. Far from it. Still, he couldn't remember a time when he enjoyed it more. He was going to get out of 'this hell hole' and go home.

Home to Louisiana. Home to American cooking, American utilities, and American women. Even the thought of fewer flies made him grin with joy.

So he just smiled at the black girl who'd just slapped him, threw the bill on the counter, and left the airport bar. He practically skipped across the tarmac to the chopper.

A green Jeep was parked right next to it.

"What the fuck?" His light step turned into his drunken version of a jog. "Get away from there or I am going to kick your fucking ass!" Gauld screamed to the black man standing by the Jeep.

The man backed away with his hands up and a frightened look on his face.

Gauld trotted up to the helicopter and tried to force sobriety into his alcohol-soaked brain cells. He stopped in front of the chopper with his palms on the top of his knees, gasping for breath. "What the fuck are you doing here?"

"I am from the World Health Organization."

Gauld was close enough now for a good look. The man was young, barely more than a boy. He kept his hands above his head and wore a terrified expression.

Gauld regained his breath. "Who?'

The young man smiled. "Yes, exactly."

The pilot looked perplexed. "What?"

"No sir, WHO." The boy answered. "I have come to take you to the organization headquarters."

"Who?" Gauld cocked his head in confusion.

"Yes. That is correct. I have fuel in case you do not have enough to fly to the island of Sao Tomé."

"Got any booze?" Gauld asked.

"No, sir, but it is imperative that you transport Miss Smith and Mr. Logan to the Island of Sao Tomé immediately." He spoke in an educated British accent and was impeccably clothed and groomed.

The boy lowered his hands, rolled up his sleeves, and began to fill the chopper's fuel tank from a large can from the Jeep. "The director is anxiously awaiting your arrival." He gave Gauld a sincere smile.

After countless hours in bars, Gauld read people pretty well and decided this young man could be trusted. He returned the smile.

"Where did you say you were from?" Gauld unlocked the door to the cockpit and surveyed to make sure everything was as he left it. He then checked several of his secret stash places in case he had forgotten a little taste of something.

"No sir, not where—WHO. The World Health Organization"

"What?"

"Not 'what' sir, WHO."

"Fucking whatever." Gauld left the cockpit and watched the young man to make sure he was filling the fuel tanks correctly. "They should be here in an hour or so. Why don't you go and get me something to drink while we wait."

"Maybe it would be best if I got us something to eat, sir," the boy said, smiling with respect.

"Fucking boring I would say, but a cheeseburger sounds really good right now." Gauld climbed in the cockpit and adjusted his seat, settling in for a nap.

"Sir, I would advise leaving with all due haste when Miss Smith and Mr. Logan return."

Greg looked at the boy with half closed lids, wondering about the sudden sense of urgency. Something about the young fellow made him recall his years at the academy. He sat up straighter and looked at his reflection in the cockpit window. Grimacing at the sight of grizzled jowls and bloodshot eyes, he climbed out onto the tarmac.

"If we are going to Sao Tomé, we'll need a maintenance check." Even the mention of food sobered him up. "Do you know anything about choppers ... um, what did you say your name was?

"My name is Efrain, sir."

"Well, damn glad to meet you, Efrain." Gauld shook his hand heartily.

CHAPTER 79

H arper and Mike hid under the wharves, their heads barely above water. Magnus was out of sight, heading upriver in pursuit.

"OK, let's go." Mike hauled himself out of the water and onto the tilting dock. He had already picked out a likely candidate for his needs. The Pharmco thugs commandeered a large and cumbersome vessel and Mike vowed not to make the same mistake.

He mentally reviewed the topography of the river and its banks he had seen while flying in on Gauld's chopper. From above, he observed the ships docked in an incredibly random fashion, like iron filings attaching to a magnet. That could be helpful. He also knew it would be much quicker to reach the airport by water than by land, even with the enemy on the river. By now, Magnus had made sure the one main road to the airport was heavily guarded.

Mike pulled out a wad of water-soaked bills from his pants and handed it to the owner of a small skiff with a three hundred-fifty horsepower outboard motor. He smiled at the man and used hand gestures and his limited Swahili to buy the boat and trade clothes.

Mike and Harper hid behind a larger vessel and quickly stripped off the filthy, drenched clothing and threw on the traditional local garb of brightly-colored cotton robes, covering their faces and skin color. Mike cast off in a slow and deliberate manner, careful not to draw any attention to the boat and its passengers.

The previous owner of the vessel waved cheerfully as he stuffed more money than he usually saw in a year into his pocket. In his boat, Mike and Harper nimbly puttered their way upstream toward the airport.

CHAPTER 80

"We need a compelling reason for these hoodlums to never return and, well," Claire looked around, "tell all their friends what they find."

Richard looked at the village elders. He stroked his unkempt beard in thought. "Tell all their friends, eh?" He glanced at Dave, who pursed his lips as he considered everything from a military standpoint: offense, defense, strategy, artillery.

"What if we put ourselves in their shoes?" Claire asked.

The men gave her curious looks.

"These are mere boys," Claire continued, "stripped from their villages, their families, their mothers." Claire looked at the boys, not one of them over thirteen years old, standing behind the elders. "We just need to get them off their guard long enough to, one, feel something, although that has been systematically brainwashed out of them; two, be afraid enough to not come back; and three, convey to their superiors that it is not worth returning."

"Thinking like the enemy," Dave said. "Excellent!"

Claire smiled. "How about witchcraft?"

"Why, Claire, is that something of which you have knowledge?" Richard smiled, but did not know the answer to his question. He found himself slightly afraid of her response.

Her whiskey eyes lit up as she laughed. "Why no, Richard, I am not Christine O'Donnell but I am positive you men can figure out a way to make it look as though I am."

Richard smiled warmly as he lowered his eyes to the lithe English doctor and kissed her on the forehead. Dave couldn't hide a slight look of envy.

Dave addressed the group in French, "Okay people, let's get to work."

A rousing reply ensued. "Salongo, alinga mosala!"

CHAPTER 81

The Mercedes screeched to a halt on the docks. Magnus leapt out and onto the boat holding the Pharmco henchmen. Once the big Dutchman was on board, it continued to chug in and out of the berths of the shipping area, scanning the river for anything remotely resembling two Americans.

Mike steered the skiff in the opposite direction and kept his head down and wrapped in a colorful scarf. Harper pretended to have a child in her arms for added disguise. It was actually a moldy buoy wrapped in an old rag, but somehow, much to her surprise, it felt natural. Mike glanced down at this scene of maternal bliss and smiled his broad, bright-white, even-toothed smile.

No one in this region had teeth that perfect. No one except Americans.

"There, get them!" Magnus hollered to an accomplice as he reached for his hand gun.

"Play time over!" Mike yanked on the throttle of the large outboard motor and began to maneuver through the docks. The engine was too large for the small aluminum skiff. Mike had to use all his extraordinary strength, skill and ingenuity to keep the skiff under control and ahead of the pursuers.

He sped upriver to the larger commercial shipping docks. The strong currents of the muddy, petroleum-laced water further complicated the stability of the heavy outboard motor, but in this situation, Mike figured they were better off with a motor too powerful than one weak and small. He steered the boat straight into the fleet of container ships and darted in between two large vessels.

Magnus barked orders into his lapel. His newly acquired boat was cumbersome compared to Mike's small craft. The gunfire paused as the skiff slipped out of sight between the ships. Mike and Harper heard Magnus yelling at someone to go faster.

Mike wove in and out of the ships, focusing on his direction. Harper was completely disoriented as the vessels' hulls towered over their heads, making even the sun difficult to pinpoint.

"How are we going to know where the airport is?" She yelled over the sounds of the engines as they popped in and out from the shadows of the giant ships.

Mike pointed to the sky.

Harper followed the direction of his finger and shouted, "Follow that plane!"

CHAPTER 82

Through the interpreter, Richard addressed one of the elders. "We need more than wasp hives to defend the village. How close would you fellows need to be to get an accurate blow dart assault?"

The tribesman thought for a moment and gestured his hand to a large boulder outcropping about ten meters away.

Dave stepped in as commander. "Fine, get your men to prepare as many darts as possible and I will select the areas of attack. We will have four spots staggered along the entry road. We will shield the men from sight using blinds made of brush and wood."

He thought for a moment. "We will get as close as we can to large rocks in the event the Mayi start shooting. If we place the men with darts in the appropriate locations, so our target cannot ascertain the direction of the darts, they will not know where to shoot."

Richard chimed in, "Brilliant, Sergeant! I agree, in the event they do start randomly shooting, our people need cover."

Dave grinned. "And wouldn't it be best if they set their darts to the 'most irritating' mode?"

"Well done! We don't want them dead, we want them to go back to their superiors and live to tell about it," Richard said, returning the smile.

"Oh, no, I have a better idea." Claire wore an unusually wicked look on her face. "Why don't we use a small amount of psilocybin on the darts for a hallucinogenic effect? That way, anything we may throw at them will seem even more terrifying."

"Excellent, my love." Richard looked at her with admiration.

Richard suddenly had an idea—an idea so disturbing he almost dismissed it. Try as he would, he could not banish it from his mind. "I know this goes against your Hippocratic Oath, Claire, but I know a way we can also magnify the 'witchcraft' aspect of this mission."

"Go on!" Claire and Dave demanded.

"Well, it is highly unethical and unsuitably immoral. But this is war. Do we agree?"

Claire and Dave nodded.

"If we also lace the darts with the Ebola virus, we not only condemn the boys in the Jeep, they will take the disease back to their camp. It could possibly eradicate much of the guerilla population in a couple of weeks."

Claire, Dave and Richard looked at the ground, each wrestling inside with the moral implications of the suggestion.

"Can you culture such a strain, Richard?" Dave asked at last.

"In a heartbeat. Unfortunately for these people, Ebola is abundant on this continent," Richard answered sadly.

Again, an uncomfortable silence. Claire surveyed the peaceful villagers attending to routine tasks. "We must instruct the villagers to make sure no one goes near the Mayi camps. Since they are isolated, the should be safe. We can't chance infection the general population."

"What if we used the 'witchcraft' aspect of our plan in addition to the infection?" Dave mentally put the final touches to his plan. "Claire, do you have any objection to nudity?"

"I beg your pardon?"

"I know this is a lot to ask, but I think if we can rig up some Hollywood-style special effects, a naked white woman may create the superstitious effect we desire. A woman who is all powerful and in control of nature may be the key to squelching their assault in perpetuity."

Dave added thoughtfully as he looked Claire in the eye, "I think that men's general fear of women may fuel the lack of civility in this world."

She gave him a glance of appreciation.

"Dave, are you serious?" Richard said with concern. "I can't let you put Claire in front of men with guns, especially with no clothing." He put his hand to his forehead. "No way."

"Now, Richard, think about it. Would you shoot a naked woman?" Claire put a reassuring hand on his.

He stopped. "Umm, no."

"Exactly!" Dave pumped his arm with enthusiasm. "We'll use a pulley system to 'float' her across the clearing, and we'll get the tribeswomen to add beads and feathers to her hair and paint her body with mystical symbols."

"I know this might sound odd, but I don't have any aversion to snakes." Claire stated calmly. "Perhaps we could add a few snakes."

Both men got the visual of Claire floating across the village with feathers in her hair, naked, with snakes writhing around her body.

"Umm, hello? Anybody listening?"

The men cleared their throats and shuffled their feet with embarrassment.

"Bloody hell—MAP!" Claire shook her head, remembering Harper's verbal shorthand for "Men Are Pigs."

"Huh? Oh, and how about some smoke?" Dave added.

"Brilliant!" Richard replied. "And while you're at it, see if you can rig up a device to make it sound like her voice is coming from more than one place."

"I'm on it," Dave said.

Again putting herself in the shoes of her adversaries, Claire had another thought. "What if we plant the information in the Mayi-Mayi camp that there is some kind of white witch in this village who protects the tribe?"

"Also brilliant!" Richard said.

"Just one problem," Dave said. "We don't know when they will attack. Perhaps we can leak that the witch only appears during a full moon, thus narrowing down our time frame for preparedness."

"And she could be looking for a suitor to assist her in her queenly duties, offering herself and the riches of the tribe." Claire grinned. "Perhaps a challenge will guarantee they will come at the appropriate time."

"Last night's moon was rising gibbous. That means we have only four days to the full moon." Richard bit his lip. "Can we do it in time?"

"We'll just have to," Dave said.

"Let's not forget about the 'education' phase of the plan," Richard added, surveying the women and children in the center of the village. "We need to prepare them to evacuate into the jungle the second the bell rings. And I mean, the second ...."

Claire watched a small boy playing with a banana slug. "I will start that program immediately. Dave, can you find the young lady who helped you interpret with the elders?"

"Will do." Dave, Richard, Claire and two of the elders put their hands together in a pile. "Salongo, alinga mosala!!"

CHAPTER 83

The skiff darted between tankers and container ships. Mike kept his eye on the skies for direction. Magnus and his henchman followed close behind, shooting whenever they had sight of the small boat, spraying bullet holes into the tankers' hulls.

Harper crouched in the slimy, filthy bottom of the boat. Despite her fear, she couldn't help admiring Mike's amazing skill as a navigator. Not only did he evade the deadly pursuers, he actually managed to lure the bigger craft into a series of near-accidents, even knocking the boat's operator off the bow. Magnus had to jump back to grab the tiller and turn around to retrieve his drowning pilot, giving Mike and Harper a small lead.

"Were lookin' good, Harp!" Mike sped away from the commercial docks and skirted the perimeter of the anchored ships, picking up more speed. Now he needed to figure out how he and Harper would get from the river to the airport where, God willing, Gauld would be waiting with the chopper.

He recalled seeing from the air one small offshoot of the river near the airport and hoped his memory was accurate.

"Look for a sharp right, a canal or estuary," Mike shouted to Harper from the stern of the small skiff, leaning forward to maximize the engine's full throttle. "If you see anything that looks like it could be a waterway, speak up!" She could barely hear him over the roar of the engine.

Harper raised herself slightly above the edge of the boat to take a backward glance. "It looks like the coast is clear," she yelled to Mike. She sat up and began searching for a canal or inlet.

All she could see was an occasional boat nestled in heaps of floating garbage. Fishermen pulled in tattered nets and debris covered the beaches.

"Are you sure you saw a way inland?" She strained her voice to be heard. "Maybe we should head in by foot?"

Mike scanned the skies and spotted a sleek, silver body of a jet headed for the clouds. "Keep looking. We must be getting close."

A burst of gunfire shattered the peace of the river. Harper and Mike threw themselves onto the floor of the skiff, as Mike pushed the throttle to the max. "Shit! We need to get out of here!"

The boat holding Magnus and his henchmen was closing in. Harper took one last look ahead before hiding below the side of the boat. "An alluvial deposit!" she screamed.

"What?" Mike shouted as he ducked to avoid a spray of bullets.

"An alluvial fan! Look!" She pointed upriver to a brown area spreading across the water, coming from the shoreline. "There's the estuary!"

Mike raised his head over the side of the boat. He tried to figure out what Harper was talking about, but just saw brush at the side of the river. It all looked the same to him.

Harper's knowledge as a botanist easily detected a difference in plant communities flanking the hidden entrance.

"Turn right here!" Harper screamed.

"Where?"

Harper motioned to the shore. "Here!" Her finger pointed to the spot where two separate plant habitats bisected.

Mike cut a hard right. As far as he was concerned, he was steering the boat directly into the dense jungle. But considering the pursuers had an endless supply of firepower and were almost on top of them, he was running out of options.

Bullets rained close to the skiff. "If you have ever been right about any scientific situation in your life, this better be it!" he yelled.

Mike navigated the invisible pathway while dodging bullets.

"There! Look!"

A waterway appeared between two large overhanging shrubs. It was only about twenty feet wide but led into a larger canal.

"You are beautiful!" Mike stood up in the boat to judge the depth of the estuary. "This is perfect!"

Magnus and the henchmen followed the skiff to the mouth of the waterway and slowed, obviously concerned about the depth. The Dutchman stood at the larger boat's bow with a revolver in one hand and a machine gun in the other. He decided the boat's propellers would not get trapped in the mud and motioned his pilot to go full speed ahead.

Mike looked to the sky where a plane flew directly overhead, descending. Their only hope was to avoid the hail of bullets long enough to get the pursuers' boat stuck in the shallows while taking the skiff as far as they could to the end of the canal. The plane above was lowering landing gear, so they must be close to the airport.

Of course, conditions had to be perfect: Gauld waiting by the chopper and sober enough to fly; Magnus failing to send more of his thugs to the airport to intercept them.

If one of these conditions wasn't met, he and Harper were toast.

CHAPTER 84

The bell clanged its warning in the early evening. The elders and tribesmen ceased their usual activities and solemnly adjourned to their positions. Per their instructions at the toll of the bell, the women and children retreated into the depths of the jungle. Even the youngest tribe members had the sense that silence meant survival.

The sound of raucous laughter preceded the arrival of the Jeep. The young men in the vehicle swigged liquor and toked on hand-rolled cigarettes, brandishing an assortment of handguns, rifles and machine guns. When they found themselves in a deserted village, their mirth diminished slightly.

"Where the fuck are the women?" the oldest boy belched in Swahili as he took another hit.

"*Je suis ici.*"

Claire floated, fully naked, across the center of the village in her hastily-painted and feathered regalia. Snakes wrapped themselves around her torso and arms and smoke wafted about her.

The youths in the Jeep stopped in their tracks, obviously recalling the rumors circulating in their camp.

"*Je sais pourquoi vous etes venu.*" Claire's voice echoed from a nearby tent. Her French was good enough for this!

As the marauders focused their attention on the white witch, blow darts descended from every angle. The hallucinogen took hold just as the Jeep tripped the release for the hornet's nest, which had been resting for several days in the net above the only road leading into the village. It immediately dropped into the driver's lap.

They made a quick U-turn, the Mayi-Mayi passengers screaming like little girls. They would not be back. They would only live long enough to relay their story and spread the scourge of the Ebola virus.

As Claire, Dave, and Richard watched their retreat, they almost felt sorry for the rest of the Mayi camp and the terrible fate awaiting them.

But only for a moment.

CHAPTER 85

Mike steered the skiff as close to the shoreline as he could without tangling the outboard propellers in debris. Speed was no longer an issue as the pursuers' larger boat struggled to avoid sand bars and floating junk. The water was so thick with algae there was no way to tell what dangers lurked beneath.

The boats randomly docked along the waterway got smaller and smaller as they headed inland. Mike took that as a good sign.

Magnus's boat again came into view. Bullets began to fly.

"OK, Harp, hang on and be ready to jump." Mike said.

Harper looked at the fetid water. "I'm ready when you are."

Mike yanked on the throttle, forcing the boat to speed to the end of the waterway. The skiff rammed onto the shore. Mike yanked the outboard out of the water at the last minute.

"Let's go!"

Harper jumped out of the boat anticipating water, only to roll in mud.

"Follow me!" Mike took off in the direction of the descending jet and found a faint footpath. His sense of direction told him it would lead them to the highway. He made one last backward glance and saw the larger boat beach itself on a hidden obstacle.

Mike and Harper wasted no time. They ran as fast as they could. When they finally stopped to catch their breath, the only sound they detected was the dull roar of the plane above and the highway in front of them.

They stumbled out of the brush at the edge of dense traffic. Everything from jalopy to luxury vehicle, tiny motorbike to huge truck, careened at speeds fast and slow in both directions on the multi-lane highway. No painted lanes or signs, just random chaos.

Harper stopped short. "You are fucking kidding me." She raised her thumb to her forehead and winced.

Mike spat on the side of the road and wiped his mouth with the back of his hand.

"Shit. Well, we've made it so far. This is the last barrier before freedom. We're just going to have to deal with it."

"Sheesh." Her wild hair whipped around in the vortex created by the traffic. "When you say go, I'll be right behind you."

Mike ran his fingers through his hair and eyeballed the oncoming traffic.

"Get ready … go!" He shouted when he spotted a slight lull.

They dodged a cattle transport, two motorcycles, a box truck with one flat tire, and six dilapidated taxis. A bobtail tractor barreled down at them as the driver yakked on his cell phone. The driver slammed on his brakes just in time, creating a giant pileup. Cars, trucks, and two-wheelers crunched into each other with a sickening screech of twisting metal and breaking glass.

Fortunately, the bobtail had decent brakes. Harper and Mike crept away from the bedlam of steam, loose animals, scattered cargo, and screaming drivers.

They'd made it halfway across the highway.

The pile-up on the northbound lanes caused enough rubbernecking to slow the southbound traffic. Mike and Harper jogged across the rest of the roadway with ease, arriving at the chain-link fence surrounding the airport tarmac.

Mike gave her a leg up and boosted her over the fence. She found enough gaps in the barbed war at the top to avoid being scratched. After a brief glance across the freeway, and seeing no sign of Magnus or his thugs, Mike quickly scrambled up and over.

They ran across the broken asphalt to the spot where they had last seen Gauld and the chopper, barely daring to hope the aircraft might still be there and the pilot sober enough to fly.

"There!" Harper shouted with joy when she spotted the helicopter. "But what is that?"

"It looks like we have company." Mike grabbed Harper's arm and shoved her into a bush next to the small, squat building that housed the airport bar. He ducked behind to get a better look.

"Gauld's in the pilot's seat," he reported to Harper. "He's not moving."

"Shit! Now what?" Harper didn't know if she could bear one more disappointment.

"I'll get a closer look. You stay here."

"Shit."

Mike crouched and duck-walked across the tarmac, staying out of the line of sight of the Jeep. He saw one pair of feet on the other side of the chopper's fuselage and decided that with the element of surprise, he could take out their owner. He spotted no one other than Gauld in the aircraft and no passengers in the Jeep.

He came up from under the helicopter and tackled the man, holding his arm hard against his back and grinding his face into the ground.

The young fellow yelled, jarring Gauld from his nap.

"Hey, Logan. Nice to see you dude!" The pilot stumbled out of the cabin.

"Who the hell is this?" Mike demanded.

"Yeah, that's right. WHO," Gauld stammered.

"What?" Mike asked.

"No, no. Not what, WHO!" Gauld once again got a confused look. "Shit, not again. Would you just let the man get up, please? He can tell you himself."

For the first time, Mike noticed the logo of the World Health Organization painted on the side of the Jeep.

"Shit, man, I'm sorry." He helped the boy to his feet. "Now what? I mean who?"

The young man dusted dirt and pebbles from his pants and re-gained his composure. "My name is Efrain. I am with the World Health Organization. I have come to take you to the director. With Captain Gauld's help, we would like you and Miss Smith to come to our floating headquarters off the island of Sao Tomé. It is near Gabon."

The boy had a serious look on his face. "It is not safe for you here."

"Yeah, no shit." Mike said with a deep sigh.

From her hiding place behind the bush next to the bar, Harper could see that Mike, Gauld and the strange young man were talking amicably. She tentatively approached the chopper and held her hand out to intro-duce herself. "Hi, I am Harper Morgan Smi …."

From the other end of the tarmac, a large troop carrier charged in their direction. "No time for formalities, people. Let's MOVE!" Mike shoved Gauld into the pilot's seat and dashed around to the cabin with Harper.

The young emissary from WHO jumped into the chopper, abandon-ing his belongings in the Jeep. Bullets flew as Gauld set the blades to rotating.

"Hold on folks, this is going to take a minute."

"We don't have a minute, Gauld," Mike said.

"I am not a fucking magician, dude!" The pilot madly flipped switches.

The bullets flew closer and began to rain on the WHO Jeep.

That's when Mike took notice of the large gas container on the back. "Oh shit! Gauld, you had better get us out of here and now!"

The plastic container of aviation fuel blew up just as the chopper lifted off the ground. The secondary explosion of the Jeep's gas tank sent the soldiers on the troop carrier flying off the vehicle. The few still conscious continued to fire wild shots at the helicopter, but it was out of range.

The four shouted in victory, barely audible over the sound of the engine.

Gauld banked a sharp right to the north. "Next stop, Sao Tomé," he announced with a grin as the river, jungle, villages and towns of the Democratic Republic of the Congo grew smaller and smaller and finally disappeared beyond the horizon.

CHAPTER 86

Harper thought the big white ship nestling in the calm cove was the most beautiful thing she had ever seen. If there were any lingering doubts as to the final destination, she was at least reassured by the large green letters spelling out 'WHO' on the chopper pad.

"Harp." Mike reached over and stroked her hair. "We made it."

Her face was pressed up against the window. She looked back at him with a radiant smile. "We made it."

Harper was halfway expecting Vandervere, Magnus, the Mayi-Mayi, or some other unpleasant weapon-toting surprise. Instead, she was greeted with smiles from a dozen uniformed crew members from all parts of the world. She hugged every person on the landing pad.

Harper, Mike and Captain Gauld were escorted to the decks below to cabins where they could "freshen up" before dinner.

"Freshen up!" Harper chirped giddily.

"Cabins!" Mike laughed out loud.

"Dinner!" Gauld chortled. "That means wine …."

The ship was immaculate, with crew members stationed throughout. It was not a luxury yacht by any means, but was modern, clean, and extremely well appointed.

"Miss Harper, this is your cabin." A lovely Asian girl led her into a stateroom with a private deck. "You will find clothing in the closet and toiletries in your bath." The girl bowed. "Please pick up the phone if you should need anything further. Dinner will be served in one hour."

Harper wanted to throw herself on the bed but resisted, knowing she would soil the linens with her filthy clothes and grimy body. Against her better judgment, she took a glance at herself in the mirror.

"Oh my God." She touched her sallow cheeks and combed her stringy hair with her fingers.

Her room had a small refrigerator. Harper was famished. This time she could do something about it.

"Oh my God." The fridge was full of bottled drinks, fruit, cheeses and chocolates, and bags of crackers, nuts, chips and cookies sat on top. Barely taking time to tear off the wrappers, she shoved chunks of cheese and handfuls of crackers in her mouth.

Then she saw it. The bathtub.

"Oh my God …."

Mike was in the next cabin making much the same discoveries.

Then he saw it. Clean sheets on the nicest, biggest bed he'd ever seen.

"Oh my God …."

CHAPTER 87

An hour later, Harper, Mike and Captain Gauld sat in the captain's dining room, silently but ravenously enjoying the best meal since leaving Dr. Merrill's tree house. Harper began to feel like a human being again.

"Who brought us here again?" Gauld asked between bites.

"Yes, WHO." Harper replied as she dotted the side of her mouth with a napkin. She was actually using a napkin, a civilized luxury she'd almost forgotten about.

"What?" Gauld crammed a half a loaf of French bread into his mouth.

"No, not what, WHO." Mike had butter dripping down his chin.

"Shit, not that again," Gauld grunted. "Whoever they are, I love them!"

"Didn't the boy say something about the 'director'?" Mike asked.

Gauld popped a shrimp, a Louisiana delicacy that brought a tear to his eye. "Yeah, the director."

Harper paused. Now that she was clean and fed, she had time to reflect, putting herself in the shoes of the African people. "Okay, let's take a look at this." She folded her neatly pressed linen napkin in her lap.

Mike, intent on fulfilling his own basic human needs, had not stopped to look at her until this moment. Harper's hair was a shining copper and her skin a dappled pond of freckles. The clothes they had provided were simple yet perfectly tailored to fit her slim, athletic body.

Green was definitely her color.

Mike relived the vision of her tied to the pole wearing nothing but her boots. He preferred that view. His thoughts were written all over his face.

"MAP." Harper whispered under her breath, but secretly didn't mind so much this time.

"Hello ...." Harper bopped Mike on the back of the head. "Let's take a look at this, guys." She snapped him back into reality. "Why would the World Health Organization want to help us?" She bit her lower lip. "How did they find us and who is the director?"

"I don't know, but I am starting to smell a rat." Mike slid a dinner knife into his newly-donned khakis.

Efrain, the young man who had found Gauld on the tarmac, emerged from the galley. "Good evening, my friends."

Mike and Gauld stood up abruptly, brandishing whatever dinnerware they could grab. Another man joined Efrain from the stairs next to the galley. This man was wearing brass buttons and the gold braid of a captain's hat.

"We understand your wariness, mates." The man had a ruddy, sea-worn complexion and a slight swagger. "I am afraid that we have not been formerly introduced."

He walked over to Harper and took her hand in his. With a cocky look straight into her eyes he said, "I am Captain Robbie. It is a pleasure to serve you." Harper immediately recognized his Down Under accent.

Mike tensed and studied the muscle-bound captain with wariness and suspicion.

"Blimey, mate, it is also a right pleasure to meet you and Mr. Gauld," Captain Robbie said to Mike. "I am the captain of this beauty and I would like to welcome you aboard."

"Why are we here? What do you want from us?" Mike demanded.

"Mr. Logan, the director will explain everything to you in the morning," Efrain said. "We realize you have been through a very difficult ordeal. Please know we are here to help you ...."

Mike reluctantly took his seat.

"Once you have had the appropriate nourishment and rest, the director will address all your questions. Please take this time to replenish yourselves and get a good night's sleep. Everything will be better in the morning." The young man bowed and retreated.

"He is right, gentlemen," Harper said. "I don't know about you, but I am exhausted. A good night's sleep after this fantastic meal sounds like heaven to me."

Harper placed her folded napkin on her plate, nodded to the pilot, and kissed Mike on the forehead. "Goodnight, gentlemen."

Mike remained wary, refusing to let down his guard.

"Don't worry, I will deadbolt my cabin door." She smiled at Mike. "I'll be fine."

"Well, I don't trust these people. I'll check on you in about a half an hour," Mike scowled.

Her parting smile was the last thing he remembered before his head hit the pillow eight minutes later.

CHAPTER 88

"Please be seated; the director will be with you shortly."
Harper and Mike placed themselves in the captain's chairs in front of the big desk. Gauld was nowhere to be seen. Harper assumed he was still sleeping.

The windows in the director's office framed the breathtaking view of the Sao Tomé coastline. The executive chair was turned away from Harper and Mike, facing the island, its back so massive and high they couldn't tell whether it was occupied or not.

"Well, this mystery is about over, I hope. If they have another 'mission' for us, I think I will tell them where to go." Mike squirmed in his chair like a child waiting for the principal.

"But what a gorgeous view!" Harper still did not feel totally comfortable, but her fears and doubts were quelled by a full stomach and a good night's sleep.

"It appears that 'the director' likes the view as well," Mike said with a smirk.

"As a matter of fact, I do." The big leather chair spun around. A beautiful black woman with hair graying at the temples beamed from its depths.

"Ursula!" Harper jumped up and threw her arms around her friend. "Ursula! Oh my God! What are you doing here? I mean, what, I mean who, I mean, um ... what?" Confusion halted Harper's tears of joy.

Ursula stood to return the embrace. "My dear Miss Harper, I am terribly sorry I could not reveal my true identity to you on our short but wonderful interlude." Ursula stopped speaking to hold Harper at arm's length and look her over, head to toe, with a critical eye.

"You are slight, my dear, but all seems to be well. You survived the fever, I see." The director smiled. "I knew you would have the fortitude to succeed if it were possible."

Harper's jaw dropped. How had Ursula known she had dengue fever? That episode seemed like a millennium ago.

"Oh Ursu ... I mean Madame Director, please excuse me. This is Mike

Logan. He saved my life on so many occasions, I couldn't even begin to count them." Harper smiled at Mike.

Ursula observed the obvious attraction between the pair. "I see, Miss Harp. The Organization chose correctly."

"Do you mean this was all a set up?" Harp looked at Mike with a stricken expression.

"How did you know where to find us?" Mike demanded.

"Now, now, you two. Please sit down and I will explain everything to you." Ursula made sure they were settled and offered them water. She walked around the back of the chair and placed her small hands on Harp's shoulders as she began.

"We knew about *Podophyllum peltatum*, of course. We sent dozens of botanists to find it. But, the World Health Organization does not have the resources that Pharmco does. When Dr. Merrill came close, finding a *peltatum* cousin, we knew the ancient myths could be a reality."

Ursula rounded her desk to view the island cove through the cabin window.

"When we heard what Pharmco was up to ... the order to exterminate Dr. Merrill, the formation of your team, and then the eradication of the plant materials, we knew the only way to squelch the operation was to infiltrate the team." Ursula looked at Harp. "I am sorry, my dear, for misleading you."

"But you rescued us at the N'djili airport in Kinshasa," Harp said. "How did you find us?"

"Well, we have been tracking you." The director seemed to be speaking more to the window than to Harp and Mike.

Mike stood up. "Tracking us?"

Harper also stood, astonished. "Tracking us?"

Ursula lowered her head.

"Do you mean to tell me we have been running for our lives, starving, burning, drowning, preyed upon by man and every other living creature and you knew where we were?" Harper bristled with anger all the way to the roots of her strawberry curls. "Why didn't you come and get us?"

"I know, and I am truly sorry. Now please seat yourselves and everything will be made clear." Ursula sat on the edge of her burlwood desk. "Now, listen to me." Ursula's voice took on a solemn tone. "The World Health Organization walks a very tight rope with the African countries. We are bound by agreements in which we do not interfere in local politics.

That enables us to operate in those countries with minimal oversight. Of course, that means we must turn a blind eye to many civil atrocities we would give anything to end."

Harper looked at Mike, seeing past her own small world into the bigger picture.

"Pharmco is very powerful and has corrupt officials in every major country in the world. Pharmco is also one of the largest contributors to the WHO. Of course, that is a public relations ploy, but please also note the entire operating budget of the organization is one quarter of one percent of Pharmco's worldwide revenue. We cannot survive without their support."

The director slid into her large executive chair.

"So we must look at our overall role in world health. *Podophyllum peltatum* could save tens of millions of lives. Now that we know the approximate location of the plant material, we must wait it out until Pharmco either changes its philosophy or gets distracted with some other possible threat to their bottom line."

Mike leaned forward toward the director. "Since it seems highly unlikely they will change their philosophy, I guess we will just wait. They burned the whole meadow anyway."

"Harp, do you have a comment to that?" Ursula asked.

Harper crinkled her nose. "Now, wait a minute. *Podophyllum* is a rhizome. Unless they had several hundred gallons of weed killer, there will be fragments of survivors underground." Harp's memory went back to that day. "But Chris and Hermann ...."

"And you were tracking us? How?" Mike demanded. "We ditched our tracking devices after the meadow. And where are the surviving team members? We were with Dr. Merrill and Claire, but the last we saw Richard, he was being assaulted by the Mayi."

"And what about Sergeant Murano?" Harp was on the verge of tears. She had not the luxury of recalling the horrors they had survived before this moment. Now terrible memories flooded back.

"Can you not think of how we were tracking you?" The director had a sly smile. "I am afraid we were not able to track Sergeant Murano or the doctors. Harp, only you had ...."

"The lighter!" Suddenly she got it.

"Yes, Miss Harp." Ursula grinned. "I know that a tremendous amount of things have transpired since our flight. I commend you for holding on to the lighter during all those instances."

"But I left it behind." Mike slumped in his chair, remembering the bar in the middle of the jungle and the need to keep Gauld well-stocked with booze.

"You left it? My lighter?" Harp turned on Mike with agitation. "That lighter saved our lives so many times. Where did you leave it?"

"Do not worry, Miss Harp," Ursula said calmly. "Mr. Logan did absolutely the correct thing with the lighter. By the time he gave it to the bartender, we already had you."

"Captain Gauld. You sent Greg to come and get us. It was not a fluke he happened to be at that bar." Harper smiled. "Thank you."

"OK, so we are here. Yes, thank you." Mike nodded. "But what are we going to do about those sons of bitches from Pharmco? We can't let them just get away with this."

"Well, our intelligence says that Dr. Vandervere has been terminated."

"Good. Fire the bastard." Harp pictured the slimy tycoon in his lair of hunting trophies back in San Francisco.

"That is not exactly what I meant by terminated." Ursula looked at a file on her desk. "My point is, to exercise any retribution against Pharmco is suicide. Even to bring the matter to the public through the media is pointless."

"But they hired hit men to kill us! And what about the plant eradication? A life-saving plant?" Harper's voice rose along with her temper.

Mike clenched his fists. "Can we prove any of that? Can we prove they hired the assassins? Can we even prove we were hired by Pharmco?

"And the Pharmco lawyers are the largest and highest paid team of sharks ever assembled," Ursula said. "Do you have any idea how many lawsuits are brought against Pharmco every year? Even with all the money and resources imaginable, we could never win."

"You're kidding me, right?" Harper said in disbelief. "They win?"

"Yes, Miss Harp. They win." Ursula slid open a drawer in her desk. "But we can make it just a little painful for them."

CHAPTER 89

U rsula placed a manila envelope on her desk in front of Harper.
"What is this?" Harper picked it up.

Ursula came around her desk to stand in front of the young woman.

"Do you remember our conversation in the galley of the jet right after we left London?"

"Yes, but …."

"Open it."

Harp pulled out the contents of the envelope. "Oh my God. The contract." She was unable to say anything else.

"Yes, my dear. The contract." Ursula beamed. "You were a clever girl to save it from that shady British barrister who obviously took everyone else's contractual agreement directly to the shredder."

"What the hell am I supposed to do with this?" Harper held up the document. "Their legal team will never honor it. You said so yourself— they're a bunch of shysters."

"Yes, my dear. They are shysters. That being said, you have a legally binding contract which our team of attorneys has reviewed." The director smiled. "It would be cheaper for Pharmco to pay out the terms of your contract than it would be to dispute it or risk any unfavorable press, even if they refuted it. Besides, a half a million dollars is a drop in the bucket to them and perhaps you could put that money to some very fine use."

Mike stood and paced to the window. "A half a million dollars? You have got to be fucking kidding me!" His mercenary's pay, sewn in his shorts, didn't even come close. "Sorry, director."

"Perfectly understandable, Mr. Logan."

"Yes, I believe I could put that money to very fine use," Harp said with a sly grin. "Do you really think they will give it to me?"

"First of all, you have earned it. However, you must demand it and threaten them with bad publicity if they don't pay up."

"What if they try to kill me like they did before?"

"That is an excellent question, one we have faced on many occasions."

Ursula tapped her fingers together. "You see, a contract kill on the African continent is one thing. There is no real law, no news media to speak of, and no accountability. That is why those poor people are so horribly subjugated. However, the American system is completely different. We must make an event out of your return so they know you pose a threat. You must also be in the public eye for a time so that if you do disappear, questions will be raised."

Ursula paused. "Miss Harp, you must prepare a platform, perhaps something you have experienced or observed that needs to be brought to the public's attention."

Harper wished Claire was with her now. The atrocities against the women of the so-called 'Democratic' Republic of the Congo were so bad, so inhumane, so despicable, Claire would be the perfect partner for this job.

Harp's head dropped into her hands with the thought of Claire. She felt like she'd lost a sister. Harp was halfway tempted to go back to the DRC to find the British doctor, or at least to find out what happened to her.

But Harper knew she had work to do. The contents of her 'platform' were obvious.

"We assume Pharmco and their henchmen are aware of your survival, so we must be stealthy in your retreat from this continent," Ursula continued. "That being said, all of our employees have seen your arrival. It would be very difficult for Pharmco to dispose of you now, but we cannot take any chances."

A knock on the cabin door caused the director to look up.

"*Entrez vous s'il vous plait. Bon jour Monsieur Gauld*, please come in and sit." The director led the pilot to a small couch. "May I offer you a beverage, Captain Gauld?"

"Yes ma'am. *S'il vous plait. Je vais prendre whiskey* if you've got it, Madame." Greg smiled at Harper and Mike. "Hey, I'm from Louisiana, guys. We speak French there too."

Harp and Mike smiled. If nothing else, the helicopter pilot was consistent.

"I am so glad you could join us, Captain. We were just discussing our return to the United States." The director filled the pilot's glass higher in response to his hand gestures. "As we were saying, we cannot take any chances. Pharmco would not dare make a move against you on our ship, but who knows what might happen if you attempt to use public transport?"

The director walked from one cabin window to another, just shy of pacing. "It appears we will have to take you all on this ship."

"Across the Atlantic?" The trio spoke in unison. They stared at each other, their faces a mixture of thoughts and emotions.

The first image to flash through Mike's mind was a week or more of letting down his guard, of not constantly keeping himself at the ready for an unknown attack.

Gauld imagined the extensive bar and that cute girl in the galley.

Harper pictured Mike's cabin right next to hers, and blushed.

CHAPTER 90

2010 September
Geneva, Switzerland

The etched glass lobby of WHO headquarters was an extreme contrast to the Congolese jungle. Harper was not quite sure which she liked best.

"Miss Smith, Mr. Logan, please come in to the conference room. Captain Gauld, we need you to fill out some paperwork for our files." The attractive receptionist in the tailored suit led the pilot into an office.

He surveyed her figure as she walked in front of him and grinned. "See ya'll."

The director stood next to a leather chair at the far end of the conference table, facing away from the entrance. She was bent over some files with the inhabitant of the chair, pointing out items on the documents.

"Miss Smith, Mr. Logan, welcome." Ursula hugged Harper and showed to her a seat near the head of the table. Other men and women in business attire filed in until the table was nearly full.

Harper's stomach fluttered with discomfort in the official atmosphere. She had survived the most primitive conditions imaginable in the depths of the African jungle; had sipped rainwater from an armadillo shell; fought her way through a volcanic mountain; staved off starvation by eating scorpions, and dodged bullets. But could she endure a formal business meeting with all these important people, and navigate her way through the politics and protocol? The return to civilization was a tougher adjustment than she thought.

Harper took her seat. A familiar-looking man in white gloves appeared at her side to offer tea. "Ezekiel!"

The kindly butler smiled and bowed slightly. "I am very happy to see you, Mademoiselle," he whispered.

"Damn, it seems like meeting you in San Francisco was another lifetime." Sometimes she felt she didn't know the girl she'd been only a month ago.

The director sat on the right of the large leather chair. "Let this meeting come to order." Ursula smiled at Mike and Harper. "I present to you the Honorary Executive Director of the World Health Organization."

A door opened and a man with a broad, white smile entered the room.

"Mr. President!" Both Harper and Mike instinctively stood at attention.

"Ms. Smith, Mr. Logan, the United States of America salutes you for your efforts and your dedication to humanity," the President said. "It is a sad thing when we are not able to save those who are in the most need, but we will do what we can. Ms. Smith ...."

"Please call me Harper, sir."

"Well then, you can call me Barack." Everyone in the room chuckled.

"Harper, you have a bigger mission ahead of you. It is imperative that you complete your doctoral degree. That will add to your knowledge and credibility for a life's work that could assist mankind into the 22nd century."

The President addressed the room. "Ms. Smith will have the funding to complete her PhD, compliments of the United States of America."

He paused to flash that famous smile at Harper, then continued. "We have lost to the corporate criminal for now, but I can assure you, this will not always be the case." He lowered his eyes and fidgeted with his pen. "As you all know, I have a special concern for the continent. Although I have not personally seen the atrocities that I have read in Ms. Smi ... I mean Harper's report, I feel that given the raw wealth of the land, usurped by corruption, and the potential of its people, enhanced American attention could contribute to change in the ways of African politics."

The Commander in Chief turned to Mike and Harper. "You two have acted most heroically and I commend you. The best of luck in your future endeavors. You are an asset to your country and the people of the world."

He shook their hands in earnest and left the room.

No sooner had Harper recovered the shock of meeting the President of the United States—not only meeting him, but receiving his congratulations and thanks, and the promise of a free education—then Ursula offered another surprise. "Harper and Mike, may I please present you with our next guests."

The door opened and a woman burst in, ran up to Harper and wrapped her in a hug.

Forgetting decorum, Harper leapt from her chair and returned the embrace. "Oh my God! Claire! You're alive!"

"Harper Morgan Smith, you gorgeous, brilliant woman!" Claire stroked Harp's curls and smiled with her warm whiskey eyes.

"But what about Richard? And Dave?" Harper's eyes stung with tears as her joy turned to sorrow.

Two men entered the room. Ursula spoke. "Please welcome Dr. Merrill and Sergeant Murano."

Harper thought she would burst with sheer happiness. Once again, she heard her father's voice.

Don't forget what happens to the organism that gets enough light, nutrients, and a little love.

What, Father?

It thrives.

The five survivors clung to each other in a huddle, barely hearing Ursula whisper the President's assurance of Dr. Merrill's funding necessary to complete his algae and other eco-friendly research. In that moment, each of them felt something intense, convergent, and humbling. Their previously empty cups felt full.

Ursula lovingly watched the teammates and wondered if she or any of the other somber VIPs in the room would ever triumph over so much adversity, or achieve so much for the good of humankind as this ragtag band of ordinary citizens.

EPILOGUE I

Smoke from expensive cigars wafted around the mahogany-walled room as snifters filled with the world's most coveted liqueurs clinked.

"Gentlemen, and of course, Madame," multiple translators murmured, "it appears that our Sub-Saharan cache remains under our control."

Low sounds of approval circulated throughout the room.

The large black man in the decorated uniform continued. "Thanks to our friends and your considerable contributions, we have been able to maintain complete subjugation of the land, the peoples, and all manners of export and commerce. Since we are all in need of the treasure trove of minerals and raw materials this part of the world holds in abundance, it is imperative that our countries and industries maintain this beneficial, albeit unilateral, relationship."

Jovial grumbles greeted this remark.

"Wouldn't you agree Messrs. Presidents? Messrs. Premiers? Messrs. Prime ministers? Oh, and of course Madame Chancellor?"

Nods of appreciation complemented raised glasses.

An invisible voice rose from a large leather wing-back chair. "Well, ya'll have done a darn fine job in makin' sure that the infightin' and immorality of those heathens are bein' blamed for the whole damn situation."

More murmurs of agreement.

"You can all expect full shipments of your orders to continue in perpetuity." The uniformed man clicked his heels and bowed as he left the intimate group.

Quiet conversations were interrupted only by the arrival of a black man in white gloves to offer refills on their drinks.

EPILOGUE II

Harper, Claire, and Richard had seated the delegates, offering whatever assistance was needed to the multi-national participants, and stood at the back of the room. The meeting turned to the topic of violence against women, and to the testimony of Melanne Verveer, Ambassador-at-Large for Global Women's Issues before the House Foreign Affairs Subcommittee on International Organizations, Human Rights and Oversight in Washington, DC.

Harper nodded in agreement as the ambassador spoke of the imperative of not relegating violence against women and girls as simply a "women's issue," but instead as "a humanitarian issue, a development issue and a security issue."

Verveer noted that the places around the world most dangerous for women also pose the greatest threats to international peace and security. Harper immediately got it: where women are oppressed, the government is usually weak and extremism is more likely to take hold.

"The current scale, savagery, and extent of violence against women and girls is enormous," the Ambassador continued. "It affects girls and women at every point in their lives, from sex-selective abortion, which has culled as many as one hundred million girls, to withholding adequate nutrition, to female genitalia mutilation (FGM), child marriage, rape as a weapon of war, human trafficking, so-called 'honor' killings, dowry-related murders, and so much more."

Harper looked over at her companions. Like her, they nodded as Verveer said, "We need a response commensurate with the seriousness of the crimes."

Some of the stories the Ambassador shared were almost unbearable for Harper to hear. "Confronting violence means being able to rewrite stories such as that of a young Yemeni girl, Najoud, a vivacious child with a big smile, whom I got to know. She was married at the age of eight to a much-older man, and she walked out of her house after two months of rapes and beatings."

Harper knew how lucky she had been to be born in a free country and given an education, compared to the young women of South Asia, Africa, and elsewhere who are forced to marry as teens, their childhoods effectively curtailed, their education terminated, their emotional and social development interrupted.

Yet Harper was able to gather hope from some of the other stories from the Ambassador, such as that of Mukhtar Mai of Pakistan, gang-raped on the orders of a local village council because her brother allegedly held hands with a girl from a nearby village. It was expected that she would commit suicide because the attack dishonored her family.

Instead, according to Verveer, "This illiterate young woman mustered the courage to take her case to court. She won a modest settlement, which she used to build two schools: one for boys, and one for girls, in which she enrolled herself. When asked why she used her small settlement for this purpose, she said she knew nothing in her village would ever change without education."

Harper came to attention when the Ambassador mentioned the Democratic Republic of the Congo. "In the DRC's Eastern provinces, eleven hundred rapes are reported each month. Rape is being used in armed conflict as a deliberate strategy to subdue and destroy communities."

I know that all too well—I've seen the evidence first-hand, Harper thought to herself. Once again, she glanced over at Claire and Richard and could tell they were contemplating the same thing.

Ambassador Verveer continued, "There is a powerful connection between violence against women and the unending cycle of women in poverty. Women who are abused or who fear violence are unable to realize their full potential and contribute to their countries' development. There are enormous economic costs that come with violence against women. Ending violence against women is a prerequisite for their social, economic and political participation and progress."

She spoke of the critical role women will play in the progress and prosperity in the twenty-first century. "When they are marginalized and mistreated, humanity cannot progress. When they are accorded their rights and afforded equal opportunities, they lift up their families, their communities and their nations."

Claire smiled softly, embracing her own intimate connection to the Ambassador's message. Standing next to her, Richard absorbed Claire's compassion, her experience, her empathy. As a man who uniquely identified with life and the power associated with love without ego, he had never felt closer to her.

Watching them as they took in the message of the Ambassador, the resolve of the audience, and the pureness of the ethereal link between Richard and Claire, Harper's feminine psyche was filled with both hope and trepidation.

She couldn't decide which was more compelling.

END OF BOOK ONE

CPSIA information can be obtained
at www.ICGtesting.com
Printed in the USA
FSHW020139170919
62084FS